MYSTERIOUS
RANCHO

Center Point
Large Print

Also by Jackson Gregory and available from
Center Point Large Print:

The Far Call
Timber-Wolf

**This Large Print Book carries the
Seal of Approval of N.A.V.H.**

MYSTERIOUS RANCHO

Jackson Gregory

CENTER POINT LARGE PRINT
THORNDIKE, MAINE

This Center Point Large Print edition
is published in the year 2018 by arrangement with
Golden West Literary Agency.

First US edition: Dodd, Mead & Company
First UK edition: Hodder & Stoughton

The text of this Large Print edition is unabridged.
In other aspects, this book may vary
from the original edition.
Printed in the United States of America
on permanent paper.
Set in 16-point Times New Roman type.

ISBN: 978-1-68324-692-3 (hardcover)
ISBN: 978-1-68324-696-1 (paperback)

Library of Congress Cataloging-in-Publication Data

Names: Gregory, Jackson, 1882-1943, author.
Title: Mysterious rancho / Jackson Gregory.
Description: Center Point Large Print edition. | Thorndike, Maine :
    Center Point Large Print, 2018.
Identifiers: LCCN 2017052526| ISBN 9781683246923
    (hardcover : alk. paper) | ISBN 9781683246961 (pbk. : alk. paper)
Subjects: LCSH: Large type books. | GSAFD: Western stories.
Classification: LCC PS3513.R562 M97 2018 | DDC 813/.6—dc23
LC record available at https://lccn.loc.gov/2017052526

CONTENTS

CHAPTER I

A DECISION IN THE DAWN

Two young men in the lounge car of "The Lark," speeding northward from Los Angeles toward San Francisco, were observing intently a third man a few seats removed.

"That's Benjamin M. Whitney," said one of the pair to his companion. "Met his Waterloo at last, I guess. Looks like he had a punch left yet in each hand, though, don't he? Seen the late papers?"

He unfolded the afternoon paper and indicated the article, the first and briefest of many which were to tell of the collapse of Whitney, the young financier, who after years of spectacular success, had been caught in the trap of a wily competitor and ruined.

Meanwhile the object of their whispered observations, noting with a sense of relief that there was no one in the car whom he knew personally, stared out into the dying day and coming dusk about the onrushing train. One with no key to his abstraction would have judged him a man who, at the end of a full day, relaxed naturally; who, probably, had had a day of it, but held much in reserve against further calls upon his strength; normally tired but resting normally. His lips were firm about his cigar; he smoked steadily; his hands were quiet. Details which, over the paper, the casual young men noted not without casual admiration. Whitney was showing himself a good sport, they thought.

For half or three quarters of an hour Whitney scarcely stirred. At last he slipped a hand into his coat pocket and drew out a small memorandum book and pencil. He flicked over page after page, frowning thoughtfully at the penciled notes. He turned to a page which held him; with pursed lips and eyes narrowed speculatively he considered it. He made an erasure; he penciled something in its place, he studied it again.

"Post mortem," decided one of his observers astutely. "Figuring out how he ought to have played it. Or tallying up what's left? Or planning on fresh backing?"

Whitney finally tore the leaf out, crumpled it and tossed it carelessly toward the waste basket near the writing desk. On a fresh page he began setting down other notes. A subtle change crept over him. He had the look of one visited by Inspiration. When a man's lips are about a cigar it is difficult to detect a slight smile upon them; when he happens to sit so that his hair and brows shadow his eyes it is hard to be sure if the eyes smile. But one, if he is very attentive to details and very astute, can actually *feel* a change of mood. At any rate he was penciling swiftly, deeply absorbed in what he was doing, and in the end obviously satisfied with the result.

When at last he got up and went in to the dining car his casual observer possessed himself of the fallen scrap of paper. His brows shot up swiftly in a look of surprise, came down slowly in a frown of perplexity. The perplexity instead of being dissipated with study became profound.

The paper had been torn but that fragment which had fallen to the floor and which by all rules which the astute young man could bring to bear on the case should have consisted of additions and subtractions in dollars and cents, read instead:

". . . bacon beans potatoes
. . . hammer wire tomatoes."

To be sure it might have been some sort of code. But to the two young men into whose hands it had come it sounded like nothing more nor less than the abortive creation of a shattered brain groping for poetic expression and achieving drivel.

Benjamin M. Whitney awoke in the early dawn; he raised himself on his elbow to look out at the oak-studded hills, green and smooth, flying by, and his eyes kindled. This was country he knew. Just yonder, a few miles over the hills, was the spot he had had so much in mind during these later frenzied months. San Luis Obispo County,

Monterey County—he felt he could find his way about them in the dark. Once they had been home. He had been born within a hundred miles of this spot. . . .

Not twenty-four hours ago he had locked up his offices, taken the keys and the keys of his safety deposit box to his attorney's office, laid the keys and a package of papers on the desk, and announced,

"I'm through. Finished. What has been done to me is what a brisk hammer, well swung, does to a plate glass window. Here's power of attorney for you. If any pieces of the wreck are worth saving let me know. I'm going somewhere but I don't know yet just where. When I do find out I'll let you know."

His train ticket read "San Francisco," and before leaving Los Angeles he had wired the Saint Francis hotel for reservations.

But now, as the dawn brightened, and with it the light in his eyes, an impulse presented itself which he considered thoughtfully. Back of the impulse was a strong urge that had long been in his blood. The purpose which had caused him to buy a ticket to San Francisco could be still better served in another way, the way suggesting itself now. To get away from people, to be left unhampered in re-shaping his plans.

He slipped a hand into the pocket of his coat and turned to the page in his memorandum book

10

which had interested him last night, reading slowly and with pleasure the list which he had made six months ago and which he had frequently altered and amended.

The next thing of which he was keenly conscious was of the fact that he had thrown a leg over the edge of his berth and was dressing rapidly. When the train stopped at Salinas in the crisp dawn he got down, and carrying his bag lightly, stood on the station platform, mildly curious what would happen next.

CHAPTER II

A LAND OF LITTLE CHANGE

The stage driver, Hap Smith, who made the trip from the little railroad station out to Toyon three times a week, took an ever fresh interest in each new passenger. At this season of the year, with roads still bad from the rains, and slow going imperative, the long ride grown monotonous from the repetition of years, Hap Smith welcomed company after a hearty manner which assured one that he was thinking less of the fare he would pocket at the end of the ride than of the pleasure of talking with someone. He decided tentatively that this fellow was all right.

"Been out this way before?" he led off.

11

"Not for a long time," was the answer. "Yes, once when I was a boy. Pretty close to twenty years ago."

"I've been drivin' only a spell over sixteen years," said Smith. "Knew I hadn't seen you before. Business out this way?"

"No, hardly. I'm chucking business for a while." There was nothing offensive in Hap Smith's normal curiosity and the stranger added lightly: "Just want a change, you know. The city sort of gets on a fellow's nerves now and then, taken as a steady diet."

"Sure," said Smith. "I know. I've always said the cities was all right for them that likes 'em. I've been there. Teamed once in San Francisco and acrost the bay in Oakland. That was before I begun stagin' down here. I went to see what it was like and I found out and I'm through."

He embroidered the fabric of his recital casually, told of an experience when he was broke and couldn't get credit, and returned to an investigation of his passenger's affairs.

"What name?" he asked.

The other for an instant failed to get his meaning. Then, with a half smile back of the seriousness of his eyes, he answered:

"Whitney, Ben—" He broke off and amended. Even people in the far out rural districts read the San Francisco and Los Angeles newspapers and it would be no strange thing if there might be among

12

them one here and there who recalled the name of Benjamin Maxwell Whitney. So he gave instead the middle name which had been crowded off his business cards. "Max Whitney," he said.

"Not a lawyer, are you?" asked Smith. And when Whitney shook his head the stage driver explained: "Just brung a city fellow out to the valley ten days ago. He was a lawyer, or anyway that's what he said. Name of *Mr.* Sheffield; never got no front name out of *him*. Visitin' the Calderon folks. Anyway, that's what he said he was doin'. Don't know him, do you?"

Whitney shook his head.

"I know of the Calderons, though," he said. "When I was a kid I went through the valley above Toyon. Where the big ranch was. I've forgotten what they called it—"

"King of Spain Valley," Hap Smith reminded him. "Likewise, King of Spain Rancho. Well, it's there yet."

"We lived down toward San Miguel then. My father sold some horses to the Calderons and I drove them up. I remember the big adobe house and the ruins of the old mission half way across the valley and a very elegant Spanish gentleman who reccived the horses and paid me and made me stay all night. Mr. Calderon, I suppose it was."

"Didn't know him," said Smith. "Dead before my time; dead more'n twenty year, I'd say off hand. Might be the man you mean is old Mentor:

13

Mentor Olivas. He runs the ranch and has run it a long time."

"Possibly," conceded Whitney.

"Goin' to visit the Calderons?" asked his questioner.

This time Whitney's ready smile broke through.

"Of course not; I don't even know them. In this roll which you're hauling for me I've got some blankets; the canvas on the outside is all the roof I'll be likely to need for a while and that only if it rains."

"Campin'," meditated Smith. "Kinda rushin' the season, Mr. Whitney. It ain't the middle of March yet and we're liable to get more rains." Again he examined his seat-mate with keen, squinted eyes, taking him in from the top of his soft gray hat to the soles of his shoes. "I guess you'll get acrost, though," he decided. "Wasn't always a city man, was you?"

"Born on a ranch; lived there until I was pretty close to sixteen." And then, not so much to switch the current of the conversation as to have a bit of information himself, he asked: "There's a store in Toyon, of course? I can get what odds and ends I need there, can't I? Camp stuff; frying pan, coffee, bacon?"

"You *can* get them things there," said Smith unenthusiastically. "Store run by a man name of Vogel." He spat contemptuously. "Me, I don't owe Vogel a bean, if pretty much everybody else does, and, me, I ain't got so many luxuries as I can afford to throw away what luxuries I do happen to have. One of 'em, first and foremost on *my* list is: My mouth's my own. Speakin' of buyin' things of A. Vogel: Don't take no change back or you'll never get the smell of it off your hands. He's a dirty skunk I wouldn't name a hound dawg after. You can buy things at Vogel's, yes. I do business with him because it's my duty I'm paid for by the United States government, him bein' postmaster, too. I take my bags and slam 'em down on his floor: I take up the mail bags I'm to fetch back to the railroad. But I don't say damn' your eyes to Vogel and I ain't said as much to him in nine years. Oh, yes, you *can* buy from A. Vogel."

"Guess I'll have to, this trip," rejoined Whitney.

"You'll pay enough," muttered Smith; and relapsed into a long silence. Whitney, glancing sidewise at him, observed that his mouth was clamped tight and his brows puckered over his squinting eyes.

When the stage driver spoke again it was with a return to his natural cheeriness. He talked of the rains; of the fine year promised the farmers who, it would seem, had suffered much of late from dry years. He explained how at this season, when the roads were bad and he had few passengers, he used the light buckboard instead of the heavier wagon. He offered Whitney a chew of Star tobacco and accepted a fat black cigar which he shoved

15

into his shirt pocket, promising to smoke it after supper. As they went along and the winding road crept upward among the steepening hills, he had many colorful scraps of information to give; he had been held up here one time by a bad *hombre*, an Indian named Felipe Moraga, only a year ago released from the penitentiary at San Quentin; a runaway had occurred there; his wagon had tipped over one winter day at a ford which today they made with no mishap, and his mail bags would have been swept away if he had not had the forethought to tie them in.

For the greater part, Whitney followed him interestedly, having no thoughts of his own to which he cared to cling. They drove through a pass in the hills, wound up a long muddy grade where the wagon wheels pulled heavily and coated themselves with adobe mud which thickened and thickened until at last from its own weight it fell away. On the hillsides were pines and oaks intermingled; the slopes were green with young grass growing lustily, sprinkled with blue and yellow field flowers; in level places were small fields of wheat and barley. Infrequently they saw a rancher's house set back from the road, old buildings for the most part and looking shabby and broken-spirited. Across barbed wire fences horses and cows watched them pass; an occasional herd of pigs rooted in the soft black soil.

"The country hereabouts hasn't changed much," offered Whitney.

"Changed?" Hap Smith lifted his brows. "It's been like this ever since I come here. No newcomers droppin' in to speak of; most of the old timers holdin' on. A few babies, a few folks dyin'. No, it ain't changed much. Good enough like it is, I guess. Strikes me, but I dunno, like some other places there's too much change goin' on."

Whitney nodded. He, too, was impressed by the thought that the country was good enough as it was. The clouds which had threatened an hour ago were drifting lazily away now, the sun poured more gold into the chalices of the buttercups, the smell of the grass was sweet in the air and the whole of the world about them, rimmed with fresh, clean hills, was steeped in peace and quiet. The only sounds across the vast silence, excepting the rattle of the wagon, were the occasional call of a quail and the faint singing of pine tops.

To one like Maxwell Whitney, resting from a long buffet with the strong currents of the active centers, such a land was infinitely soothing; it was the Lotus-land of the storm-tossed mariners; it was pervaded by an atmosphere which certainly had held on from the earlier Spanish days of large contentment; it was all that the American cities are not, hence the necessary complementary part to

17

make a perfect whole. It was easy to fancy, if you closed your eyes, that the little warm wind brought from afar the faintest of sounds of a distant, slow-ringing Mission bell. A cowbell maybe; maybe downright imagination; but certainly the hills and valleys were as if still asleep under the spell of old time.

Smashed all to fragments, broken financially like glass under a hammer—so he had put the case to himself and to his attorney. Naturally that was a consideration of vast significance, of an importance magnified by the habit of years, a matter which had its place somewhere in the man's mind during all his waking hours. But today, removed by so few hours from the accomplishment of the fact, already the consideration was thrust back from the fore of his thoughts, to lie shadowily on the rim of his consciousness, something without clear cut form though sinister, something tingeing his fancies rather than dominating them.

Whitney was not one given to introspective musings and analyses. There was a golden look to him. His skin had never lost the look of a country boy's; the golden bronze seemed lying just under the surface, lightly glossed over.

His health blessed him in many ways. It gave him a clear brain, a cheery, white-toothed smile, a hearty appetite, good sleep of nights, generous impulses by day. It brought him friendship. It afforded him vast funds of energy and endurance. In one guise or another it opened many doors for him.

The world is a very fine place for its young animals who take it as they find it.

CHAPTER III

THE ROAD INTO
KING OF SPAIN VALLEY

Toyon was a tiny flock of houses, rather than a town, lost there in the quiet world, and, like a flock of birds which had been dismayed by a circling hawk, it held its discreet silence as it hid itself away among the little hills. A couple of the buildings, old adobes, had the detached air of having flown away as far as the bend in the road; others, since the old Mission days, had quite fled away and disappeared, leaving behind them here a broken, fast dissolving wall, there a stone chimney, of no more importance in the eye of man or beast than so many handfuls of fallen feathers. Long ago Toyon had dreamed its dreams and danced to its own music and held its place in the young state as a link of the chain which was *El Camino Real*. Now even its memories were blurred and it heard but faint echoes of outside noises. Its one roadway, which no one ever thought now of naming the King's Highway, was deep in dust during the long hot summer and thick with black, sticky mud when it rained, a place given over to Toyon's many dogs, and the occasional ranch wagon or saddle horse. As the stage came in, bringing Max Whitney, there was no man, woman or child to be seen.

Down the empty road Hap Smith's horses, their ears pricked forward and their slack traces tightening at the first sight of the barn where they would be stabled, trotted straight to Vogel's store. Whitney marked the two buildings which they passed; one was Mrs. Dominguez' "hotel"; the other a blacksmith shop.

Vogel stood in the doorway of his house. Above him, painted by his own hand many years ago, was the all but illegible sign "Store & Post Office." The building itself had originally been a small adobe affair of two rooms. Vogel had added to it a shed-roofed adjunct which served him and his boy as kitchen, bedroom, living and dining room. Vogel himself was a dirty-looking man, small statured, perhaps sixty years old; he had a short, carelessly trimmed beard, a rusty black with some straggling lines of soiled gray; a low forehead over which crept a few straggling wisps of the same black and gray hair; a pair of shrewd black eyes.

He disregarded Hap Smith who, true to his word, threw down the mail bag without speaking.

20

But Whitney, being a newcomer, claimed all of Vogel's prying interest. He was seeking perhaps to stare through the stranger's eyes and his clothes, into his pockets.

Whitney's bundle thrown out, the stage driver drove off to the barn and Whitney followed Vogel and the mail bags into the store. Here was a rough counter with shelves behind it extending to the ceiling and well crowded with various sorts of homely merchandise; there were tinned goods, all of the cheaper variety, sides of bacon, hams, odds and ends of dry goods, even a few bolts of cloth, shoes, boots, overalls. There was also a six feet square space in the corner with a tiny window opening on the porch where Vogel had already dragged his mail bags.

"I wanted to get a few things," said Whitney. "I suppose you won't be long with the mail?"

Instead of answering him, Vogel called out shrilly, directing his voice toward the rear of the store.

"Henry! Hi, Henry! Get a move on, can't you?"

A tall, scrawny youth of nineteen or twenty, Vogel's boy-of-all-work, came in answer to the call. He looked at Whitney, ducked his head as Whitney greeted him casually, and dragged his large, thick-soled shoes across the bare floor to the corner devoted to the mail.

"Henry'll sort the mail," said Vogel. "I'll wait on you now. It ain't my way to keep folks waiting."

While Whitney bought this and that, such camping utensils as frying pan, coffee-pot, tin plates, cups, knife and can opener and spoons, such articles of food as coffee, bacon, sugar, salt and pepper, all of which he checked off of a list in a memorandum book, he made his lunch of crackers and cheese. He helped Vogel put the things into boxes. And, toward the end of the negotiations, he asked where he could hire a horse and wagon. He explained where he was going; somewhere at the farther end of the King of Spain Valley, in the hills clustering about the base of the Santa Lucia mountains.

It appeared that Vogel had only a horse and cart; that the Dominguez woman had an old mare and a ramshackle buckboard; Vogel said that the mare was thirty years old and the wagon likely to rattle to pieces.

"You'll go by the Calderon ranch house," said Vogel. "Someone comes in every mail day. It might be young Juanito; he'll come on horseback. Or it might be Vidal with the big wagon; old Mentor told me yesterday he would be sending Vidal for some supplies. He could haul you far as the ranch house and you could get a team there for the rest of the way."

It was Juanito who came first, racing up to the door on a fine red-bay colt, setting his mount up on all four sliding hoofs, throwing himself from the saddle to the porch with something of a flourish. For at least a suggestion of the extravagant went into everything which the gay young Juanito did or said or thought. Whitney, watching him enter with jingling spurs, could not entirely repress a smile. Not a smile of amusement, quite; Juanito did not so much amuse as he pleased. Were such occurrences permissible in the scheme of human events, one would have felt sure that he had skipped down through a generation or two, emerging direct from his own grandfather's times and making himself at home in this latter day. He was the one son of Mentor Olivas; he was twenty-one, and his heart would never be a day over twenty-one. He wore his loose black coat with an air; at the throat of his fine silk shirt was a fluttering scarlet tie; about his monstrously large black hat was a silver chased band and today, no unusual thing with Juan Olivas, a large rose was thrust into the bright buckle.

"It is Juanito Olivas," said Vogel. "He will tell you about a horse."

Young Olivas nodded pleasantly to Vogel and went to sit on the end of the counter while he rolled a thin cigarette with white rice paper. He nodded as pleasantly to Whitney and said a gentle-voiced, "*Buenas días, Señor.*"

"He don't talk Spanish, Juanito," offered Vogel. "He wants some stuff hauled up by your place. He's going—"

Whitney cut in for himself.

"Rather," he said, "I am going to ask permission of Mr. Olivas or of his father, to camp at the head of the valley. My name is Whitney; I am a stranger to you—"

Juanito jumped down from the counter and came forward, his hand out. His lean brown fingers closed firmly about Whitney's.

"It is one great pleasure, Señor," he said warmly, "to meet you. The Calderon lands are broad and fine; there are ten thousand spots for a man to camp, they are all yours." He waved his hand in a wide gesture. "For my father I speak as he would speak were he here."

It was all low music when Juanito spoke. And, weaving in and out among the English words, like a bright thread of another hue, was the intangible stress which indicated the Latin tongue; to his speech was given that which is not rightly an accent but rather a flavor. To designate Juanito's speech as flowery is to employ an apt figure. It was as though each word he spoke was an exotic blossom still steeped in its own fragrance.

"I told him," said Vogel, addressing Juanito, "that if Vidal drove in with the big wagon—"

But again Whitney interrupted, having no need of a go-between and little taste for Vogel's manner, that of suggesting that aid be given rather than of asking for information and then paying his way. But Juanito caught the case before Whitney had more than opened his mouth and said lightly:

"Vidal is coming. You will see him already from the door. He will bring Señor Whitney's boxes to the rancho. There we have what you please of wagons and horses; all kinds; you will choose. And one of the boys to help."

"I had planned," said Whitney hastily, "to have hired a horse and wagon here in Toyon."

Juanito laughed at him, understood that the stranger did not wish to seem to have presumed, and decided on the instant to like his new acquaintance. Juanito's great black eyes were always smiling when they were not wet with a sudden change of his quick emotions.

"I will help you with your things," said Juanito, "when that Nuñez *flojo* shall arrive. Nuñez will load on some other things for the rancho from Vogel here. Then you will ride with him. I will be first at the house and will tell my father that you will need a boy to go on with you."

"I had no intention," said Whitney, "of making a nuisance of myself." Again Juanito laughed.

Nuñez arrived, swaying upon the high seat of the big wagon, sent his four horses through a wide circle and slammed on his brake in front of the store. He was what Whitney would have had him in order to complete the picture; a Mexican whose strong white teeth glistened under his heavy, curled, black mustache, a slouching figure of a man who crawled down from his place as though he had all day for the thing and was already much wearied in body and soul.

The boy Henry finished with the mail; he and Vogel and Nuñez loaded on the heavy sacks of grain, the barrel of sugar, the flour and the several cases of groceries. Juanito drew on a pair of gauntlets which until now had drooped from a hip pocket, and gave Whitney a hand with his own things. Then he called for the mail, received a couple of papers and several letters, and swung up to the back of his red-bay mount.

"Wait a minute," called Vogel. "You didn't get the bill."

Juanito's horse was already dancing and fighting the heavy Spanish bit. The boy waved his hand carelessly.

"Another time, Vogel. You, Señor Whitney, I shall see again." He caught sight of Mrs. Dominguez at the hotel, a fat, swarthy Mexican woman, lifted his hat to her in a wide, graceful sweep and shot away, headed toward the mountains which stood a blue barricade against the western sky. Whitney climbed to the seat beside Vidal Nuñez, the brake was thrown back and they followed on the road which led into King of Spain Valley.

CHAPTER IV

A WELCOME TO
THE HACIENDA CALDERON

Now more than ever did Max Whitney experience the sensation of having stepped from one world into another, or of having found an ancient roadway amid romantic relics and vestiges of other days leading his willing feet backward against the flow of time and into an older order of things. Now did the bonds between him and the outside centers of commercial and financial endeavor strain almost to the snapping point. It was so hard to breathe the air of this still, sequestered valley and continue to harbor thoughts of dollars won and lost. For the King of Spain Rancho, than which there is none lovelier throughout the scope of the southern counties of California, is part and parcel of the past rather than of the present; it is a bit of the earth in which time itself has loitered, progress drowsed, so that today it would seem to belong to the day of the pastoral kings and mission fathers.

Half a mile out of Toyon, Nuñez stopped his horses and Whitney got down to open the gate across the road. There would be no other gate though the ranch house was still ten miles distant.

They went on, the horses trotting, the way leading up the gentle slope of the valley floor. Already was Toyon lost behind them. Scattered across the level lands, marching up the slopes, were ancient oak trees festooned in long streamers of gray moss which wavered like countless banners in the March wind. Shadows ran across the green meadow lands, cast by the clouds which again were gathering and darkening with rain. The little river which wound among willows, gushing from springs in the flanks of the Santa Lucias, augmented by the recent downpours in the mountains, flashed by glinting when the sun struck it, looking dark and ominous in the shadows, at all times reaching them across the stillness with its murmurous singing. Cresting the ridges to right and left were nut-bearing pines wherein gray squirrels quested and leaped, blue-gray flashes against the gray-green of the pine needles, wherein briefly paused the wild pigeons on their annual hungry flights. Along the roadway and in gay splashes of color here and there in the fields grew tall mustard stalks with bright yellow flowers through which black birds, many with red-spotted wings, flitted.

The wind in a sudden gust, sharp and chill, put a scurry into the fat drifting clouds and a few big, scattering drops of rain fell. Nuñez turned his head sidewise, like a bird, squinted upward and under his breath sang melodiously:

"Copa-ting-ting-ting-ting,
Esta noche va llover."

Whitney buttoned his coat collar about his throat and smiled; he remembered the lines of the stupid little song which announced with many ting-tings that "tonight it is going to rain." Then he considered seriously. He was still far from the spot where he meant to camp, the afternoon was drawing on and he knew the discomfort of pitching camp in dark and rain.

The sudden wind passed on and was gone, rustling through the oaks, singing through the pines; the clouds broke once more and let the golden sunshine sift through; the murmur of the little river grew insistent again and the mustard stalks now merely stirred as with a quiet breathing. A rainbow extended its triumphant arch, spanning the valley, based in the hills. Nuñez swore at his horses with Spanish oaths as pleasant sounding as caresses; the horses, to the last animal of them, shook their heads as though they understood and mildly disapproved; the big wagon creaked and groaned and rattled on, all of the little down slopes taken at a trot.

"Que bonito el mundo!" Nuñez exclaimed softly.

Whitney nodded and made no other answer where none was needed. Yes, the world was beautiful; especially beautiful here, where everything

29

was quite as it had come from the hand of God. The oaks which might have been cut long ago for wood and fence posts stood unmolested, inviolate. Long had the forests of the rancho been a pride of the Calderons. The river ran in its ancient course since none had lifted a hand to turn it aside into unsightly irrigation ditches. But few fences scarred the fresh purity of the landscape; but few necessary acres of the whole magnificent extent had been put under the plow. Here and there of necessity were grain fields, sturdy and vigorous spears already driving toward the sun. But one hardly noted them, so dominant were the original features of the valley, the wooded hills, the spreading oaks which dotted the fields themselves, about which the plows must detour. Now and then a small herd of cattle or horses; once a band of pigs. But only one head where ten might have grazed, just as there was one acre of land cultivated where ten might have been in labor to put gold into men's pockets. From end to end the valley gave the one outstanding impression that those who owned it had their thoughts set upon something else than getting richer than they already were; that the descendants of the older Calderons had a way of enjoying their princely estate without making it over into a commercial venture.

Whitney knew in advance that he would like these people, Calderons and Olivas. He had the index to their characters all about him as he rode with Nuñez; he counted on finding them large of soul, kind of heart, open of hand, simple and genuine of mind. In his present mood, that of a man wearied with the unsleeping stress and striving of the cities he found a rich contentment in everything about him. The ranch of the King of Spain was too beautiful to spoil and, thank God, no hand had been raised to profane it. The Spanish family which had owned it while still the native-born Indians hunted through its forests and which in an unbroken line of succession proudly called it theirs on well into the twentieth century loved to keep it as it had always been.

As an hour passed and as they crept ever deeper into the heart of the ranch Whitney found more and more evidences of yesteryear. He glimpsed the ruined mission down in the valley, its adobe walls crumbling wherever the sun-baked red tiles were missing and the rains washed down. Some columns stood intact, some arches spanned them outlining old corridors down which musing priests had strolled; fragments of outer walls indicated enclosures, garden plots, outbuildings where the scores of dark-skinned neophytes were housed. Olive trees, far older than any man or woman who came beneath them now, stood like messengers of peace in front of the august pile, their gnarled roots driving deep into the soft, rich soil, the hardy trunks thick with lichenous gray moss. Beyond the olives was what time had left of the old orchard; two tall pear trees, brought here as striplings from Castile, planted with tender care, stood like Baucis and Philemon, lacing their shadows across the broken walls. A grapevine, as thick as a man's thigh, spread its fruitful branches over an oaken trellis which was giving away with time and the growing weight it supported. Roses were already blooming in many a corner, the red roses of Castile, the yellow roses of Spain. As the wagon rattled around the last bend in the road a flock of a hundred pigeons rose, circled and disappeared beyond the ruin.

Here was another orchard, younger, planted only a generation ago. Already it took on the air of age. It was unplowed; thick grass and tall yellow mustard grew everywhere among the trees. Here was no trim, spick and span grouping of trees in mathematical rows, pruned to one shape that they might produce heavily in ultimate minted coins; here rather were ragged trees growing as they pleased, some with branches broken down by last season's yield, many already graying with lichens, all seeking unrepressed expression in a natural reversion to the ancestral type. They fitted into the same picture with their wild brethren of the rugged hills. They were the final word of the tale told of the Calderon distaste of commercialism. At least, so today did Whitney consider them and their silent message.

And then, crowning a gentle knoll, the old home burst upon them. Scarcely less ambitious in size than the vanishing mission, the Calderon home breathed spaciousness. Everything was ample—doors, windows, chimney stacks. The thick adobe walls, which had not been whitewashed recently, nevertheless gleamed whitely as the midafternoon sun struck them. The building recalled to Whitney a certain old De la Guerra home in Santa Barbara; he was certain of the shady patio though he could not see it; knew how the walls were not less than three feet thick and how they gave to the doorways through them a certain, indefinable, romance-pervaded atmosphere of a hundred years ago; knew that a man entering those venerable walls would feel for the first time and ever thereafter a strange, half-religious veneration for he knew not exactly what that had entered into the building from hands now long at rest. The most splendid oak tree which he had seen during the day's ride grew in front of the house. There was, at the side, a long grapevine arbor; near the grapes grew an ancient pear tree; beyond it some scattering olives. In little plots about the front of the house outlined by whitish earthenware bottles, sunk neck first, grew the homely, old-fashioned flowers; violets and pansies, rosemary and geranium and mignonette.

An old man, very erect, dressed in boots and black cloth, his hair, mustache and beard as white as his shirt front, stood upon the porch between two of the columns supporting the red-tiled roof.

"Mentor Olivas," said Nuñez.

He flung out his long whip with a crack over his horses' heads, wound up the gentle slope by the orchard and to the open level space near the house and stopped his team. Whitney climbed down over the wheel. Already was old Mentor Olivas coming to meet him.

His straight slender figure, too sinewy and hale to bend under the whitening years of sixty-five, was carried with that graceful dignity which is a birthright of his people; even his boots, as small and neat as many a fine lady's, assuring you that Señor Mentor still adhered to the use of the all but obsolete bootjack, harked back to a younger day.

His little chin beard was drawn to a needle point; his mustaches were nicely curled at the ends; the natural waves in his fine head of hair had been pampered. He was smiling; his eyes, like the eyes of his son Juanito, were bright with welcome. In his youth, one knew, he had been very splendid in costume and manner, he had kissed white hands inimitably, he had been followed by many soft eyes and softer sighs. He had perhaps serenaded under windows across which there were cruel iron grilles, he had carried in his breast a wilted flower long after the faded petals began to wither and fall; in his heart he still carried memories of flowers and moonlight and long dead señoritas. In a word, he was very elegant and very antique.

"Juanito told me you were coming," he said, and extended his hand. The skin was soft, yet under it there were quick, hard muscles.

"I had not meant to presume," said Whitney hastily. "I did count on your kindness in the matter of allowing me to camp somewhere among the upper hills of the ranch. But I expected to get someone in Toyon to haul my things."

Señor Olivas smiled and inclined his head in comprehension.

"Since our wagon was driving out anyway," he said, making nothing of the favor, "of course it would bring you this far. The rancho, *gracias á Dios*, is still large; I trust you will make yourself at home upon it. We do not see so many strangers here, Mr. Whitney, that it is not a pleasure to see new faces. You will come in?"

Whitney demurred.

"If you have a light wagon and horses to spare me for the rest of the afternoon—"

"At least you will come in for a little? Coffee is ready and I am alone."

"Gladly," said Whitney heartily, though since it still threatened rain he begrudged any time lost against getting himself settled for the night. "You are very kind."

Together they went up to the house while Vidal drove around to the rear. On the long porch were several chairs, a couple of old, rudely carved benches, a home-made, oak table.

Señor Olivas dragged chairs forward.

"When the pleasant days begin to come," he explained, "it is our custom to have coffee here. Josefa!" he called without turning. "We are ready, please."

His English was correct and exact and yet, like Juanito's was pervaded by the vague softness of the Spanish tongue. He did not say "leetle" when he meant "little"; not quite were his vocal cords to trick him into calling a sheep a ship or a ship a sheep, but his English words were indefinably different from the speech of the latter day American, much softened, more musical.

Josefa came with the tray and both she and her burden briefly held Whitney's attention. She was an Indian girl of sixteen or eighteen, her hair as black as night and straight, her skin dusky, her eyes hidden under her lowered lids and, when glimpsed, night-black and so shy as almost to be furtive. The tray in her slim brown fingers was as old as the pear trees in the yard and of heavy silver. Of silver and old, too, were the massive spoons, and the three-handled sugar bowl and tall cream jug.

Josefa set down her tray, shot one long, curious look at the stranger and slipped away. Within the house a voice spoke to her in Spanish, a woman's voice querulous and old; Josefa answered briefly; the house grew silent again.

"That is Señora Antonia Loreto," explained Mentor Olivas. "With us she is Tia Tonia—Aunt Antonia. She is an invalid; she does not drink coffee. It is bad for her."

Whitney appreciated the impulse which led the old gentleman to this much of the household's private affairs; the Olivas graciousness which held no courtesy above hospitality took care even in small things not to give the impression to a guest, though chance alone brought him, that he was an outsider.

They drank their coffee and smoked, Whitney offering his cigars which Olivas politely refused for a deftly made cigarette; they chatted pleasantly while their eyes roved down the valley, across the mission ruins. The younger man had also an eye for the march of the clouds; they dragged their shadows ominously across the meadows.

"Although you do not realize it, Señor," said Whitney, "we do not meet for the first time today. The other time was fourteen or fifteen year ago. I was a small boy and drove some horses to the rancho from my father's place down by San Miguel. I have never forgotten. Somehow that day you made me feel quite a grown-up man. Also you saw that I had something to eat before I started back."

"So?" said Mentor interestedly. "You drove up some horses from your father's place? San Miguel?" He had gathered his brows in seeking to recall so trivial an episode of so long ago. Suddenly his eyes brightened as he exclaimed: "Whitney of San Miguel! But, Señor, then your father was Benito Whitney?"

"Benjamin Whitney," nodded the son.

Old Mentor was on his feet, his two hands out, his eyes brighter than ever.

"But, Señor, I knew your father like a brother! I called him always Benito; me he called Don Diablo, making fun of something which happened long ago. He was killed; I know. A horse fell on him. I was sad, very sad, for I loved Benito Whitney who was a man of high honor, a gentleman always, one of *la gente.*—You speak Spanish then?"

"A few words. As much as any farmer's boy raised hereabouts must. If I have not forgotten it all here of late."

"*Seguro que sí,*" continued Mentor Olivas absently. He regarded Whitney with a fresh, frank interest, measuring the size of him, taking stock of the look in his eyes. At the end he slowly nodded his approval. "You are like Benito's son. Not only the man outside," he amended, "but the man inside. You are like him, no?"

"I'd like to be," smiled Whitney.

"It is going to rain," said Mentor abruptly.

38

"A moment ago I was about to offer you our hospitality for the night. Now," and his old eyes crinkled about the corners and lighted with one of his quick smiles, "I can speak differently, no? It is the son of an old friend and I have a duty, a responsibility. You must not be allowed to catch cold in camp on a night like the one we have coming. You will sleep here."

"But, Señor—" began Whitney.

Mentor laughed and waved aside all objections with one wide sweep of his arm.

"*Pero nada, Señor*," he countered. "A man who comes down here to camp in our woods has no such urgent business that he cannot postpone it a few hours to humor and oblige the old friend of his father. You will stay the one night if no more; you will come often and we will have coffee together and smoke and talk of your good father. You will see; we are not dull here. There is Juanito, my boy; he is gay always; he will play for you. There is a young man from San Francisco now visiting us, our lawyer, Señor Brooke Sheffield. You will meet him. You will meet Señora Antonia Loreto—Tia Tonia. You will meet Señorita Calderon. She, Teresa Calderon, will make you welcome when she comes in, as I do now in her place until then. She is riding now somewhere with Señor Sheffield. At supper we shall see them all. Come, I will show you our horses. We are proud of them here."

He caught a wide black hat from a peg in the wall near the door and led the way. Together they went to the corral behind the barn to look at the horses.

CHAPTER V

AN OLD WOMAN
AND A YOUNG GIRL

Though the rancho was unmistakably down at the heel, no matter how picturesquely so, here in the Calderon stud was the exception to the general condition. Mentor, as he and his guest leaned over the corral, pointed out with a childlike pride half a dozen young horses, any one of which would have drawn admiring eyes in a city park of a Sunday afternoon. Saddle animals, all of them, creatures of flaring nostrils and erect ears, of proudly lifted heads and intelligent eyes, of trim, glistening bodies, deep-lunged chests, thin and dainty forelegs.

The oldest of the lot, a noble black gelding with more than a drop of racing blood in him, was still four months distant from his seventh birthday; this was Mentor's favorite saddle horse, *El Tacano*, "The Rascal." The others ranged from two years and a half to six; all had been broken by Mentor himself or by his son, Juanito. Three were of the same deep red-bay color as the horse which Juanito had ridden into Toyon, and had the look of brothers; the remaining two were sorrels, both mares and both of the same strain.

"El Tacano," explained Mentor, "is the son of Dixie, whom I will show you someday; she is out on pasture now. She is a highborn lady; of the best Kentucky strain, from the old Pat Murphy stud. Tacano's sire is Black Prince. That means fine breeding for my little Rascal. There is no swifter horse in the county. He is all endurance and speed and intelligence."

"He has the look of it," answered Whitney. He recalled the days when, a boy, he had ridden whatever horse came to hand and always longed for such a mount as this. Or as any one of these!

There was a flurry in the corral; El Tacano shook his head, putting it low down to the ground and blowing through his wide nostrils, and the three red bays, shoulder to shoulder as though harnessed abreast, trotted toward the fence.

"Those fellows," added Whitney; "they're dead ringers to the horse your son rode today. There is speed in them, too, isn't there? And endurance and intelligence as well?"

Mentor smiled.

"*Pero, sí, Señor,*" he laughed softly. "I have said that we are proud of our horses! Those are all half-brothers of Juanito's horse, all out of Red Comet and each with a worthy mother. Would

41

you like to ride one of them with me? I believe," and his old eyes twinkled and the many little lines about them creased into traps for a humorous good nature, "that the clouds but gathered in order to lend weight to my invitation to stay with us tonight. Now that you have promised to do so—Look! It will not rain before night. I had thought of riding over to the Judge Belden place this afternoon. Or tomorrow, it is all the same. If you—"

"By all means," said Whitney heartily. "I'd like nothing better if you'll let me come along."

"Choose your horse then," said Mentor. "It is only four miles and we can be back before Teresa and the others."

Max Whitney felt, as he looked over the corral, that Mentor's twinkling eyes were still upon him, that Mentor was interested in seeing how he would estimate horses in a snap judgment, and sensed that in a tolerant sort of way he himself would be judged by the result of his decision.

Suddenly Whitney decided.

"That bay in the middle. I like the look of him."

Mentor clapped his hands.

"*Bueno*," he said delightedly. "That will please Juanito when I tell him. You have singled out *El Sol*. Juanito and Teresita together named him 'The Sun.' Juanito says he is a better horse than my Tacano. Juanito is a good boy and is no fool about horses, but here is one matter over which we quarrel. *Venga.* We will saddle and you are going to try him."

They went through the gate and the horses in the small enclosure pricked up their ears, flung aloft playful heels and scampered to the farther side. Mentor stepped in at the side door of the barn and came out with two coiled *riatas*, one of which, again with that pleasant twinkle in his eye, he gave to his guest. Again Whitney felt, though in his heart he knew it to be no disgrace if a man from the cities failed to drop his noose prettily over an alert head, that Mentor was trying him out. He accepted his *riata* with misgivings; he had not thrown a rope in more than a dozen years. Subconsciously, while he watched Mentor step out into the corral, his mind held the consideration: "What have I been doing all these years?" For, at the moment, the ability to capture his own horse and do the job with off-hand assurance, struck him as a more valuable accomplishment than being able to make ten dollars out of one.

Mentor, with the coil in his left hand, the loop dragging from his right, moved on. The horses fell apart at his approach. El Tacano appeared to realize that it was he who was being sought, drew back, came up with his rump against the corral, essayed a sudden dash across the enclosure. Mentor's loop rose from the ground, seeming inspired by its own volition rather than by the action of a supple wrist, widened as it rose, circled once only, became a large, slightly compressed capital O and with absolute precision fell about the defiant running neck. El Tacano snorted and came to a dead halt without awaiting the tension of the rope.

"I hope that when I am of your age I can do that," said Whitney.

Mentor chuckled as he led El Tacano away from the other horses.

"Your father, Benito, grew to be good with a rope," he said. "And, before you grow as old as Mentor Olivas you have many years for practice."

Whitney, not without misgivings, made his first throw. He had awaited his opportunity when El Sol had been separated from his fellows. But as luck had it just as his circling loop left his hand the other horses broke and ran, he missed the alert El Sol completely and his noose fell about the neck of one of the sorrels. Mentor's laughter at the result was as ready as a child's and had as little sting in it.

"If it had only been one of the bays that I caught," said Whitney jokingly, "I could have said that that was the one I wanted. But being a sorrel, that is literally a horse of another color."

Mentor looked at him sharply. He was as ready for joking as another but one did not jest about a point of honor; a gentleman did not lie, even in small things. But he saw the candid look in Whitney's eyes, knew that his guest would not have tried to avail himself of an accidental happening like the one suggested, and his smile came back.

Whitney removed his rope, patted the sorrel and let it go, and made his second attempt. This time his rope fell across El Sol's back, and the animal crouched like a great cat and slipped out from under it.

"I know what it is to be out of practice," said Mentor. "If you like, Señor—"

"Three times and out," laughed Whitney. "Give me one more shot at him and, if I make a clean miss again, I'll let it go for this time."

Mentor nodded. Whitney again drew in his *riata*, coiled it, made his loop and confronted El Sol. Because of a grim determination along with a certain modicum of skill gained in his boyhood, making the feel of a rope a familiar sensation, and added to these a bit of luck, this time he was successful and the tall red-bay gelding yielded to captivity and followed him docilely to the barn.

"*Muy bien*," said Mentor.

From several saddles hanging from pegs in the barn, with bridles slung over the horns, Mentor took down his own and indicated one for Whitney. Here again, as in the matter of horse-flesh, was the King of Spain Ranch particular; the saddles were of the type called Mexican, the leather select and carved tastefully, the horns of steel and at once graceful and serviceable. The bridles with their cruel-looking Spanish bits were fine with silver, the reins being either of soft black leather or of thin but stout round-plaited rawhide. The spurs, as bright and untarnished as any young knight's, with their musically jingling chains and silver buckles, were properly in keeping with the entire caparison. A saddle horse from the King of Spain Rancho, though seen fifty miles away, could be recognized by any knowing eye as a Calderon animal; first the look of the horse itself, then the order of its accouterments, made the identification unquestionable. Surely in its pride in its stable the Calderon household was within reason.

They mounted and rode down the slope into the valley road, Mentor swinging up and striking his saddle as lightly as his son had done. He saw the look in his guest's eyes.

"With us, Señor," laughed Mentor, "death strikes at the top first, as he does among the pines in the forests. I am white up here and my full sixty-seven years. But the heart is still young! And the feet—when Juanito plays *La Varsuviana* or *La Cachucha!*—they remember and dance."

The Judge Belden place, to which they were riding, he explained had originally been a portion of the Calderon lands. There had been two big holdings, joined by the late Señor Don Pablo Jose Antonio Maria Calderon; the original *Rancho del Rey de España*, consisting of eleven leagues or

46

forty-eight thousand acres, and the *Pajaro Azul*, or Blue Bird, rancho, of only sixteen thousand acres. These two ranchos, together, after the merger, were known as the King of Spain Ranch, and had been held intact until twelve years ago.

"At that time," said Mentor quietly, "we sold to Judge Belden a certain part of the Pajaro Azul, some eight thousand acres."

Whitney, glancing up at him quickly, his attention caught by a vague something different in the old gentleman's inflection, marked also the hint of a shadow in the musing eyes.

"Judge Belden until recently lived there," continued Mentor. "It is a fine place; there are big open meadows watered by the Pajaro Creek and also, lower down, by the river. There are some fine trees, oaks and pines, and the outlook is excellent. You will see the house in a moment."

"I have heard of a Judge Belden, formerly of Santa Barbara County."

"The same. A most admirable gentleman." Mentor sighed and added gently: "But the world has been hard with him. For two years he has been forced to live in the cities in order to have medical attention. He is no older in years than myself; and yet he is less young. About some gray hairs cares flock like ravens. He is not a very happy man."

They followed the wagon road up the valley for a mile before striking off into a trail across the grassy meadows leading toward the hills across the valley. Whitney marked everywhere a rich promise of feed for stock, and here and there a few head of cattle, looking fat and lazy. They forded the river where the muddy water widened and shallowed in a lazy bend, deep enough only to wash against the horses' bellies.

The Judge Belden house, hidden at first by a long, low ridge thick with a diversity of timber, appeared suddenly, crowning a slight knoll very much like that on which stood the old Calderon adobe. But in no other particular did a common resemblance exist. The Judge's home was a modern structure, in the style of the typical Southern California bungalow, a somewhat artistic superstructure of rustic timbers and rough log pergolas upon a foundation of brown field stone. The barn at the rear looked newer and altogether more square of corner and straight of line than the old Calderon barn, the fences were of tauter wires upon more generally vertical posts. In a word, the Judge Belden place, in so far as the handiwork of man upon it went, had not yet existed long enough in this land of indolence to acquire the untidy picturesqueness of age.

"That the Judge should not worry about the conduct of affairs here during his absence," said Mentor, "I have been accustomed to ride over once a week; he knows that today, unless something has prevented, that I will be passing through his gate, and that if not today, certainly tomorrow. He has left a most excellent man in charge, his old foreman, Pedro Valenzuela. But I feel that it is a gratification to him to know that his old friend Olivas keeps an eye open."

They turned into the Belden roadway, now grass-grown from two years' disuse, and galloped up the slope. In the foothills were browsing cattle, probably a hundred in all. Before reaching the house they skirted the young orchard, some ten or fifteen acres of eight or ten year old trees looking sprucer than the Calderon trees though not recently pruned. Then the driveway split to encircle the house, bordered with young orange and lemon trees. The rose garden was a tangle, grown high in wild oats.

Returning by another trail, they pushed on into the hills at the upper end of the Belden ranch, rode among the cattle, found a trail winding among live oaks, and came out upon the top of the low ridge shutting this property off from the larger valley. Here Mentor reined in to indicate to his companion the view of the long sweep of King of Spain Valley with the mission and the Calderon home standing out boldly under the late afternoon sun.

"We of King of Spain Valley love this view of it," said Mentor.

From where thcy sat their horses the ridge, thick with timber, ran down to the valley which stretched away, mile after mile, in slightly rolling, rich, velvety lands, brilliantly flooded with sunlight. A drowsy silence filled the valley and made the world seem a place of quiet peace. On all sides the hills with their groves of oaks and pines shut out the outside world. The old adobe house, the crumbling mission, gave significance rather than dissonance to the serene solitudes.

"Teresa shall show you the picture painted at this spot by an artist priest who came here from Spain in the first mission days," said Mentor. "In our eyes that painting is very precious; we are prouder of it than of anything else, I think. For it has its history and it has its part in our lives. A duplicate was sent by the father of Teresa's father to the King of Spain. And the king was much pleased and sent a royal letter back to Señor Calderon in which he said, 'Were I not a king but a man who might wander, I would cross the ocean to California to dwell in your valley.' "

"And so you call it, from the king's letter, King of Spain Valley!"

"*Si, Señor*," said Olivas.

As they rode slowly homeward through the fringes of dusk and lengthening shadows Whitney marked that Señor Olivas lapsed often into silence, that he appeared preoccupied. He, too, spoke little for after all in the country day's ending is a time of hush, of human voices stilled into silence or dropped to slow quiet monotones, the hour given over to the singing creatures of the grass whose shrill notes are like bright needles weaving in and out through the diaphanous fabric of the hour, stitching the lacy dusk to the embroidered garment of the advancing night.

"The Judge is going to sell the Pajaro Azul," said Mentor abruptly, and Whitney had the definite clue to the somber meditation. "He regrets the necessity; we regret the calamity. It is our hope that the old place may fall into hands such as his—rare hands in these days."

While he was speaking they saw the first light down the valley.

"It is Josefa hanging out the lantern," explained Mentor and they broke into a gallop. "It is an old custom with us." As though the tiny glow had kindled its counterpart in his breast he spoke again cheerfully. "It gives a look of brightness and happiness, *no, Señor*? If a stranger were passing, belated and in need of shelter, it would be good to see. Also, you and I know that supper is ready."

When Señor Olivas and Whitney, having left their horses with Vidal at the stable, stepped on the porch where the lantern hung, the house within was but dimly lighted. The big dining room, into which they looked directly, but half retrieved from darkness by the one coal-oil lamp suspended from the ceiling, was peopled with shadows which shifted eerily. They entered. That there was no one in the room was Whitney's first impression. Then, as Señor Olivas led him forward for the first introduction, he noted the wheel-chair drawn back a little from the square window, and its occupant who turned quickly at their tread.

"Tia Tonia," said Mentor gently, "here is an old friend. It is the son of Benito Whitney of San Miguel."

She was a very little, very old, terribly emaciated woman whose burning bright eyes peered upward into Whitney's face. Even though now the lamp light fell directly upon the withered features he could read in them no expression; they were as void of any sort of animation as those of a mummy. Her eyes, where alone there was life, appeared less windows of the soul than pits in which flickered smoldering fires of some inner conflagration. Here was one, thought Whitney immediately, who lived with her memories alone, memories which consumed her, over whose fires she was used through the long hours to bend her hidden spirit and which in the end of time would leave to her only, in a little heap, the white ashes of despair.

Tia Tonia stirred slightly and put out her hand, much fine black lace falling away from a frail, thin wrist. The hand was cold and for the instant that it lay in Whitney's was as inert as a hand of carved ivory, offering itself lifelessly, making no effort to respond to his clasp, withdrawn and folded again with its fellow on her lap. About her pinched face fell the loose folds of an antique black *riboso*. Her lips moved and Whitney heard but indistinctly a few words in Spanish which he accepted as a conventional acknowledgment of the introduction. She withdrew her eyes from his face, plainly unconcerned with his presence; her interests were without young tendrils to cling to new things.

He felt his dismissal and drew back; his eyes marked the old-world environment into which he had stepped.

He had known in advance what the interior of the house would be like but, even so, its individuality presented a charm not dulled but stepped up by anticipation. The whole establishment created in the mind an impression of the faith of the padres, the largeness of the Spanish heart, the wide generosity of the men who had builded, the romantic spirit of their age—all of these ghost-images in slow procession like monks with cowled faces stirred noiselessly or stood still at his elbow. No one stood out distinct and prominent; the message of each was confused with that of the others; but together the impression was harmonious and eloquent.

The quick gay laughter of Juanito Olivas sent all these fancied shadow shapes scurrying. Juanito and two others were coming into the room. He saw

Whitney and came forward impulsively to shake hands. Then he stepped aside, yielding place to his father in the privilege of making Whitney known to the others, saying only a pleasant and respectful, *"Buenas tardes, papá."*

"Teresita," Mentor was saying, "here is an old friend. He is the son of my best good friend Benito Whitney of San Miguel. Mr. Whitney, my ward, Señorita Teresa Calderon."

After having only a moment ago met Tia Tonia, now to meet Teresa Calderon! It was to have looked through ancient eyes into a heart whose fires were yielding to ashes and then to be confronted by a young breast in which white and pink rosebuds were swelling. It was to have stepped from the tragedy of sorrowful age into the presence of that bright land of faery which is girlhood.

The touching of hands, as Señorita Calderon greeted her guest, so soon after he had held the hand of Tia Tonia in his own, did nothing to lessen his impression of the contrast. Instead of coldness and bony fingers he had to do with warmth and a friendly pressure in return for his own which were definitely pleasant.

Behind Miss Calderon came a young man, nonchalantly awaiting his turn in the ceremony of introduction, who was doubtless the San Francisco guest whom Mentor had mentioned. He was perhaps thirty, slender, neat in the conventional gray outing suit, his plaid cap in his hand, his glistening puttees showing to the world the outward seeming of a well-shaped calf; a man as unmistakably of the cities as was the adobe room in which he ill-fitted a product of a pastoral people. At a first glance Whitney marked the puttees, a tiny light-brown mustache and a pair of keen, purposeful eyes.

"Mr. Whitney," Teresa Calderon said, "this is Mr. Brooke Sheffield. Mr. Sheffield," she explained, "is our lawyer."

"Only that?" challenged Sheffield when the two men had shaken hands. Teresa laughed; Whitney did not catch her bantering reply; they all went to the table. Juanito was first at Teresa's chair, drawing it back for her, making her a little bow in return for her nod of thanks; something in the manner in which the courtesy was extended and accepted bespoke long custom. Then Juanito ran to Tia Tonia—it did not appear that those feet of Juanito Olivas had ever learned or ever could learn to walk like other men's—and rolled her chair to its place. Already, when he sat down, Josefa was serving.

"*Pobrecita Tia Tonia,*" said Señor Olivas gently in Whitney's ear while Juanito was bringing her. "She is not merry, but God understands; if she is silent, Señor, you will forgive her? She has not walked for twenty years when she had a bad fall; not a step. One grows sad like that; it is like being a life prisoner."

Presently Whitney found himself watching Teresa Calderon and listening whenever she spoke. In her speech was that same quality which marked Juanito's. She could never achieve the harsher Anglo-Saxon sounds simply because her birthright of a Latin tongue forbade. There was that liquid and caressing tone when she spoke which is utterly Spanish.

She was like two girls at once, he thought; he could fancy her having an ancestress who was very grave, very demure, who kept her eyes lowered under long lashes, who had given her that magnolia white skin and that blue-black hair; who, perhaps, in more than one deep religious moment thought to forsake the world for a nunnery; and he was sure that there was another ancestress who had bequeathed to Teresa Calderon the ripe red of her lips, the sparkle of her eyes, that manner of looking at a man as though she were coming forth to be friendly and then laughing a little and drawing back; that tender, haunting music of her voice.

Josefa placed the glasses of red wine and withdrew to the kitchen to whisper with the old Indian woman, Uracca, her grandmother, who aided with the cooking; Mentor explained how for many years the King of Spain grapes had filled the cellars; Whitney listened and at the same time marked how in the household drama there was at once the obvious and the veiled. It was very obvious that Brooke Sheffield was interested in Teresa; several times he cut into what another was saying to address her, always with his eyes flattering and his voice taking on the quality of excluding all but her from what he had to say. It lay on the surface that Juanito's gaiety was clouded by Sheffield's attentions; that Juanito adored Teresita and was just the one to consume his merry soul with fiery jealousy, no matter how imaginary the cause. One need not look a dozen times to see that Teresa knew this quite well and had no objection to the little comedy running on. For the sheerest of comedy it was since Juanito, who thought to cast himself for the tragic figure, was the gayest of them all.

CHAPTER VI

THE TREASURE BOX

"Look," said Teresa. A long ray of yellow light reaching through the window lay across the begonia leaves. "The clouds have passed and the moon is out. Will you have your cigar with Padre Cipriano?"

Mentor, whom she addressed, nodded. Padre Cipriano was the old pear tree in the garden, named in memory of him who had planted it so many years ago, and Señor Olivas with the coming of the fine evenings had the habit of pacing up and down between the pear tree and the olives or of sitting upon the garden bench, while he had his *"buenas noches"* cigar. Teresa got up and brought the box from the smoking table in the corner; Señor Olivas handed it to Whitney and Sheffield before taking his own. Juanito was already making his white paper cigarette.

"We have not had so fine a night for a month," remarked Señor Olivas from the window. "It would be wrong to stay indoors and not taste it. Señor Whitney," he smiled, "perhaps your coming to us brings us good fortune since you bring us so fine a night."

"Mr. Sheffield brought us a big storm," said Juanito quickly. "Rain and cold wind."

Sheffield laughed easily at the innuendo.

"Rain makes your pasture lands and grain fields green," he answered lightly. "All that will put money in your pockets later on. There are times when storms are better than sunshine."

Juanito shrugged.

"Money is not everything," he retorted. "And sunshine makes the little flowers open in the grass. Also, an empty pocket is not so bad when one has a full heart."

"You speak after a hearty meal," said Sheffield. "Do you not confuse the heart with the stomach, Señor Juanito?"

He was immensely good humored in his

bantering but in Juanito's cheeks there was a faint dark flush. Teresa interrupted them, saying:

"While we are outside, tasting the moonlight, will you play for us, Juanito? Your new piece?"

Juanito's flush deepened but was now eloquent of pleasure which made his expressive eyes mistily bright. Mentor and Whitney strolled toward the open door; after them came Brooke Sheffield chatting with Teresa. They went down the long veranda and to the spot where under the arms of Padre Cipriano, outflung as in benediction, was the bench, a twin to that against the wall on the porch. The moon, though not at the full, filled the valley with its subdued splendor; in the meadows the mission ruin, surrounded by the shadows of their own walls and the trees about them, gave its mystic touch to the spell of a fragrant night. There was never a cloud in all the starry sweep of the sky; grass and flowers and trees, their leaves still wet from the day's showers, glistened and twinkled as the faint evening breeze stirred them softly.

Juanito appeared on the porch wheeling out Tia Tonic's chair, his violin under his arm. The old lady sat in the moonlight, her still hands in her lap. Juanito lifted the violin to his shoulder, tuning softly and swiftly. You knew when he was ready to play by the sudden gesture into which his whole being seemed to enter. With a jerk he threw back his head so that his long black hair was tossed back like a mane; at the same time he bent forward a little and threw up his bow-arm. Then came the first of the brilliant notes which, even here in the open, were full and rich.

It was Juanito's "new piece."

Whitney, who knew no great deal of music, knew only that Juanito was not the one to confuse his stomach with his heart and that it was now his heart singing through the bow and the strings, leaping with the notes which seemed to reach out groping for the stars, dancing with the quickened measures, sighing and singing again. He filled the night with a delirium of joy; he hushed a string to a murmur of regret. He drew a mood from the music; it passed into his blood, it blossomed at his fingertips; he made it his own and transferred it across the stillness into other hearts.

When he had done with a swift sweep of the bow and stood as rigid as if his own magic had charmed his body into stone, Whitney heard old Mentor's deep sigh and a quick gasp of delight from Teresa. They were all clapping their hands, he with them. He saw Juanito bow deeply as he might have bowed to a triumphant applause of a concert throng.

Then the boy tossed back his hair again and set the violin strings to laughing, flirting with melody, dancing through the refrain of a little ballad.

"It is the air of *Teresita Mía*," laughed Señor

Olivas. "Now he plays alone for Señorita Calderon!"

"He plays wonderfully," exclaimed Whitney. "And that violin—"

"Sí, Señor. It is not everyone who can play like my little Juan. The violin? It was Teresa's grandfather's; it is very old and those who know say there are few like it."

They called "Encore!" but Juanito shook his head. Besides, he explained, it was too cold for Tia Tonia; she did not feel well and, if they would excuse her, would go to bed now.

"And I," said Brooke Sheffield, "must get a couple of letters written in answer to some which came today." He drew from his pocket some letters and showed how they remained unopened. "What say you, Olivas," he added jocularly, "of a young lady who makes a man forget his important mail?"

He clapped old Mentor upon the shoulder, nodded to Teresa and went off to the house, the letters in his hand. Already Juanito was wheeling the chair in through the front door; they could hear him calling to Josefa to come to Tia Tonia.

For a little while the three under the pear tree were silent. Señor Olivas paced up and down, his hands clasped behind his back, his cigar smoke rising serenely through light and shadow. Whitney stood looking out across the valley while Teresa seated herself upon the old bench and, with a light shawl thrown over her hair, was enwrapped in the mysteries of her own reflections.

Even that bench, in character with the various appointments of the house and garden, had its history. Señor Olivas, coming presently to stand with one hand resting on its back, began to tell his guest something of it; twin to the one on the porch, it was a relic of the mission. The fathers had taught the Indians, Uracca's people, forefathers of Josefa, the homely, useful arts. This had been made by one of the more intelligent workers under the supervision of Padre Cipriano himself. If Señor Whitney but stooped closer, even in this light, he could make out the carvings. Teresa moved a little—

From the house burst a shrill scream. Teresa jumped up and Whitney marked how wide her eyes had flown open. Mentor whirled and started toward the house. Already, however, Whitney was before him, running. He had never heard a cry like that one which, though unrepeated, still rang in his ears; he did not know if it were an utterance of terror or of anger or of pain. He did have time to wonder if something had happened to Josefa or to the old Indian woman in the kitchen. Oddly, he did not once think about Tia Tonia.

In the dining room was Tia Tonia's chair— empty. There was an open door, a white bedroom beyond it, another open door to a second bedroom.

It was in this second room that he saw what looked like a black bundle on the floor.

Though he paused but briefly, Señor Olivas and Teresa Calderon were at his side. The three went on; old Mentor stooped, went down on one knee and lifted the frail bundle in his arms.

He looked up at them with a white, startled face. "Tia Tonia!" he said like a man dazed. "Dead!"

"Tia Tonia!—Dead!" Teresa repeated after him.

"See," said Mentor excitedly. "Tia Tonia who has not set foot to floor in long years, has run this far herself! Thirty steps, forty steps! Into her own room! And is dead!"

"Look!" exclaimed Teresa suddenly, in a queer, hushed voice.

She pointed to the window near which stood Tia Tonia's little table. The table was half toppled over, leaning insecurely against the wall. The few books on it were all awry.

"Tia Tonia's *Cajon de Tesoros* is gone!"

"You mean that someone has robbed the room?" said Whitney. "Someone has taken her Treasure Box?"

He went swiftly to the window and looked out. There was only the empty garden with the moonlight sifting through the shadows. He turned and saw both Juanito Olivas and Brooke Sheffield burst into the room, their faces looking startled.

Queerly enough both men carried something in

63

right and left hands; Juanito his bow and violin, Sheffield a letter and a pen.

"Outside, quick!" called Whitney. "Someone has robbed the room. He can't have gotten off yet."

He went out the shortest way, through the window. As he did so he heard Teresa's frightened voice:

"Juanito! In the closet! There is someone there! I saw the curtain move!"

The closet was but a recess in the wall behind a curtain. Juanito ran across the room and whipped the curtain back so that it came away in his hands.

Inside was Josefa.

She came out, her head lifted, her lips a tight line, her eyes already blazing defiance as they swept the faces about her.

"Josefa!" cried Juanito.

"I was fixing her bed," said Josefa. "I saw a man slip in at the window. I was afraid and hid."

"Who was it?" demanded Juanito sharply.

There was the briefest of hesitations before the Indian girl answered, but a hesitation marked enough to make them all believe she lied when she said curtly:

"I do not know."

Mentor gently placed the wasted body of Tia Tonia on her bed. Then he and Whitney and Juanito and Sheffield went to make a fruitless search of the gardens and outbuildings.

CHAPTER VII

DEATH STRIKES
OUT OF THE SHADOWS

When again figures approached the carved bench where Padre Cipriano cast a thin pool of shadow it was as though this were not the same night but another which had descended upon the *Rancho del Rey de España*. The air seemed stiller than before; perhaps the faint night-breeze had fallen off, perhaps the hush was but bred of the new stillness in the bosoms of those who were suddenly reminded that life itself is a mystery whose solution lies in that other mystery, death. Down among the mission ruins a little owl lifted its small, weird cry timidly through the immensity of the silence; when it ceased, the hush was as deep as infinity; when it called again the notes were as soft, as plaintive as those of a mourning dove. It might have been the uncertain cry of a lost spirit, dazed by the suddenness of transition from a material into an immaterial sphere. . . . They had not heard the tremulous notes until just now.

Again Mentor Olivas paced back and forth between the olive tree and the pear tree. His hands were behind his back, his head was bowed save when, now and then, he stopped and lifted his sober eyes to the sky as though seeking to read something among the stars. Max Whitney, sitting motionless on the bench, listened to the owl, waiting during its silences for a repetition of the cry. A little way from him sat Juanito Olivas; on the boy's cheek was the crystal gleam of tears.

"*Pobrecita Tia Tonia*," said Señor Olivas thoughtfully. "Poor little thing. Not to have walked in all these years—then all of a sudden to jump up, to run into the arms of her death like a girl running to wrap herself about in her lover's cloak. It is sad, Señores. And it is strange."

"All these years," said Juanito, his voice quiet with that awe which death creates in all breasts but most of all in the breasts of the young, "you have smiled at Tia Tonia's secret box. Now, because of it, she is dead!"

Mentor resumed his slow pacing. Juanito sat shrouded in the gloom of his meditations. Presently he spoke again, his hushed voice taking on a new quality of bitterness.

"The man who robbed Tia Tonia, killed her," he muttered. "He is a murderer."

"No man laid hand on her," said Mentor gently. "She was spared that violence, my son."

"The violence of hands at her throat, *sí, Señor*," cried Juanito. "But not that of a hand tearing her heart out! For her treasure box held everything

66

that she loved; her heart has lain there for many years."

He turned to Whitney, with an agitation which arose from sources which could not fail to move the soul of such as Juanito.

"That box, Señor," he said softly, "is, to you, nothing. But you are a friend; God has brought you among us when this horror happens." Impulsively he put his hand on Whitney's knee; frankly he lifted his wet face. "In twenty years but two persons other than poor Tia Tonia have glanced into it. One was Teresita when she was a little girl; she remembers. One was I, not meaning to pry, only last year when I startled Tia Tonia, running in on her to tell her something—what it was I forgot when I saw the box open. A little box, not so large."

He indicated with his hands held first some ten inches apart for the length, then separated by less than half that distance for the width.

"And in it, I saw—what? Some letters, old and yellow; something which might have been a rose when Tia Tonia was a young girl; a lock of black hair. A man's hair," he barely whispered, his romance-imbued soul weaving the tender vision of an old love story. "When tonight she saw a hand stretched out for that, Tia Tonia ran again, as papa says, like a girl. When it was lost to her, what was left? She died. What man would rob her like that? And why?"

"But, my son," Señor Olivas reminded him, "tongues have wagged in mouths of those who have not seen as you and Teresa have seen. Idle tongues making mysteries and mischief. There are those who have thought that there was gold in that box. Or, better than a mere handful of gold, a certain paper—"

"Yes," said Juanito eagerly. "That is so! And," he added thoughtfully, "perhaps, among the yellow letters, there was that paper? *Quien sabe*?"

"He who stole it knows now," replied Mentor. "If he can read, which I doubt! And if there is such a paper—which I doubt very much more."

Juanito started up, caught by the insinuation in his father's words that the box had been stolen by one who could not read.

"You know who it was?" he demanded. "You have a suspicion?"

Mentor hesitated, then shook his head.

"The words came when I should have been silent," he answered. "I have no right to think them, Juanito. It is a crime to suspect a man simply because—"

"I know!" cried Juanito. "You think it was Filipe Moraga! You are right! He would do that!"

He began running toward the house. But Señor Olivas, a certain sternness in his voice, checked the flying footsteps with a curt command. Juanito returned though reluctantly.

"But you were right!" insisted Juanito. "We have

forgotten Moraga's past; we have taken him back. And then he does this! Oh!" The boy clenched his hands and his voice trembled. "It is a duty we have before us. Why do you call me back?"

"I had not the right to speak," said Mentor calmly. "It was wrong of me. It may not have been Moraga. Now, as I think of it, I feel certain that it was not. We have befriended him; he is not without gratitude—"

But in Juanito's shining eyes shone unshaken conviction.

"Josefa saw!" he said excitedly. "She hid, not from the thief, but from us rushing into the room. And she would not tell! Why? Josefa has a lover and that lover is Felipe Moraga!"

To Whitney, when the name was first spoken between them, it had a shadowy familiarity. Suddenly he remembered; the stage driver had told him of a robbery, of a man named Moraga who had gone to the penitentiary for the offense. He, with Juanito now, wondered at Mentor's tarrying instead of hastening to accuse the ex-convict.

But, whereas in both Whitney and Juanito there were the heady impulses of youth, in Mentor Olivas there were those qualities of greater dispassion which are commonly attributes of white hairs.

"I regret having voiced a passing thought," said Mentor, though in the moonlight his face looked uncertain. "It was unjust and unkind of me; you will forget, Señor?"

"At least," answered Whitney, "I leave everything, where it belongs, in your hands."

Señor Olivas inclined his head gravely and moved away to resume his steady pacing back and forth. Whitney knew just how many steps he would go, how he would pause a moment, how he would turn, just how many paces before the next pause, the next turn. Juanito, playing a silent tattoo upon the back of a still clenched fist with the nervous fingers of the other hand, frowned at the ground, restive under the restraint of his father's command to inactivity. When he could hold his tongue no longer he burst out:

"But think! Mother of Christ—Only think! In there lies poor Tia Tonia alone, helpless, stricken down; and somewhere through the night goes Moraga—"

"Or another," interrupted his father firmly. "It may be another, Juanito."

Juanito sprang up, vibrant.

"What matter *who?* It is someone who slips away with all that Tia Tonia clung to in life! Her little box—Why, it is sacred! It should be buried in the same grave with her. And we do nothing, we who surely she would have thought—"

"Juanito," responded Señor Olivas gently, "you will remember that we have not been entirely idle. We have searched all about the house and barns. A moment, my son," and he lifted his hands as Juanito was about to interrupt. "I have been indiscreet enough to mention Felipe Moraga. You will forget that I have done so. It would be very unkind, if he is innocent, to set tongues wagging. In the meantime, however, I will be sure to have a word with him. Will you bring me a horse?"

"But, is it not for me—"

"My son," and Mentor's voice, without being lifted, grew very stern. "It is for me."

Juanito bowed and turned away. They saw him going swiftly toward the stable.

"When a man has made one mistake in life," said Olivas, "we are too ready to find him guilty of whatever happens. Felipe Moraga has done wrong before now, but in his heart he is not a bad boy. If he has done this, greedy for gold, he will be sorry and will tell me and give back poor Tia Tonia's little treasures."

Whitney with no part to play in the matter sat without answer.

"Señor," Olivas said thoughtfully, "since it has happened that you were with us at such a time—"

Whitney rose and said quickly:

"There has hardly been the opportunity to speak with you since your kinswoman's death. If there is anything which I can do to make myself of service—and I am afraid that there is not—If I could borrow a horse I would ride back to Toyon for the night."

"There need be no talk of going," said Mentor. "Unless you prefer? But—From the heart, Señor, I should like you here."

He spoke genuinely; his next words gave Whitney a clue to the thought which had shaped an invitation almost into an entreaty. Mentor said slowly,

"I shall ride for a word with Moraga. I may be gone several hours. I have given him a little cabin at a far part of the rancho." He pointed toward the hills into which the upper end of the valley was broken, the hills seeming to lie at the foot of the Santa Lucia mountains. "He is cutting wood there and mending fences. While I am gone there is Juanito left; Juanito is a good boy, the best in the world, but he is so young, so quick! Of course there remains Señor Brooke Sheffield. But—"

He hesitated; a certain fine, almost childlike, simplicity was never more apparent in old Señor Olivas than just now. To Whitney, with no wish to pry into the old man's heart, it was nevertheless as though the innermost thought of Mentor's mind was a white stone to be seen clearly in the depths of a clear pool.

"I shall stay very gladly," said Whitney.

"You speak of Tia Tonia as my kinswoman," said Señor Olivas. "She is not that. She is a Loreto, the last of her line, a third cousin of Señor Calderon, father of Teresa. I have in me no

72

blood of the Calderons, but am distantly related to the family of Teresa's mother.—*Pobrecita* Tia Tonia," he continued amusingly. "There are sad little lives, Señor; hers was one. Her poor box of treasures, as Juanito has said, that was all that she had. And what was it but a sad memory? Once into her life came love, one of those terrible and beautiful loves which make gay spots and black burnt-out spots in Spanish lives. One man only did Tia Tonia love when she was a young girl; him has she loved always. And when her destiny ruled that he look elsewhere, marrying gaily under Tonia's eyes, never marking all she offered him, she turned old in a day."

Juanito came up with his father's horse and the gallant old gentleman mounted and rode away.

"I should have gone with my father," said the young man gloomily. "Moraga will lie to him; Moraga might even kill him. Men do anything for gold."

"But you have told me yourself," objected Whitney, "that the treasures were merely those of sentiment. Letters, a rose—"

"If that were all!" exclaimed Juanito. "But, though others laugh and pretend to disbelieve, I know there is gold hidden somewhere on the rancho. And in my heart I know that that was Tia Tonia's secret. Why did she keep the secret all these years; why did she hold her silence even when we were forced to sell the Pajaro Azul? Who knows, Señor, the throbs in a woman's heart? Come, sit here with me and I will tell you of wonderful things."

CHAPTER VIII

A TALE OF VANISHED GOLD

"You will understand, Señor," began Juanito circumstantially, "that in the good old days of Teresita's father there were not banks everywhere in California and that many men, even when the banks came, preferred to keep their own money in their own hands. Of such was Señor Calderon. *Bueno*! When he dies, where is his treasure chest? No one knows for it has never been found!"

He made the announcement triumphantly as though to say: "What more would you have? That proves it, *no*?"

Whitney hid his smile.

"But certainly," he objected, "Señor Calderon would have told."

"Ah," cried Juanito. His assurance was but the more triumphant. "But how did Señor Calderon die? You have not heard that! Well, it is I who am going to tell you. And, mind you, Señor, I am not being indiscreet; Juanito can be as close-mouthed as Vogel himself when need be. What I tell you everyone knows; Vogel knows; Moraga knows; the latest corner to the valley and the oldest resident know. These things are in the wind which blows across the old mission there; they are in the whispering of the grasses and the singing of the birds and the shine of the sun. Come, Señor; look back with me, through my eyes, and see what happened:

"I am a little boy, five years old; but I remember. Teresita is not so old, about four; she does not remember. It is one fine day; the summer is beginning. It is one fine afternoon. Tia Tonia is not an invalid at this time; she is an old woman though. Ever since I can remember she is an old, very sad woman. She is on the porch, standing, looking down into the valley where the shadows are beginning to run down from the hills. I hear her scream; that is what makes me remember this day so well, I think. It is a scream like her last one; never for a man or a child to forget.

"She had seen what happened; perhaps she was looking for his return? It was Señor Calderon riding home. He, the finest rider in the world, was killed by a horse. That happens, Señor. He was galloping, sitting loosely in the saddle as was his custom. Behind him he heard someone call; it was one of his Indian *vaqueros* of whom there were many in those days on the King of Spain; the Indian called out about some trifle, maybe a broken fence or a strayed steer. Señor Calderon

75

turns in the saddle. At that moment his horse gets a foot down into a squirrel hole and falls and Señor Calderon, with an answer in his throat to the *vaquero* behind him, is thrown over his horse's head.

"No; Tia Tonia is no invalid then! You should see how she runs! I am afraid. You know how it is, Señor, with a little child, not many days from God; he feels things which other people do not, like a dog at night about the old graveyards. I do not know at my five years of age what death is but I know it has come. Tia Tonia runs down into the valley; when the *vaquero* is stooping over the fallen Señor Calderon, Tia Tonia is already at his side. I see Señor Calderon with her arms about him; I see him struggle to sit up; I see her cry out to the Indian to ride for my father.

"Does Señor Calderon speak? *Quien sabe ahora, Señor*? Only Tia Tonia knew, and she is dead. And when my father rides furiously to them, Señor Calderon is past speaking. Teresita and I are clinging to each other, crying. He is dead and we little ones, we know before anyone tells us.

"Now, everybody knows that Señor Calderon was his own banker; everybody remembers that only a few days before this he had sold a big herd of cattle. And everybody knows that if he had his chests of gold and silver they have never been found by us."

Juanito's tale was quite the sort of recital

Whitney had counted on hearing, a torn fabric for the wind of sane disbelief to pierce, of fine texture and bright colors only where the boy's imagination supplied the golden threads. The talk had begun with Tia Tonia and her box; it had ended with the implication that Señor Calderon had spoken to her before he died.

"Surely," said Whitney, "if she knew—"

"Have I finished?" cried Juanito. "Tia Tonia was always strange since I first knew her. After that day she was what you saw her tonight in her chair. She too had an accident, a fall. It was when she was standing on a chair to catch back a curtain which had fallen. My father came to her and picked her up as you saw him pick her up tonight. She never walked after that. She was very ill for weeks; she was delirious. In her wild talk there was much of a secret and something which she and Señor Calderon alone knew! *What was that secret, Señor?*"

And again Juanito's voice rang out triumphantly; in his own mind his point was proven.

"But she could have had no reason for concealment."

Juanito sighed and shook his head doubtfully.

"Who can look into a woman's heart? He who can spell out the words in the whispers of the wind, and no other. To look into her eyes and know her mind is to look at the stars and read the riddles of the universe.

"It is I," Juanito went on, after the abstracted fashion of one who dreams in the moonlight, "who one day will find the gold of Teresita's father, Teresita's gold. You will see, Señor!" He thumped his breast dramatically. "In here, I know. And other treasures also, perhaps. For is the earth not ancient with secrets and stored with treasure as an old tree with the acorns of the *carpenterias*? As the little woodpeckers have stored away their wealth, and more often than not, have not come back for it, so have men done. There was once a certain Joaquin Murietta; you have heard of him; everybody has."

Certainly everybody in California. For here the name of the bandit of the earlier days grows as romantically and colorfully invested with the passage of time as any Robin Hood.

"Joaquin Murietta was killed and his head pickled in alcohol for the reward; so say some," continued Juanito. "Joaquin escaped, another paid for him; he and his beloved Rosita lived out their lives elsewhere; so say others. But what all men know is that Joaquin amassed much gold; that whether the head was his or that of a man who looked enough like him to gain the five thousand dollars' reward to Captain Love, in either case what man has ever spent Joaquin's gold? There is an old tradition, Señor, that Joaquin Murietta, shortly before his death or disappearance, was seen here in the valley; that he came with a wagon and three men; that he went out alone."

The moonlight shone softly over the valley; the mission ruin half hid among its shadows; a little owl cried out timidly through the stillness; Mentor Olivas was riding to have a meeting with Felipe Moraga; on the bench under an ancient pear tree bearing the name of Padre Cipriano sat Juanito, steeped in romance, telling tales of buried gold! The quaint atmosphere of the old days, seeming complete before, was perfect only now.

Teresa came out from the house. She stood on the porch, her figure clearly outlined in the moonlight, her face hidden in the shadows of the lacy shawl thrown loosely about her head.

"What think you, Señor?" Juanito was demanding.

Whitney started. He was not thinking; just dreaming.

"Strange tales, Señor Juan, I should answer, if you were telling them to me at the club in Los Angeles. Not so strange, somehow, here in the King of Spain Valley."

For he felt instinctively that from such conditions as held here golden legends must arise as inevitably as fragrance from roses.

CHAPTER IX

IN CAMP

Before six o'clock the next morning Maxwell Whitney was riding with the teamster, Nuñez, toward the Santa Lucia mountains. He had breakfasted with Señor Olivas and Juanito, heavy-hearted and bewildered at the tragedy of the night before and the failure of all efforts to solve the mystery of Tia Tonia's fright and death. Since her passing could mean little to him, a stranger, it seemed best that he remove himself from the house in which she lay awaiting the coming of a priest. And he was eager to be gone.

In the buckboard which was to carry him and his canvas roll and few parcels over the little-used roads, he and Nuñez were drawn swiftly by two trotting young horses toward the sources of the valley river. In a little more than two hours they came to the spot where Whitney meant to make camp. Nuñez gave him a hand at unloading, stopped to make a cigarette, said a brief "*Adios, Señor*," and was gone back down the steep road. And Whitney, once Nuñez was lost to his sight and the rattling noise of the buckboard was no longer distinguishable above the faint murmuring of the pines all about him, filled his lungs full of the sunny air of the woods and knew a moment of deep serene content.

"Eight o'clock," said Whitney, "and all is well."

He was all eagerness to get to work. But when he had an ax in his hand, having changed to rough khaki suit and laced tan boots, he grew suddenly still and for a long time stood looking, listening. He heard the faint splash of the little creek, hardly to be distinguished from the music of the trees; somewhere in the woods he heard a squirrel scurrying up a tree trunk; every few seconds a quail called from a mountainside thick with sage and chaparral; far away, down in the valley, the sweet, cooing voice of a dove mourned for an absent mate. Little voices rose out of the grass; a brownie bird made a racket worthy of one ten times his size in some dead leaves among the bushes.

He looked off toward the mountains; there the hills rose ever more steeply, massing and lifting to defy ocean winds and fogs an entrance into this happy valley from the twenty mile distant Pacific. He looked down into the cañons on either side; live oaks, laurels, alders and willows made a shade there which would be deliciously cool during the hottest days of summer.

He moved up the slope a score of paces to a spot where a great boulder, standing secure through the ages, wore the nonchalant look of extreme insecurity; at first glance one might have thought that at any time its hundred ton weight needed only a spring freshet to send it toppling and crashing down through the trees. He looked at it with interest; his interest was ready this morning in answer to the tiniest call; he noted how at the rear, whence it sloped up gently to the top, it was deeply embedded.

"You'll be on the job, old fellow, with never a budge," he thought, "when all of us three-score-and-ten boys have gone on."

He dropped his ax and climbed up. At the very top was a level place from which he could look through a vista of the nearer trees, over the tops of others, and down into the valley. Wooded hills in the distance broke his view, however, before his eyes could travel the ten miles to the Calderon home; the Judge Belden place likewise was hidden by a ridge, but the ridge itself was already familiar to him; upon it the old padre artist had made his painting for the King across the ocean. Again Whitney turned toward the mountains; thickly timbered slopes everywhere within the nearer foreground, a spot of lush grass and tall stemmed flowers, and willows ringing the spring.

Into his nostrils rose the smell of the earth. The black soil was damp from the rains; the golden sunlight pierced through everywhere, flooding all of the open spaces, seeming to glide in a warm, life-giving stream down the tree trunks. Like an invisible mist there rose from the ground that sweetest of all fragrances, the subtle fragrance of the earth itself. He filled his lungs deeper and deeper; he put back his head; he drank in the breath of the morning through his parted lips.

"God, it's good," he muttered.

If below in the valley where Mentor Olivas guarded the interests of the last of the Calderons the world had been held back to the time of the early Californians, here in the woods time had loitered and lost itself since the day long before the outer world knew that there was a California to conquer and name. One might seek all day through these leafy solitudes and fail to find a man's track or that of a shod horse. By nighttime here you would see no light from another man's hearth; in the dawn no other stain of smoke. Here was what Maxwell Whitney craved, what he had sought: solitude absolute.

He wondered how long it could hold him. Just now, with the deathless ancient youth of it all talking to the spirit within him, he felt that he could forget the world he had turned his back on and never ask again the sight of all that which modern cities offered the modern man. For the moment, at least, he hearkened to faint voices singing in his blood, and his blood-beat caught the tempo of the world about him. At any rate, he thought conservatively, he would tarry here until, with no clamor in his ear to distract him from the main issues, he could think out a number of matters; when one day, if that day should come, he remade his canvas roll and departed for the double iron trails which carry men into the heart of their own jungles of traffic and progress, he would know what he wanted. And he would go get it.

But today, with certain necessary duties before him, was sufficient unto itself. He climbed down the big rock, patted it like some grotesque, giant brother, caught up his ax and strode back to his belongings. He had chosen already the spots for both bed and kitchen and meant to have them in a fair state of order before the sun went down. There was a small grove of young pines, the tallest of them lifting its aspiring pointed crest not over twenty-five feet from the ground; among them he would sleep. A few manzanita bushes must come out; he slashed away at them with a will and in short time had made his clearing. Then he went to work on the bed itself. And in the manner of its construction was ample evidence that the new visitor to the Coast Range planned on a number of nights here.

For a night's lodging, or for as long as a week, he knew that nothing surpassed for easeful slumber a bed made on springy branches piled on the ground. But Maxwell Whitney, a man whose heart was big enough to embrace much of the natural world, had no place in it for spiders and other crawling things, and knew from past repeated experiences that it would not be long before such a retreat invited them in numbers. Ground spiders would be coming out to bask in the warmer weather; he could regard them from a distance with sufficient charity to let them bask to their hearts' content but had not come to the pass of the simple-hearted Ancient Mariner that he could invite them in to share his couch. Therefore he devised his sleeping quarters with an eye to privacy. Having made his clearing he cocked a thoughtful and measuring eye at the young pines grouped about it, marking how closely they stood together and thus estimating how long a timber would be required to reach from one to another. Then he carried his ax off into the wood and sought two straight saplings which might come down without being missed. He swung his ax at them vigorously, taking a joy out of the flying chips which under the keen blade were as soft as butter and as white as milk, and having old boyhood memories stir vaguely in him, riding down through the years on the smell of resinous wood. He got down two baby pines some ten feet tall, lopped off the branches each with a single smooth cut, and dragged them back to his "bedroom."

The next task was that of climbing and snaking a timber up after him. He got the butt end of one of his saplings secure in a crotch, braced himself, swung the lighter end across to the near-by tree and got it placed similarly so that now he had one horizontal rough beam in place something higher than his head above the ground. He clambered down, regardless of various scratches upon the skin of hands and forearms, grown tender with too many years of a sheltered existence. The second timber he placed next so that it rudely paralleled the first at a distance from it of about eight feet.

Now he went back into the wood for two more saplings; he dragged them to camp; these were to be the side-boards of his swinging bunk. In his carefully selected outfit was a plenitude of rope: a few minutes' work only was needed to sling the two smaller saplings so that they swung a couple of feet from the ground, parallel, horizontal, a yard apart. The "bedstead" was complete; it but required the slats across, the springs and mattress. And these he was above an hour getting fixed to his satisfaction. He placed many of the lopped-off branches across, tying the ends to the swinging saplings; at this stage his bed looked as much like a side of a chicken coop as anything. But when he had enough of these springy branches rigged crosswise to support his weight, he began covering them with leafy boughs laid lengthwise. He went down into the south fork for armfuls of laurel; he stopped to crush and smell the spice of many a handful of leaves before he was done. When the cross limbs were all hidden he placed other layers of pine, making a thick, springy, odorous mat.

Over the whole of it for warmth he placed a folded bit of canvas; upon this his blankets, drawing a flap of the canvas over the top. And then, with both hands on his hips and a smile of genuine happiness not devoid of pride of workmanship, he stood back and regarded his handiwork. Before he had done contemplating it he even drew back a few yards to mark its appearance from a short distance; in the little grove it was almost hidden, without conspicuity, creating no ugly dissonance in the woodland note.

"It's a good job," he thought, glowing. "I'll sleep like a top in it. Later on I'll rig up a screen of foliage. Now for the kitchen."

The first step in this direction, before he began actual work, was an engineering calculation. He went up to the spring and, returning slowly, estimated just where he could best run the water to bring it into his house. He saw that it could easily run by his bed—right under it, if he chose—and across a little clearing where there were a number of loose stones. That suited him exactly; among those stones he would make his stove; his larder would be swung to a branch of a pine outflung over it; his fire would be just far enough from the tree to scorch and smoke none of the branches. He went whistling about his work of gathering stones; he selected them with as much care and interest as Benjamin M. Whitney would have chosen a secretary last week. He found here and there just what he wanted; some he brought from a distance; some came from the bed of the river, some from higher up the slope, of varying sizes all were alike in the matter of having flat surfaces. He placed a first layer in a horseshoe shape; on these he laid others, building up. He regretted briefly that he had not thought to bring a couple of flat pieces of iron to lay across the top; but then one going camping and assembling his outfit in haste, could not think of everything. And then, too, there was a certain satisfaction in making suffice just that which the forest offered. By thickening the walls of his fireplace and then searching out some longer flattish stones, he managed so that they protruded inward at the top so as almost to meet; a frying-pan would sit nicely on them over the fire. And always a coffee-pot in the coals is as pretty a sight as a bird in its nest.

He sat on a log in the shade, mopped at his face and rested. He glanced up at the sun in the clear sky and hazarded a guess at the time. Pretty close to noon, he judged; say, eleven forty-five. He consulted his watch. Eleven forty. He chuckled. He had missed it only five minutes; pretty good, he called it, for a man who hadn't watched the sun and shadows in the woods for a long time. To eat now or to bring the water down to camp; that was the question. Just now the only, the supreme question in his life! He chuckled again. Life was what a man made of it—sometimes. More often than not it was what man let it make itself. Well, today he was on the job as chief director of destiny and he was shaping it into a mold which pleased him. Here came one question at the time; he would make it his system to get that answered before another came along. He jumped up and went to the spring; he could stave off his hunger another hour and he had the hankering to eat his lunch right in camp with the water of his own direction running by where he could scoop up a bucketful to douse out his fire.

A shovel was another article which he had not brought along; a shovel in camp is a luxury, after all. Where the spring emptied itself in its own way through the ring of willows to spill down into the river, he constructed a rude dam of rocks as big as he could carry, with bits of turf packed into the cracks between them. He muddied the water and got both boots soaking wet but he waged a winning fight. The water rose against the obstruction, backed up, sought a new exit. He got his ax and cleared away a few willows; with a sharpened stick he gouged in the soft earth to make the desired channel; he removed impeding rocks that were loose in their beds, made detours about others and in the end saw the muddy current obeying his will and beginning a wild escape down the slope. Now he gave it its head and allowed it its own way as much as was possible, merely striding along and checking a dash to the side now and then by cleaning out the proper way, kicking stones and dead limbs aside, making a shallow trench with his stick. The stream showed a decided penchant for wiggling into the pine grove where his bed was; he let it have its way. Before it reached the first of the four young trees to which his hammock bed was hung, a fresh inspiration made him forget utterly that he was hungry. He divided the stream here; its two separate arms flowed to right and left of his bed-post pines; thus he made a little island of the ground about his sleeping quarters. It was the moat about his castle walls; let ants and other ground creeping invaders puzzle over that!

Again, though forced to dig one of his trenches rather deeply now, he reunited the waters. They ran on with little aid from him, almost in a straight line, close to his fireplace. Here he unearthed a boulder, rolling it down the slope. The hole rapidly filled; he stood by it and watched the water clear, having no further interest in the stream which continued on down into the ravine. Here was his supply of cooking and drinking water needing only to be scooped up without a man stirring two steps from camp. What better service did the man in town have who paid for pipes and faucets and all the folderols? Whitney considered himself the proud possessor of a *cuisine de luxe*.

But there would be little cooking for this first meal. His hunger, held in abeyance until long after the noon hour, whetted keen with long hours of exercise which spared no single muscle, was not the patient sort to wait upon lengthy preparations. He did make a fire of pine cones and dead wood, largely for the sake of using his new fireplace; he did set a pot of coffee to boil, rather for the sight of it and the smell of it than because of any great thirst for the beverage itself. But the remainder of his meal was ready for the eating the moment the papers were torn off packages. He cut himself a slice of cheese as large as his hand; he opened crackers and ate cheese in the meantime; he ripped open a tin of beans which he found quite the best he had ever tasted though taken cold. He had forgotten neither salt nor pepper nor dry onions. Nor yet sugar and milk in cans; he discovered both by the time the coffee began to send out its aroma to mingle with the woodsy smells.

He stretched out on the ground and dined like a king.

All of the time his mind was busy with other camp details; things to be done this afternoon and tomorrow and the next day. The recent occurrences at the *Rancho del Rey de España* wcre of too grave an import to be excluded entirely from his thoughts; he thought of poor old Tia Tonia; of the puzzle confronting Mentor and Juanito and Teresa Calderon; of the vanished box. But all this seemed vague today and far away; more vital matters were the larder he meant to make safe from inroads of squirrels and chipmunks; the table which he was determined to have. He saw that a few great, sluggish clouds drifted across the sky; the springtime had come and yet there would doubtless be showers: He would rig up his other square of canvas with ropes at the corners; he could draw it up like a sail if it rained, making it shelter him, and could furl it for fine weather so that when he went to sleep it would be under the stars. He recalled Brooke Sheffield's boastful plannings and his friendliness with the valley vulture; he regretted that such as these two were sinking their claws into the fair throat of the valley. But he forgot both immediately as his coffee began to boil over. For the instant boiling coffee was the largest consideration in life.

"It's not so bad being broke," he mused complacently. "There are a lot of worse things; being without matches, for instance. Or out of tobacco."

He filled his pipe and lay back with a deep sigh of satisfaction.

He smoked in serene enjoyment for a few minutes. When his pipe went out he did not notice. He had drawn his hat over his eyes to shut out the sun; he felt lazy and "good." The word in his mind struck the keynote of one of those delightful bits of verse in one of the Vagabondia books. The lines ran through his mind:

"I want to find a warm beech wood
  And lie down and keep still,
And swear a little and feel good,
  And loaf on up the hill;
And let the spring house-clean my brain
  Where all this stuff is crammed,
And let my heart grow sweet again,
  And let the Age be damned."

Through lowering lids he idly watched the play of light upon a wild lilac bush; broken fragments of thoughts brushed through his drowsy consciousness. He wondered if the gay Juanito were sighing or singing; if the priest had come; if it had been Felipe Moraga or A. Vogel or another who had pilfered Tia Tonia's little box; if there were anything in it of value; if Teresa Calderon would one day become Mrs. Brooke Sheffield and thus bring about the old order of the Pajaro Azul ranch and the King of Spain governed by one hand. No, not entirely the old order, since the hand of Sheffield would in no way be comparable to that of the Calderons. Trifling with such speculations his lids lowered still further, the light on the lilacs quivered and went out, and, here in the land of siestas, Maxwell Whitncy went to sleep.

He was awakened by the sound of a lively commotion in his provision box. Startled, he sat up just in time to see a chipmunk bolt with a cracker in its mouth. The little rodent, whose race is a combination of timidity and curiosity, the latter quality always fighting to the top, raced off a dozen yards and there sat up to divide its attention between Whitney and the loot in its paws. The sharp teeth nibbled, the quick black eyes were glitteringly full of interest. Whitney laughed at his visitor, named him the "Senator" on the spot, and got up to make the most of what was left of the day. The chipmunk's visit was but a reminder of what he had to expect; the larder must be made rodent-proof.

With an end of rope he swung his largest box from a limb of the pine near his kitchen and at a convenient height for his reach; into it he put such articles as cheese, crackers and sugar. His matches, stowed in the can from which he had taken his beans for lunch, he set on top. Only the food which was protected by tins he left, for the present, on the ground in another box. For his butter he meant to improvise a cooler: he had a two pound roll and no love for that article gone rancid. Among his most valuable possessions he counted a square biscuit tin into which, at his request, a number of small articles had been packed. These he now emptied out; the tin itself he buried in the damp ground leaving the lid flush with the grass roots. He had now but to drop the butter in, close the lid and set a stone on it, to have as cool a refrigerator on a hot day as any visited daily by the ice man.

"I've got now a bed, stove, larder, ice box and running water," he congratulated himself. "Not so bad, Mr. Whitney, for a first day's work. We can begin to think of a luxury or so. First comes a table."

The greatest of the luxury lay in the making of it. A triumphant philosopher created the line: "I made it and it's mine!" That which a man makes himself, alone and unaided, is the thing he is proudest of whether it be a hung canvas, a fortune or a two-by-four vegetable garden in his back yard. Whitney went about his table-making with as deep a deliberation as he would have given to a business deal ten days ago; when the job was done to his approval he drew from it as much quiet satisfaction as he would have known after a successful coup. He went down into the ravine with his ax; he cut branches for the top. He brought them all back to his fireplace, cleared a little level space and worked with a diligence full of profound gravity. He left crotches at the upper end of the larger sticks; the lower ends he sharpened and thrust down into the soft soil, spacing them so that the enclosed rectangle was about three feet by six in dimensions. Then lengthwise he laid straight limbs from crotch to crotch; the other sticks, cut to three feet lengths, he laid across these, close together, running a string about the ends and the supporting cross pieces to hold them securely in place. Thus his table top became a series of ridges with small cracks between; but it would hold plates, tin cup, coffee-pot, frying pan; even knife and fork, though they might slip a little way through, would hang by the handles. And, the final test, it amply suited Maxwell Whitney and there was no one else in all of the limitless universe who had a single thing to say of it! There was something glorious in that.

He set an ample table, say what you please of the manner of setting forth and the skill in cooking. Nor was he entirely lacking in ability as a rough and ready chef. There was a platter of bacon which, served in any one of the big city cafés, would have cost a man a day's wages; there were two giant potatoes baked in ashes and coals; he recalled at the last moment that a potato was not to be done thoroughly in half an hour and so thrust them back into the ashes to cook until next day: There was coffee again; a man in the woods is good for coffee three times a day and never the worse off for it. There were scrambled eggs, three of them, dark hued from bacon fat but of an astonishingly fine flavor; eggs wouldn't keep indefinitely and he meant to make sure that none escaped him. There was a big onion sliced and doused with oil, sprinkled with vinegar and salt and pepper. Half a tin of beans from lunch. A slab of chocolate and canned peaches for desert. And an appetite which many a man long on money and short on stomach, would give a thousand dollars for. For light in his vast banquet hall the stars which had begun slipping into the sky one by one and now, as though grown bolder after the advance of their bigger brethren, came trooping out everywhere; for companionship his crackling fire which, with an ancient voice which all men remember and understand, talked to the soul within him. And for his orchestra the little trickle of water from the spring, the music of the river down in the cañon, seeming to grow more distinct, more melodious as the earth went to sleep, pure liquid notes piercing through the hushed but mighty breathing of the woods. As the gloom thickened among the trees their boles where the flickering firelight found them out were indistinct in outline and assumed grotesque resemblances; they appeared to stir in a sort of guarded restlessness; one could fancy them bewitched personalities chained to inertia under the rough bark which an enchanter's spell had woven about them, but of power to free themselves somewhat during the night when there were no eyes to see. If one but mused in preference to reasoning as one was prone to do, swayed by the hour, it was so easy to imagine the whole forest moving, wherever fell utter darkness, not alone as to quivering branch but as to deep-thrust, gnarled roots. Even now, while a wall of ebony ringed about the fireplace, the tree trunks seemed to be huddling together companionably. Certainly a new quality crept into the gurgle of the running water; its melodious fall is ever the more sparklingly musical under starlight. Now the two voices of the river tributaries, lifted above that of the spring over-flow, were a clear fluted duet against the rising accompaniment of the forest; the night wind, drawn lingeringly through the woods, was a magnificent symphony as the tuneful needles vibrating like a million million strings in unison gave forth the tremulous *susurro* of innumerable pines.

The man who had heard and heeded the ancient call, forsaking the haunts of habit for those of instinct, shook himself out of a reverie and rising, piled his fire high with dead wood and pine cones. The flames leaped and licked at the fresh fuel; the incomparable incense of wood burning swept through the forest, triumphing over the smells of earth and grass and flowers; tongues of light shot out, briefly retrieving recesses invaded by the dark among the tree trunks; a shower of sparks rose and broke, swirled against the stars like lesser earth-bound stars, snapped and crackled and were gone. A night bird called from somewhere up the slope, pure notes out of the invisible. As though in answer, as though the universe sought to unite in spirit, as the trees had appeared to approach one another, as the sparks of the camp fire had given up their short little lives in emulation of the eternal stars, an owl down in the valley sent up his dove-like response. Now indeed was the voice of the night rising in the noblest of all symphonies; gurgle of stream, merry chanting of the fire, wind in the pines and notes of night-waking birds.

The fury of the flames reached its crisis; little by little as no further sticks were thrown on and the faggots settled into a growing bed of coals, the fire lost its frenzy and grew more quietly companionable again. Faint sounds which had been lost in the fierce snapping and cracking now insisted and became the dominant note of the fire's altered mood; imprisoned sap in some of the fresher fuel hummed and sang in thin-voiced cadences and Maxwell Whitney, with the half sad smile of reminiscence, thought of his mother's tales of the Fire Fairies. When a brilliant spark flew upward and vanished with an air of triumph in the surrounding dark, there was one of the fairy creatures who, long ago, had been bewitched and immured in the bark of a tree and who now, as the flames wrought their own bright countermagic, was free again.

CHAPTER X

VISITORS

For a fortnight Max Whitney had been in camp, with no thought of descending from his hills into the lower valley. Here he had found such content as but dimly had he realized existed in the world. His wants were simple and simply supplied; he had ample provisions, bedding, tobacco and matches. For companionship his was that "vast society where none intrudes." He took many long walks, penetrating farther into the wooded ravines or climbing higher into the Santa Lucias, gone from his headquarters many a day from before dawn until after dusk. For hours at a time he lay under the interlacing branches of the trees, full of ease, free from all restless thoughts. He did not read during these days; he did not plan on when he would return to the city nor yet on how he would begin again the old fight. He merely felt that he was soaking in the soft, bright sunshine, resting, quietly enjoying a lull in the series of battles and buffets which so largely constitute certain lives. He was as one of the mariners storm-driven into the serene haven of the Isle of the Lotus. Large financial transactions seemed so far away as to be included among those quiet ashes heaped in an urn of brass.

At times from an open spot which he had discovered upon the flank of the mountain he looked down into the valley. Twice only he saw a *vaquero* riding after cattle; frequently he watched grazing cows pass from meadow to meadow. But these did not concern him; they were not of his world. They were of the Enchanted Valley down into which he looked from his aloof place in the solitudes. The valley itself, however, had a quiet voice for his inner ear. How mightily the old-world peace of it rose and reached out to him! It soothed. It made its eloquent plea for life lived calmly, for the secure enjoyment of the present, a long glittering chain of golden days, for oblivion of needless, useless striving and strife. It broadened a man's heart to look down upon its placid smiling acres; it purged of mean ambitions. It was that

"Sleepy land where under the same wheel
The same old rut would deepen year by year."

Next morning standing before his tent, his eye trailed away across the valley, finding it amply perfect, left as it was. No progress here; no struggle to make the old over into the image of the new. He wandered away into the woods, lost all sight of the valley, all thought of the outside world. As he passed under the oaks, among the never-still pines, down into the ravines, through the thick-leaved bay trees, out into the sunshine, across swards springy underfoot, sprinkled profligately with wild flowers, it struck him that the world about him was so abundantly filled with life that something of the sparkling elixir spilled over and drove onward into his own veins; that it mounted upon the vague woodland mists and poured itself into him through his breathing. The earth throbbed and pulsed and quivered and swelled with life; life expressing itself through laughter was in the play of the running water; life was in the very heart of the ancient boulder clothed in moss of a vivid green; life danced in the sunshine. That was the great significant fact of the universe; it was everywhere, teeming in the clod, flowering in a man's breast. What had he to do with other and lesser considerations? It was enough to live, to move, to breathe, to eat and sleep, to bathe in the cool pools, to lie and look up at the blue of the sky through the living, stirring leaves. Life was the gift of God—or the manifestation of God—or the finger pointing to God. One could see life here. In time, perhaps, he could see God—

"A man doesn't think overmuch of God in town. I wonder if ever a man wandered seven days alone in the woods with a shut mind?"

A long halloo recalled Whitney to his camp. Making his way down the steep slope, his first inkling of whom his visitor might be was given him in a glimpse through the trees of a satiny red-bay of a horse's hide. An animal from the Calderon stable, perhaps Juanito's. He hurried on; the hospitality which the ranch had offered him had affected him rather deeply and, now that in a way conditions were reversed and he was host, he was keenly alive to the slight obligation. He saw that there was a second horse, Mentor's black, El Tacano. And only then he saw that it was not Juanito who rode the red bay, but Teresa Calderon and that Mentor was with her.

Mentor Olivas reached down to shake hands, calling him "*Mí amigo*." Whitney raised his hat to Teresa and briefly paid her full homage with his eyes. He had failed to remember her as so beautiful. In his memory she was the Magnolia Girl; the connotation of the magnolia was every bit as strong as that of the mere word girl. But now, from having ridden through the morning sunshine, there had crept into the pure creamy whiteness of her cheeks the suggestion of the blush of a wild pink rose. She was warmly, femininely human.

And her eyes were the eyes of a young country girl, bright and interested, neither demure nor shy, neither bold nor challenging, but as vaguely mysterious as are the eyes of all young girls to whom their own bosoms are mysteries. Further the eyes were faintly amused. Whitney recalled that he had not shaven; that his hair was rumpled; that his clothes were all right for a man camping alone but hardly the garments in which to receive a young woman groomed like this one, garbed in so perfectly becoming a riding costume.

"She doesn't appear borne down mourning for her Tia Tonia," he remarked inwardly. An indication, had he but stopped to analyze, that for some reason he was not regarding Miss Calderon so impersonally as the other day. What he was doing now was obey an ancient and utterly human impulse; if her attitude, though ever so subtly, was one of amusement, he retaliated with criticism. But since very frequently impulses are plants of inadequate roots and blossoms which fail to fructify, he admitted within himself that, so far as he could see, there was no more reason why Teresa Calderon should mourn for Tia Tonia than he himself should do so. Rather less, if anything.

"We began to wonder if you had forgotten us," Mentor Olivas was saying. "If you had even gone away without a farewell."

For an instant Whitney made no response. Miss Calderon's eyes and his own had met and were interestedly making their polite observations. Where he had read her amusement two seconds ago now he was not sure what to read. Now he must fail of interpretation because the look was willfully veiled. For the first time Teresa Calderon was taking stock of the man; she had finished with the clothes which did not matter. She was aware of the virile strength of him, of that "golden look," of his lusty youth, his clean and healthy male manhood. To Teresa men had meant little apart from the clothes which they wore, the speeches which they made her, the glances which their eyes shot at her. Now, Maxwell Whitney moved her as no man had ever done; she was interested though she herself did not understand that interest.

"I have been reverting to the ancient order of things," Whitney smiled, turning toward Señor Olivas. "Playing barbarian, you know. Guess I was rather hungry for the woods."

"*Comprendo*," nodded Mentor. "When one has been long away from it, especially if he be as the son of *mí amigo* Benito must be, he needs the woods. As a lover yearns for his sweetheart."

Whitney laughed.

"I am no authority on the requirements of Romeos," he replied lightly. "But I do know that every man living owes it to himself to get away from the cities at least a couple of weeks every year and to dive deep into the solitudes. But I have not asked you to get down!" He transferred his quick smile to the girl. "Even though it be your own land on which you allow me to trespass, may I not invite you into my home? The only home which I can lay claim to this fine morning."

He indicated his camp just behind him. Her eyes went interestedly the way he pointed. In full view were his fireplace, table, larder and chair. Everything was in order because he was a man who abhorred the defilement of the woods with scattered cans and scraps. From here one failed to see his bed among the pines.

"Before you go back we are going to have coffee and sandwiches," he added.

Already Señor Olivas was dismounting; he would have tarried on a friend's invitation for a cup of coffee even at a time of haste and full stomach. Teresa, though accepting the proffered aid of Whitney's hand, came down lightly, scarcely touching it. Yet that little pleasurable thrill, ever in attendance upon youth, passed between them.

The three, leaving the horses tethered, approached the camp. "Aha," said Señor Olivas; "here is one who knows the way to make himself comfortable in the woods." Whitney was pleased with his approval; was pleased to have Teresa's. She exclaimed that he had not made the forest ugly as she had seen other campers do; rather the added note of coziness had worked an improvement. The overflow and directed trickle of the spring was a delight; she sat in his chair and asked him if by trade he was a designer of period furniture; this was so obviously and line-perfectly an Adam chair. . . .

Her moods were quick; there was sparkling vivacity in her glance; she was less just then Señorita Calderon, Spanish heiress, than Teresa, a girl. There was nothing left to Whitney of that impersonal attitude of the other night in which he could consider her as merely something contended for by Brooke Sheffield and Juanito Olivas.

"Is Mr. Sheffield still visiting with you?" he asked abruptly. The girl looked at him curiously as though seeking to discover what mental process had suggested Sheffield.

"Yes," she answered carelessly. On the instant Whitney regretted his mention of the other man's name; an intangible something of stiffness or restraint had crept into her voice. He himself had no wish to bring Sheffield into the conversation.

"And how is Juanito?" he said hastily, accomplishing the usual result of bumping into Charybdis. "Sometime I want to hear him play again."

Teresa Calderon flushed. Unwittingly he had given her the clue which a moment ago she had been baffled for. Sheffield and Juanito—

"Oh, Juanito is quite his gay self," she replied coolly. "There is no more alteration in Juanito than in the wind which changes every minute and yet is always the same."

Whitney, seeing how he had inadvertently been guilty of an innuendo, switched talk another way. He showed them his "ice box," explained how he worked his canvas flaps over his bed—there had been one light shower, more windy threat than downpour—how his kitchen reservoir was kept continuously and freshly filled and, finally gave a demonstration of his stove in action. He put coffee to boil, opened a last tin of sardines and a tin of milk.

"Had you come a few days sooner," he explained, "I could have given you something better. As it is I am low in provisions."

"And here come Señor Mentor and I to eat that up!" laughed Teresa.

"Oh, I was going down to Toyon tomorrow anyway for fresh supplies," he told her. "First, however, I was going to drop in at your house to make sure that my presence here would be tolerated a bit longer."

"I trust," she answered, "that you will feel perfectly free to stay as long as you like." But she looked at him curiously and added, "Doesn't it grow lonely? And are you contented to live here a long time—like this?"

"Life should have an aim, you are thinking, and I have none here? Having loafed two weeks on end I should normally be looking about for purposeful activity again? Well, I am not so idle as you might think. I've been busy getting things in shape. And I've had some glorious long hikes and am planning on others. I want to cross the mountains and go down on the other side; I have the hunch," he added lightly, "that the view one would get of the Pacific from some peak up there would be something to remember."

She reverted to his previous remark.

"It is twenty miles to Toyon. You were not going to walk!"

"Why not?" he retorted. "It's just that sort of thing that I am getting my fun out of."

Señor Olivas regarded him in wonder. That a man, through preference, should walk a mile, let alone twenty, transcended comprehension.

"We were speaking of that," he said. "You should have a saddle horse."

"Not at all," said Whitney, understanding that next would come the offer of one of the Calderon horses. "Why, I can leave camp early, be down in Toyon before noon, have Vogel pack up an order for me and send it up by his boy Henry. I can ride back with him. And in most of my travels back in the hills I'm better off on foot."

Mentor, though he said nothing, shook his head. That a man should have a saddle horse always at his disposal was not to be discussed.

Whitney gathered some dry twigs and a handful of dead branches and got his little fire blazing. While Señor Olivas and Teresa sat watching him with that interest which always the simplest of camp matters evokes, he placed his coffee-pot on the rocks over the flames. He was explaining how only the lady could have a real cup when from the trail below floated up to them the noise of horses' hoofs and then voices.

"It is Juanito coming," said Mentor in a tone

which made clear that Juanito's arrival was expected. "But the other?"

The other was Brooke Sheffield. Whitney saw the two dismount, and saw further that Juanito led the third saddled horse, one of the red bays.

"It is for you while you are here," said Teresa. "Both Señor Mentor and Juanito declared that we had been very bad neighbors, allowing you to go so long on foot."

Brooke Sheffield, without waiting for Juanito to tether the led animal, came on ahead, his polished puttees shining brightly in the sunlight across the trail. His hat in hand, his fingers pushing back the fair hair from his forehead, he looked about him interestedly.

"Oh, here you are," he called breezily. "Hello, Whitney. How's the cave-man stuff progressing?"

Whitney experienced a quick feeling of resentment at Sheffield's presence. Into the solitude of the woods had come Olivas and Teresa and the solitudes had accepted them with himself and there had been no ripple in the serenity. It would have been the same with Juanito. But Sheffield with his infernal glib tongue and hideously gleaming puttees was for a second time guilty of smashing the picture.

Behind came Juanito, running uptrail like a boy of ten, crying out in extravagant delight at the beauty of Whitney's selected spot, at his joy at the meeting, even welcoming his father and Señorita

Teresa as though he had not seen them for a year.

"You all slipped out so quietly," Sheffield was saying as he seated himself on the ground near Teresa, "that I began to wonder what was up. Then I spied Juanito riding away leading a *caballo*—note how my Spanish accent is improving, Miss Calderon?—and I rode to overtake him."

Juanito made a wry face. Everyone there, perhaps including Sheffield, understood that he would vastly have preferred to ride alone.

From the beginning Brooke Sheffield directed conversation. He was breezy and cock-sure; he was in high spirit and accepted the situation and the company into which he had inserted himself as if made for his own advantage and delectation. Juanito sat dampened by Sheffield's unending talk, chafing and fuming. Whitney was content with silence for the most part, interested in watching now one, now another of his guests. Mentor answered politely when addressed but at such times lifted himself with visible efforts from abstraction. Since, as time passed, the greater part of Sheffield's observations were meant for Miss Calderon, she, like Señor Olivas, answered almost monosyllabically. It struck Whitney that her attitude toward Sheffield was one of unstudied indifference.

"His glib tongue hasn't shoved him ahead much during these few days," was Whitney's satisfied decision.

"It is pretty here, *no*, *Señor*?" observed Juanito once when Sheffield was silent. "You have made it charming. The trees will look sad when you are gone away."

Sheffield chuckled, fancying Juanito was attempting humor.

"You were cut out to be a comic poet, Johnny," he laughed. He cast a quick look about the camp, and exclaimed with a little grunt: "Lord, what a life for a man! Fussing around making toy tables and chairs." He let his eyes drift on to Whitney, frankly continuing his appraisal. "A man would say that two weeks of this ought to be enough for anybody. Got enough by now to last you a while, eh, Whit?"

"Good God," cried Whitney within himself, "I've got such a tingling in the toe of my boot as Cyrano felt in his sword!"

But aloud he remarked indifferently:

"No. I'm still happy here."

"I, for one, can't understand it," admitted Sheffield. "With man's work waiting to be done in the world, how can a fellow drop out of everything like a hobo? Say, old fellow, you must have come an awful cropper in town!"

"I imagine," Whitney told him bluntly, "that the others are not interested what I did or did not do in town."

Again the San Francisco lawyer laughed good-humoredly.

"I get you. Hands off, eh? Well, I wouldn't have referred to it if you hadn't been so frank about saying you had gone broke yourself."

Mentor frowned. Teresa flushed up hotly. Juanito stirred restlessly. Whitney alone seemed unruffled by the man's insufferable way.

"It is not the first time I have gone broke," he said as though touching on some matter of absolute indifference. He gave his attention to his fire, saw that his coffee was coming to the boil, and set forth his one cup and some makeshift cups on his "toy table."

"I'll not take any, thanks," said Sheffield. And, being Sheffield, he was constitutionally unable to let it go at that. He was urged on to explain how regularity of habit was, with him, one of the big things in life: he ate at mealtimes, not between meals: he had never allowed coffee or tobacco to break his mathematical perfection of schedule.

The others perhaps had the greater zest in defying his law. They accepted Whitney's little lunch eagerly and enjoyed it, complimenting him on his skill as a cook. Again Sheffield's laugh jarred unpleasantly.

"One of these fine days," was Whitney's premonition, "if he and I both tarry hereabouts, I am going to pull Mr. Brooke Sheffield's nose and slap his smug face for him. Just as sure as water runs down hill."

Whitney fancied that if only Señor Olivas and Teresa had come today, or even they and Juanito, there would have followed a pleasant half-day loitering in his woods, bright hours of common understanding, a step forward in the growth of real friendship among them. Now, however, such a thing became a sheer impossibility. Sheffield rose and poked about; he was restless and his restlessness disturbed the others. When a silence fell, during which the others hearkened to running water and whispering trees, he broke out suddenly with talk of what he meant to do. He was already in touch with Judge Belden's lawyers. The Judge was too sick to attend to business matters, he announced triumphantly, and very clearly up against it for money. Of course he was stalling at first, as any man would, seeking to drive a bargain. Well, Sheffield was in no hurry. In another week or another ten days or a month at most—what mattered a few days when he was making money by waiting?—the Pajaro Azul would be his and at his own figure.

"We must be returning," said Señor Olivas abruptly. His fine old face had contracted with pain while Sheffield spoke. "You were going into Toyon tomorrow, Señor Whitney; perhaps you will ride back with us now instead?"

He looked toward Teresa to give authority to the invitation. She responded by saying warmly:

"We should be glad, Mr. Whitney, if you would

do so. And stay with us tonight? Juanito will play for us."

"If our good Mr. Nature-lover can remain away from his hermitage that long?" bantered Sheffield.

Whitney, ignoring him, thanked both Miss Calderon and Señor Olivas. At least he would certainly ride back with them; he sought to make them understand his appreciation of their thoughtfulness in supplying him with a saddle horse. All rose and they went to the horses. Sheffield managed to be at hand to aid the girl in mounting: he assayed a few words in Spanish, calling her his teacher. As they rode down into the valley he kept at her side; Mentor rode with them in silence. Behind came Whitney and Juanito.

CHAPTER XI

WHITNEY MAKES A DECISION

Out in the bright warm sunshine Juanito's mood was all effervescent gaiety again. He hummed a lively little air as they rode single file down the narrow trail; once in the open valley, reining his horse in close to Whitney's red bay he immediately threw at least all but the very innermost corners of his heart open, talking rapidly as though he had no end of things which must be said before the end of their ride. Juanito's words gushed forth like a mountain torrent, flashing in the sunlight, bubbling and boiling over obstacles, sped by a perfect frenzy of eagerness.

Nothing had been discovered of the robber who had violated Tia Tonia's cherished secret; the thing still remained a dark mystery! (The exclamation point was Juanito's; in punctuating his utterances it was always much more in demand than were mere humdrum commas and periods.) Vogel had been seen with Felipe Moraga—aha! There was a man to watch and to mistrust! Did not Juanito know? He sighed and shook his head and grew infinitely sad in an instant and for an instant only. Another tick of a watch and the shadow passed and he was all quickened speculation again. Also, he ran on, another man who was black-hearted, a certain Nig Chorro, had been seen with both Vogel and Moraga! Was there a conspiracy? A Trinity of Evil?

Maxwell Whitney, though he smiled now and then, was interested.

"Did Señor Juan think that the thief, whoever he might be, had discovered that hidden gold which was thought to be spoken of in Tia Tonia's papers?"

"My father and I have decided this way, Señor: Undoubtedly the writing was in Spanish. Vogel would not be able to read it; Moraga, the ignoramus, can read nothing at all. But both have talked with Nig Chorro. He can read and write, hardly more. He has a wife, Nella, and a step-daughter, Rosita, who are smart women. The thief would hesitate before exposing his secret and his crime to another. That is true, *no*? *Bueno*! After such hesitation, lasting many days, has the robber at last gone to Nig Chorro? That is the question! Perhaps. And yet, it is my belief, not yet have they dared move to set the paper's statement to the test of truth. But that test must come soon, Señor! Who knows but that tonight—now . . ."

He broke off, soberly considering the baffling question. But his fancies, having caught the wind of his favorite golden quarry, were off on the luring track; his soberness passed and he fell to speaking sweepingly of the Calderon treasure and then, of course, of his theories of the loot of the famous bandit, Joaquin Murietta. He made of the whole a tale to catch anybody's ear.

"Tales of love and tales of gold
  Tales of earthly happiness.
Sighs and smiles—the southern soul
  Makes through these its sunny quest."

Juanito went from one to the other as a child may skip among plots in a flower garden. Was not Señor Whitney his friend? Juanito was sure of it. And must not one friend speak out his heart to the other? All that Juanito had imagined hidden—Whitney wondered if he could hide anything—

117

he now set into the music of his extravagant speech.

He loved Teresita; God, how he loved her! He put his hand on his romantic heart and sighed profoundly. He spoke of her in superlatives, naming her an angel at the least. Then he named Brooke Sheffield and scowled darkly; he raised his hand and drove it downward as though it clenched a knife.

He spoke bitterly. Teresita had smiled now and then at Señor Sheffield: what did Whitney suppose she meant by it? It could not be that she cared for the man to the extent which Juanito indicated by snapping his artistic fingers! Surely not! Did she but seek to vex her true lover? Should Juanito defy his rival openly? Should he slap his face and denounce him and drive him away from the ranch? Was there danger, perhaps, in allowing Sheffield to buy the Pajaro Azul and thus become a neighbor? Was the man minded to remain eternally under the Calderon roof, where he had invited himself, where there was no excuse for his long tarrying? Was Juanito to tolerate it that Brooke Sheffield should call Teresita his "teacher," that from her sacred lips he should learn to say *ojos prietos*, *la boca bonita* and even perchance, *novia*? All of this was intolerable! Juanito swore softly in Spanish. What would his *amigo* advise him to do?

That one man should come to another with his love burden was something which Whitney had never imagined possible. And yet it did not appear so strange a consummation now that Juanito bestowed his confidences full-handedly. Whitney understood that Juanito, half boy that he remained, would never be all full-grown man with the self-reliance the term connoted; he understood further that Juanito's love was deep and true, despite the froth of words, the spray of iridescent imagery at all times cloaking it. And to the young fellow's outright questionings he responded sincerely:

"I do not think that Miss Calderon will find Sheffield her type. Perhaps a girl does like to tease her lover. In the end I hope that she is going to look your way, Juanito."

When Juanito brightened and thrust out his hand impetuously, Whitney shook hands with him soberly enough and, in his heart, wished the gay Juanito all success. . . . Just ahead, between Señor Olivas and Brooke Sheffield, Teresa Calderon rode on through the golden spring sunshine. It happened that she chose this moment to turn and look back. She was not so far ahead that they could not hear her call laughingly:

"What dark plottings, Sir Conspirators? You have the sinister air of two desperados sealing a terrible pact!"

Juanito waved his hat.

"It is the ratification of understanding between friends!" he cried. "Behold two sworn allies for a great purpose! Wish us success, Señorita!"

"I do," laughed Teresa. "All success, you two terrible plotters."

Down in the valley where there was a fork in the trail, those ahead waited for Whitney and Juanito. Here Señor Olivas was turning aside to cross the river and ride by the Belden place. Whitney, willing for a chat with him, promised to rejoin the others at the ranch house for lunch and he and Mentor rode away. Juanito hesitated, turned his eyes questioningly upon Teresa and then announced with something of defiance in his voice that he would accompany her and Señor Sheffield.

"Unless," he suggested blandly, "Señor Sheffield, being interested in the Pajaro Azul, would prefer to ride with the other gentlemen?"

Sheffield laughed.

"The Pajaro Azul is not the only thing I am interested in," he said. "I am taking a lesson in Spanish adjectives, Johnny."

"Johnny!" muttered Juanito disgustedly. "Bah for Johnny. That is not my name, Señor."

Again Sheffield's easy laughter rang on Whitney's ears as he and Señor Olivas rode down to the ford. He wondered that the fiery Juanito had so long hesitated to slap the face and pull the nose of his rival.

Once on the Pajaro Azul pasture lands, Señor Olivas's face grew more sober than ever.

"It is a shame," he muttered, and Whitney understood his thought. And later that thought was expressed again and more plainly. "See," Mentor exclaimed. "Here is a holding which is worth much, much more than it is going to sell for. All because my friend the judge is sick and unfortunate. All because of a paltry two or three or four thousand dollars!"

Whitney was surprised at the smallness of the need. Mentor caught his look and explained succinctly.

"The judge is on his back. He has expenses, bills. His place is mortgaged. Vogel will advance no more money and it is difficult, on an outlying property, to get a man to take a second mortgage. So, I suppose, the judge will have to sell."

Whitney regarded Señor Olivas sharply. The fine old face was clouded, the eyes, unmindful of Whitney's look, were dark with sorrowful abstraction. Plainly, merely unburdening himself to the son of his *amigo* Benito, Olivas had not the slightest suspicion of the sudden inspiration he had given his listener. But before Whitney's mental eye rose the smug face of Brooke Sheffield. And Sheffield was going to succeed in gobbling up Judge Belden's acres simply because of the judge's urgent need of a few thousand dollars!

Now in all sincerity Whitney held himself "broke." Like a plate glass window under a sledge hammer, as he himself had put it. But even

121

of a broken plate glass window there would be certain fragments. Of the wealth which he had piled up for himself, there would be something left. He was certain that his creditors would have been satisfied by now and that, after his lawyers had done with the job, there would be some few thousands left. The lease on his offices might be disposed of, even to advantage; rents were higher now than formerly and his was a choice location. There was certain personal property, among other things an expensive car. He had not thought much of these matters since coming to the King of Spain, postponing their consideration until that vague "after a while" when he would go back to town. . . .

Mentor addressing him got no reply. Looking at Whitney's face he saw an absent look and a queer smile. Whitney was thinking of treating himself to a small luxury, to putting a spoke in the wheel of the most cock-sure, insufferably complacent individual it had ever been his lot to meet.

"Since you have been kind enough to put me on horseback," he said carelessly to his com-panion, "I think I'll ride into Toyon this afternoon. I have a letter to get off."

. . . He thought how pleased Juanito would be if he forestalled Sheffield!

On leaving the Belden place, jogging on through the genial noon-day warmth of the valley, both men were silent. Mentor's thoughts were his own; Maxwell Whitney, for the first time in many days, pondered upon matters of finance. But such matters passed from his mind long before the ranch house came into view. More sleepy than ever seemed the land about him now that the season was advancing with its growing drowsiness; in its quiet peacefulness he sunned himself contentedly; he began to wonder if he were done with ambition and its ceaseless "climbing up the climbing wave." Suppose that where his camp was he builded himself a cabin with his own hands. That he got himself a dog and a horse; that he had a fireplace and a reading lamp and surrounded himself with books; that he lay out a few dollars in guns and fishing rods; that he devoted a great part of the quiet years to come in tramping through the Santa Lucia mountains, climbing a peak to make sure that the Pacific was still where it belonged, returning homeward to watch the sparks shoot up the throat of his own fireplace. . . . He said to Mentor:

"I have evolved a theory."

"Yes?"

"That, when your forefathers came into the King of Spain Valley, they introduced into this golden California climate a certain germ which has thrived here, nowhere better! The germ of Content. It's in the air."

Mentor laughed and stretched luxuriously.

"It is good to take life easy," he said smilingly.

Teresa was on the porch waving to them. Behind her, one on each hand, stood Juanito and Brooke Sheffield. Whitney smiled as though anticipating a pleasant adventure. Then he put a hand to his unshaven chin.

"Is there a barber in Toyon?" he asked.

And somewhere, among the many merging reflections which may throng a man's mind at one and the same time, was the vague thought that he would be taking a purely friendly, though important, part in the contention between those two men for Teresa Calderon.

CHAPTER XII

THE KING OF SPAIN PAINTING

A sun-flooded land of abundance . . . as such did the King of Spain Valley impress itself upon Maxwell Whitney as he and Mentor Olivas rode through the wide fields, by the Mission ruins and on to the Calderon home. Young wild grass and upthrusting grain were lusty, driving their roots deep into the black, fertile soil, rearing their spears toward the life-giving air and sunshine. What grazing stock was to be seen was fat and sleek. The orchard was in full, shining leaf, promising a rich yield when the summertime should work again the ancient alchemy, putting pure golden deliciousness into swelling satiny skins, plumping with sugary sweetness and delectable juices. The domestic pigeons rose and wheeled and settled, filled with peace and the content of morning hunger appeased. Under the oak tree at the rear of the house, waiting for a hired man to lead them away to the stable, were three blooded horses; five when Mentor and Whitney dismounted, animals vying with one another in equine beauty and aristocracy. All was in harmony, striking the full rich note of generous sufficiency.

Within doors the same refrain repeated itself in a minor key. The furniture, though old, was massive, dignified, worthy of accommodating *la gente*. The floors, though mostly bare according to tradition, but served to accentuate the fineness of what few bits of covering there were; a rug, woven long ago somewhere on the north coast of Africa, sold to a Calderon on the south coast of Spain, brought hitherward a full sixty or seventy years ago, was of a sort to please those who may happen to understand that a rug may be something other and more than a mere convenience for muffling scuffling footfalls, quite as a picture may serve other purposes than that of hiding a bare wall. The table was set; the linen was pure and shone; the silver was worn but in keeping. . . . Even the spring breeze, wandering in from the kitchen where old Uracca and young Josefa were busied about the stove, brought such a tale of savory viands as to assure any newcomer that the old days of bounty still held on. Through dusky bottles the wine was a rich ruby red. In the center of the table was a tall vase of yellow roses from the Mission.

It was Juanito who bore Maxwell Whitney off to his room, the same which he had occupied that other night. And it was Juanito who, seeing the gesture of a hand passed ruefully over an unshaven face, suggested the loan of a razor. Barber? He laughed at Whitney's enquiry. There was none within twenty-five or thirty miles. Hereabouts one must be his own valet entirely. There would be time before lunch.

When Whitney returned to the others in the dining room it was to find everyone there excepting Teresa. She entered a moment later, the cause of her delay both obvious and excusable. She had changed from riding togs into a filmy little house dress of pale blue; she had done her hair up afresh; in it was a rose, blood red among the lustrous strands of her hair. She looked cool and fresh and summery; her eyes were soft and bright and, as they drifted fleetingly to a meeting with Whitney's, friendly. And, largely because she continued to surprise him and because he had

had no thought to bide his appraisal of her, a little pink flush again made of her something more of a wild-rose girl than the magnolia señorita he had first held her.

. . . It is a matter of extreme difficulty to say which are the great, which the small happenings in a man's life. A spider web may conceivably save a Bruce and steer history down another channel; a clumsy guide in a rain storm may lose a Waterloo. Certain it is that Maxwell Whitney, hearing Teresa's light footfall—she had pretty round ankles, black silk stockings and French-heeled slippers—had expected to see her now as he had seen her a few minutes ago. Certain it is that in a very brief time a decided change had been wrought in her. Whether this was the work of the little blue dress or of the red rose or of some subtle change emanating from the young woman's thoughts, becomes a consideration beyond speculation. Thoughts are things; they do travel amazingly from one person to another. Also, to be done with what is no more a trifle than was Bruce's spider web, the change of the outer dress works in the human breast, perhaps particularly in the feminine, a subtle chemistry. At any rate, the time was passed when in any way whatever Maxwell Whitney could regard Teresa Calderon the least bit impersonally.

After lunch Whitney had a brief tête-à-tête with her. As chairs were pushed back he said something about riding into Toyon that afternoon, thanks to the loan of a horse, to order some supplies. Sheffield at once hurried off to his room to get a couple of letters written for Whitney to mail. Señor Olivas wanted a word with Juanito about some ranch business; during the day Whitney began to understand that Mentor's hopes coincided with his son's, that one of these days he would hope Juanito to be his successor as manager of the King of Spain Ranch *ex officio*.

Whitney turned to the girl.

"Señor Olivas has told me about the King of Spain painting," he said. "I wonder if you would show it to me?"

"Of course," answered Teresa. "Gladly. We are proud of it and are perhaps a little eager to have it seen. Only—"

"If it is any trouble," he said hastily.

Teresa laughed.

"It still hangs in the room which was once my father's bedroom. To come to it one must pass through my bedroom which was once his study. And I am afraid that my room is not always as tidy as it should be. Especially when it is a case of a hurried change for lunch. Josefa!" she called.

Josefa did not at first answer though she was in full sight in the kitchen and must have heard. Teresa called again.

"*Sí, Señorita*," said Josefa without looking up.

Teresa spoke in Spanish; but Whitney understood

enough to know that she was asking Josefa to run, like a good girl, and set things in order. Josefa seemed in no haste to obey; she mumbled something about doing the dishes. Teresa called sharply and Josefa came. But the Indian girl's eyes looked sullen.

"I don't understand Josefa of late," said Teresa, looking wonderingly after the departing figure. "She used always to be so quick, so willing. Now she resents being asked to do anything." But she shrugged her shoulders quite as Señor Olivas would have done and turned back to him smiling. "As though you would be interested in our domestic perplexities! Come, let us go into the library which is also a smoking room. I'll give you one of Señor Mentor's cigars and a big, soft chair and we'll wait for Josefa to pick up a pair of shoes and smooth out a rug."

He went with her into a moderately small room at the cool side of the house where were many books in ancient bindings, a couple of tables littered with books, and some deep leather chairs. She selected a chair for him, watched him sink deep into it, gave him a cigar, and then seated herself in a smaller chair facing him. For a while he sat in silence and she was content to be as silent, watching him enjoy his cigar. The first, by the way, for above a week. But his eyes were busy enough; when he knew they must not tarry longer with her piquant perfection they traveled about the room interestedly and appreciatively. On the walls were two paintings only; both were seascapes, both charming. Beyond himself and his companion, the clothes they wore, the cigar he smoked, the lamp on the table, and perhaps a score of books, there was not an article in the room which was not the product of another age. One felt here, as when entering the living room for the first time, that he was stepping back a full hundred years.

"Miss Calderon," he said, "do you realize that you and your home have a way of putting a spell over a fellow?"

"Have we?" she smiled. "You put me first? Just by way of being gallant?"

"I'll strive not to presume upon kindness and become personal," he laughed. "So I'll confine myself to the home. Do you know it is, in its way, quite the most wonderful home I've ever entered?"

She brightened with pleasure.

"We feel that way, too," she admitted. "It is not so modern, not so rich and elegant, not so perfectly convenient, perhaps, as others. But somehow—"

"It harmonizes!" He took the words out of her mouth. "It's as though the valley were a living entity and in this home it found its soul. It is quite perfect. Any other sort of dwelling here would be an anomaly."

"You are very kind to us." She smiled under his enthusiasm. "We love our valley as it is, our home as it is. When one suggests cutting down oak trees, hundreds of years old, to plant prunes or seed barley—Ugh!"

"Fate has chosen you custodian of a priceless gem," he answered seriously. "You have a responsibility to the past."

She nodded, musing. Suddenly she lifted her eyes and surprised him by demanding bluntly:

"What do you think of Brooke Sheffield?"

He hesitated. He did not think very highly of Sheffield and, he was rather confident, she must know it. But after all the man was no doubt merely the common or garden variety of complacent nuisance and Maxwell Whitney saw no need for him to express an opinion.

"The connotation," he evaded, "is that Sheffield has been after you to slash into your forests and make the soil produce?"

"You have heard how he speaks of what he will do with the Pajaro Azul."

There came, swift and urgent, upon Whitney then the impulse to lean forward confidentially, to tell her that he was going into Toyon today with the future fate of the Pajaro Azul in mind and perhaps in the palm of his hand. She caught something of his impulse for she looked at him with quickening expectation. But long years of business training in the way of keeping a shut mouth until after a deal was safely turned, caused him to sit back, keeping his own counsel.

Teresa looked her disappointment.

"You haven't answered," she reminded him, giving him a first glimpse of that insistence which later he found to be an essential part of her character. "What do you make of Mr. Sheffield?"

This time, with his thoughts in order, he answered her.

"He impresses me as a young man who has gained at least a modicum of what he, and the world with him, names success. The sort who believes in his own destiny and hence, if for no other reason, travels far in the direction he maps out for himself. One who has his wits about him and who, true to his pledge, will perhaps some day make a certain Asa Vogel take a place farther up stage."

She laughed softly.

"You do not make any strong case against him!"

"Why should I?"

"Because you dislike him."

He drew at his cigar, met her eyes steadily and in the end smiled. But this time she regarded him gravely; her eyes, as they had done this morning when she rode into his camp, mystified.

Josefa came noiselessly to the library door, looked in, nodded to her mistress in taciturn preference to speaking three words to say her work was done, and slipped away to the kitchen like a slim, brown shadow.

• • •

"Unless you would rather finish your cigar first—" suggested Teresa.

"By no means," he answered. "I have been looking forward to seeing your painting."

She led the way, back into the living room, into a dim hallway, through a door and into her own bedroom. He glimpsed filmy white curtains at the windows, billowing gently to the soft spring breeze, a dressing table with its dainty accessories looking to have borrowed from Teresa's femininity, a music stand and an open guitar case, in a corner an old-fashioned bed shut in by its own alcove of drawn curtains. Then, across the room a door standing open; through this another room which had once been the sleeping quarters of Señor Jose Calderon, father of Teresa. As Señor Calderon had left it, so had it remained during the years; the same tables and chairs, unused, unmolested. And upon a wall where Señor Jose Calderon had hung it, was the King of Spain painting.

But, before Whitney came to stand absorbed before the painting itself, certain details of the room intrigued him. There were two windows, like the others in the particular of being deep-set in the thick walls, with the customary wide window ledges; unlike the others in the matter of the bars across them. Each window was heavily grilled from top to bottom with iron bars twice the thickness of a man's thumb, the ends set

133

into thick slabs of seasoned oak which, in turn, were embedded in the adobe of the wall. Teresa, catching his eye, explained.

"The picture, in its day, has created much discussion. Collectors of rare paintings have sought several times to purchase it; I believe, in part because of the story of its duplicate in a royal palace in Spain, more, I hope, for its own intrinsic merit, it is held very valuable. Twice, in my father's time, attempts were made to steal it. It was he who had the windows barred."

The picture itself filled a large canvas; the whole, including a wide frame which the padre-artist himself had made of oak and had stained a soft gray-green, covered a wall-space of perhaps three by five feet. Instead of being hung by wires, it was held in place by four sturdy oaken pegs, one through each corner of the frame. As Señor Don Jose Calderon had placed it, as he had liked to see it, as he had left it, so had it remained until now.

Maxwell Whitney, though knowing nothing of art's technique, understood that the painting was out of the ordinary, above the mediocre, perhaps a thing to draw much attention, praise and criticism in a distinguished gallery. From the ridge up which he and Mentor Olivas had ridden from their first visit to the Pajaro Azul, the padre-artist, with easel before him, had looked out across wide sweeping meadow lands with timbered ridges beyond; had seen in the distance the young Mission, the new Calderon home. He had perhaps brought from Spain a heart to thrill responsively to the spaciousness of California; he had seen God's promises through his colors. He had caught and immortalized the very day in which he had worked with the fine, final frenzy: that day when the sky had been its most perfect blue, when there was but the one slow drifting white cloud, when spring was verging on early summer, while yet the earth was carpeted in green and gold. One could stand here looking at an old picture and fancy he heard the trickle of water, the sough of the wind, the song of a bird.

. . . Whitney's one quiet comment when at last he withdrew his eyes was: "Thank you for letting me see it." Teresa's eyes sparkled with pleasure and then went suddenly wet at the sincerity of his appreciation which she understood lay under the words.

"Hello, in there," came Brooke Sheffield's voice. "Worshiping at the shrine, Miss Teresa?"

"Come!" said Teresa quickly. "Let us go!—You will want to finish your smoking."

"If you asked me right now," muttered Whitney, "what I thought of Sheffield—"

But she hurried on ahead, and with a last glance at the painting and then about the room which had the air of awaiting the return of a departed master, he followed her. Sheffield, licking the flap of the second of his two envelopes, they found at the open door of Teresa's room. The three went to the library. Sheffield gave his letters over to Whitney exactly as he would have handed them to an under-tipped messenger boy and, with an air which seemed to shut himself in with Miss Teresa and away from all others, remarked,

"How about our Spanish lesson? I know four lines of Johnny's little song, *Teresita Mía.*" He appeared to recall Whitney fleetingly. "It's quite a ride into Toyon," he observed. "You'll be hitting the trail right off, won't you, Whit?"

Whitney stared at him. But before he found the fitting answer Juanito interrupted them, saying from the door,

"Vogel's coming. He'll save you the ride, Señor Maxwell. He can take your order for supplies and you can spend the whole day with us."

"Vogel?" said Sheffield. "He'll have some mail for me." He caught back his letters from Whitney and went out, calling back over his shoulder: "Our lesson's postponed, Miss Teresa; business before pleasure, you know."

Since the coming of the mail to the ranch was always an occasion of interest, the others went out to the porch to greet Vogel. This time he came in his rickety cart; the wide shafts between which was imprisoned a very narrow-gauged horse, swayed with the lurching of the wheels after a fashion to make of Vogel's vehicle an unsteady craft lurching across the green sea of the valley floor. Juanito laughed, saying that once when he had ridden with Vogel the voyage had made him seasick.

Vogel, looking more soiled and crafty than ever, distributed what mail he had brought.

There were letters for Sheffield, one for Teresa, one for Señor Olivas; this letter was a large envelope for which Vogel asked a receipt since it was registered. Whitney, knowing there would be nothing for him since not even his lawyers knew as yet where to address him, idly watched. Thus he noted for the first time a certain contradiction of terms in the details going to make up Asa Vogel. The man looked as though he had never washed behind the ears; his face was grimy, his beard and hair repulsed one who loved cleanliness; certainly the undershirt showing at the throat, and the hairy neck itself, were unwashed. But Vogel's hands were as clean as anyone's, even cleaner than most respectable outdoor folks'. Not white; hard and leathery, but clean after a fashion bespeaking more than a bowing acquaintance with soapsuds. Whereas he might have achieved very gratifying results by bathing eyes and ears, he was content with going no further than the brief way from nails to wrist. That was because Vogel loved his ledgers and liked to keep them neat and clean.

"Then there's a package for you, too, Mr.

Sheffield. Some books. That stupid Henry of mine picked it up by the string and busted the package open. But I guess he didn't do the books any harm."

Sheffield, deep in a letter which he had opened eagerly, jerked his head up impatiently and muttered, "Curse your Henry for a stupid fool," and then swinging directly upon Mentor Olivas and from him to Whitney as though he sensed that these two would most strongly feel the import of his words, he announced triumphantly:

"I'm to get my definite answer on the Belden place in a week! The old judge hates to let go," he chuckled. "Likes to dribble it out through his fingers. But in a week it's mine! And at my own price! Pretty slick, eh?"

Mentor looked distressed. Whitney, turning to him, making no answer to Sheffield, chanced to observe the contents of Mentor's registered letter. In his hand were a number of bank notes, perhaps several hundred dollars. Mentor, his face still clouded, put the money into his breast pocket. Whitney, though he sought not to interest himself in his host's private affairs, could not but wonder what on earth he meant to do with so large a sum here in the uncommercial King of Spain Valley. . . . He saw that all of the craft within Asa Vogel was peeping out of his slitted eyes; he wondered further if Vogel had any particular designs on that money or if it were merely that he could not look upon any man's gold without that glint of avarice?

"No mail for you, Mr. Whitney," said Vogel sharply. "Don't you ever get letters?"

For answer Whitney shrugged. He turned away with Teresa, seeing that Vogel's gaunt beast was being led off to the stable for a real feast, and sincerely hoping that Vogel and Brooke Sheffield would have much to say to each other. But even as he rejoined Miss Calderon and she began to show him her pet roses, he was considering that if Sheffield was to have his answer within seven days, there was no great deal of time for one Maxwell Whitney to let slip.

Not if he meant to have a try at the Pajaro Azul himself—

CHAPTER XIII

JUANITO'S THEFT

Señor Olivas excused himself and went immediately to the library which served him also as office. To Whitney he explained:

"Once a month, Señor, I become a clerk; I make entries in my books, calculations; I debit and I credit and I balance things up." He sighed as he turned away; for all the world he looked like a little boy masking in the features of age, who now suddenly forgot the disguise at the call of a teacher and the bidding to a task. Mentor Olivas, struggling with ink and ledger, was an incongruity. "Juanito, you can help me."

Teresa laughed.

"*Mira*," she exclaimed. "I become an enchantress!" The long-stemmed rose in her hand she waved toward Señor Olivas, touching him lightly with the fragrant petals. "Presto! The manager of *El Rey de España* disappears; in his stead behold a mathematician!"

Mentor's smile responded; he raised his broad hat as he went into the house. Already Sheffield was drawing Vogel aside for a confidential talk, obviously of the ranch over which Vogel held a mortgage.

"It is funny," said Teresa when she and Whitney were thus left together, "when Señor Mentor and Soap-bubble Juanito smear ink over themselves! They are very dear fellows, but a good God did not intend them to be bookkeepers."

Whitney moved at her side. It was a delightfully warm afternoon, more pleasant outside than within doors. Under a rose arbor where was an old oak bench from which one might look out across the sunny valley Teresa sat down and with a glance invited Whitney to a place at her side.

"You are all so kind to me here," he said. "You ride to see me, you give me a horse, you make me feel at home, like an old friend."

"With us," she returned, "life is not full of variety. It is pleasant to have new faces. And, at least to Señor Mentor, you are like an old friend, since you are the son of his *amigo* Benito."

"I wonder what you would have to say of me as a neighbor? If I decided to prolong my little camping trip and stay on indefinitely somewhere on the fringe of your valley?"

She looked up at him swiftly.

"What a stampede of the outside world into the sleepy old King of Spain!" she exclaimed. "Men from outside, like yourself and Mr. Sheffield, suddenly forsake their old paths for our older ones! It is not that somewhere you have discovered gold? Or oil even?"

"Neither," he answered. And then, tempted by the nearness of her tempting self, he bantered: "Are there not other, more compelling things than gold?"

Teresa's eyes flashed a quick understanding and the hint of a carefree invitation to dare further. Her gay Spanish heart, he read in that glance, was ever ready to accept an hour of flirtation, of course within the ever looming bounds of the discreet. Little country girl she might be, but none the less serene mistress of those inherited instincts with which a just nature has armed her sex. The look sparkled and passed; Teresa was all that was demure. She said lazily,

"You, too, would turn rancher?"

Again came the impulse to speak of his intention regarding the Pajaro Azul; again through a business habit of long standing he kept his own counsel. He merely answered:

"Perhaps. If you would tolerate me in my camp a little longer? And if I could find a little place somewhere?"

Teresa sighed.

"If only you were in a position—" she began. But she ended there abruptly.

He thought that he read her thought and a quick thrill of unanalyzed pleasure danced through his veins. Just to have her prefer him to Sheffield as neighbor was gratifying.

"You mean the Pajaro Azul?" he demanded.

But she elected with her eyes to baffle him again.

"What!" she cried in mock alarm. "Am I in danger of having my thoughts read by Señor Maxwell?"

The knowledge that he was a second time pleased, now by having her call him by his first name which he did not even suppose she knew or remembered, set him thinking: He was starting out in great style to boost the game of his young friend Juanito!

A half hour later, as he was strolling about the garden and lawn, Mentor's voice, with now and then a word from Juanito, floated out to him through an open window in the library. He saw

142

a man in the corral doing something to a horse's foreleg; he elected to watch the placing of a liniment-soaked bandage rather than be bored with Sheffield or breathe the same air as Vogel. When Mentor and Juanito finished in the library he would go in and write a letter.

Whitney leaned idly against the corral gate; his shadow fell so that the man with the horse, who had not heard his steps, looked up. It was the swart-faced Felipe Moraga. Certainly he had a face that went with all that surmise and proven accusation had ever laid at his door. He was today more sullen and ugly than when Whitney had first seen him.

"A sprain?" asked Whitney.

"Cut," said Moraga. "Barb' wire."

By now he had finished his task and straightened up, feeling for tobacco and papers, his eyes drifting back to the foreleg which the animal held gingerly lifted.

"You a fran' of that man Sheffiel'?" demanded Moraga abruptly.

"No," came the cool rejoinder. "I am not."

Moraga grunted and turned away.

"He's pretty frash guy," he said over his shoulder. "You tell him he betta look out."

"Tell him yourself, *compadre*," laughed Whitney. "And while you're at it, you might give him the same sort of message for me."

Moraga made no response and slouched away

into the stable and out of sight; Whitney, with nothing better to do, wondered how Brooke Sheffield could have gone so far out of his way as to incur the enmity of a half-breed Indian ex-convict.

When at last Señor Olivas and Juanito came out of the house, Vogel was squatting alone on the steps. He looked up quickly; Whitney saw how he called to Juanito and how, though Juanito hesitated, in the end he stopped for a word with the storekeeper.

Señor Olivas, looking flushed and worried, joined Whitney for a smoke.

"*Caramba*!" From his lips the polite oath fell bursting with eloquence. He mopped his forehead with his handkerchief. Then he filled his lungs with a deep breath of air. "Matters of dollars and cents, Señor, make the head of an Olivas ache. Pouf! It is done for another month."

But though he sought to have done with the monthly episode, boasting of it forgotten, the puckered lines of his brow did not relax. Frequently his eyes ran to Juanito; Vogel's claws were on the boy's coat and the two appeared to have a good deal to say to each other.

Mentor frowned.

"Juanito should have more companions. Of his own age, his own station." He sighed wearily. "I do not like for him to be friends with that man Vogel," he concluded bluntly.

144

"I hardly imagine there is any deep friendship between them," said Whitney, reassuring him. "It would be incongruous."

"Come. We shall have a glass of wine, you and I. A bottle set away since 1897. Today I feel old, Señor Maxwell. *Venga.*"

"*Muy bueno.* And then I will ask you for paper and envelope. I should write a letter."

Fifteen minutes later Whitney sat alone in the library where Señor Olivas had conducted and left him. The afternoon sun flooded the table in the middle of the room and so he withdrew to a corner and with a tablet on his knee began a letter to his attorneys which he never finished. He had sunk deep in one of the big leather chairs; another chair, between him and the door, half screened him. But even so Juanito, coming in swiftly, must have seen him were it not that he had been so sure the room was unoccupied and were it not that he was so eager and swift about the errand which had brought him and which monopolized his every thought. He went to the table; every gesture of lightning speed, he lifted a vase of roses, drew from under it the small flat key, unlocked a table drawer, drew something out, slipped it into his pocket, and hurried out of the room. The whole series of smaller acts making the greater one required scarcely more than a moment. Whitney, at first abstracted by his own thoughts, then puzzled by something furtive in the boy's manner, sat silent and motionless. He saw what it was that Juanito had taken from the drawer. It was the pad of bank notes which had come today for Señor Olivas. In the neighborhood of a thousand dollars, he had already estimated. . . .

CHAPTER XIV

THE SCORN OF TERESITA

Whitney tore from the tablet the page on which a never-to-be-completed letter had begun, slowly crumpling it in his hand. Suddenly other considerations interested him more than a note to his lawyers.

He sat very still, frowning with unseeing eyes at the table whose drawer had been so hurriedly rifled.

A first strong impulse was to go straight to Juanito and put the thing up to him and he half rose from his chair. Then he forced himself to drop back; he lighted a cigar and held in check the wild horses of a man's impulse.

"Go slow, old boy," he admonished himself. "This is none of your affair—at least as yet. And you've got no call to go muddling things."

Juanito a thief? A predatory animal even in the

lair of his own kin and kind? Well, then, how about Tia Tonia's box of little treasures?

"By the Lord," muttered Whitney, his mind stunned by a fresh shock to his understanding, "if he's the one who did that, too, then I lose all respect for my judgment of humanity. I'll be ready to accept that cursed Sheffield as a most estimable and honorable gentleman and Vogel as a philanthropist."

And yet—

"I don't believe it," he told himself. "That a boy, seeming as transparent as glass, should get away with a play like that."

And yet again—Juanito had taken the thousand dollars. Whitney sprang up and hurried out of the library. He'd have a look at Juanito; he'd look deep into the boy's eyes, seeking a shadow there; he'd make sure that after all Mentor had not sent for the money.

As he hastened out of the room he met Teresa Calderon coming into the living room. She looked at him, first with a half-smile, then curiously.

"You seem in a tremendous hurry," she laughed. "There aren't any trains to catch here, you remember."

"I was thinking pretty fast," he told her, "and I guess my legs were trying to catch up with my thoughts." He still held crumpled in his hand the sheet of letter paper; he thrust it into his coat pocket, saying abruptly: "Tell me something:

147

Have you any suspicion who took your Tia Tonia's box?"

She looked at him in unmasked surprise.

"What a question," she exclaimed, "coming this way—all of a sudden!"

"I know," he admitted. "But I have been thinking and I wondered. I know it is hardly a matter which I should bring up; it lies so entirely within your own private affairs and so utterly beyond the rim of mine. But I can't help asking. And—do you mind answering me?"

He puzzled her. She held silent a moment; he marked the shadow of perplexity on her brow.

"Yes. I have a suspicion," she said at last. "But it is only a suspicion and I am rather ashamed of myself for holding it. So, you won't ask me to say anything more?"

"No," he returned. "Of course not."

"And you? What makes you speak of it now? Do you, too, suspect someone?"

"If I do I, too, like you, am rather inclined to be ashamed of myself for the suspicion!—Which, by the way, makes me wonder if you and I do not have the same person in mind?"

Teresa moved on a few paces so that she stood at the window looking out into the gardens. He waited for her to speak. At last she said, without turning her head,

"If so, what then? I am not at all sure, Señor Max, that it now makes the least bit of difference who took the box or who keeps it or destroys it. Poor Tia Tonia is no longer here to care. That there were papers of importance is only a possibility. And it is a very serious thing to accuse one of theft; a very terrible thing, if the accusation is unjust. I rather think we should forget it all; I have tried to do so."

In old houses floor boards creak with the slightest provocation. Whitney turned and saw that Josefa standing in the kitchen door was listening. Teresa also saw and her eyes flashed with displeasure.

"Josefa," she said, "I did not call for you."

Josefa stared back briefly, her jet-black eyes sullen and defiant. Then she returned to the kitchen without making any answer.

"I don't understand Josefa here of late—"

"Where is Vogel?" He was not thinking of Josefa; his thoughts were developing a way of flying fast and far, speeding on tangental lines.

"He has just gone."

"Did Juanito have a word with him first?"

More than ever he puzzled her. But she answered quietly:

"Juanito came out of the house only a few moments ago. He stopped for a word with me. Mr. Vogel was already leaving. Juanito waved good-by to him."

"And where is Juanito now?"

"With Señor Mentor. Outside.—You wanted to

send your letter by Mr. Vogel? He has not gone far—"

"No. I'll let my letter wait a little while. I am not sure that I'll not ride out to the railroad myself and send a telegram instead."

She smiled as she observed,

"You appear to have a way of changing plans quickly, Señor Max."

"Nowadays men are learning to play their hunches," he told her. "What would you say," he continued, "if I told you that whether I determine to remain in the King of Spain or go on about my business, depends on—"

She waited.

"On who stole Tia Tonia's box!" he blurted out.

"But—I do not understand!"

"No. You would not understand."

But it was clear enough to himself. Why had he thought of interfering in the destiny of the Pajaro Azul acres? For one reason, he did not like Brooke Sheffield and he did not want Brooke Sheffield to succeed in that which he very obviously meant to do. For another reason, he had liked his new friends here, Juanito and Señor Olivas and Teresa. In the beginning he had even said within himself: "I hope Juanito wins out in the rivalry for Señorita Calderon." And now? What had he to do here? He should go back to his mountains until he was surfeited with idleness and solitude. Then he should return to Los Angeles and get his feet

150

again in the old familiar trail. There lay that high wisdom which men carelessly name common sense—as uncommon a quality as a man may chance upon in a long pilgrimage.

"I think that perhaps I do understand," said Teresa thoughtfully. "And that you and I do suspect the same person. But it does so little good to mention names in a case like this, when after all it is nothing but an intangible suspicion, at least on my part. And I rather think that it will be best to forget the whole thing."

"Perhaps."

"One thing is certain," she ran on lightly. "You were hurrying somewhere and I stopped you." She nodded to him and went on to her room. Whitney went out on the porch, seeking Juanito.

Señor Olivas was strolling back and forth under the branches of his old friend, Padre Cipriano, his hands behind his back, his eyes on the blue mountains across the valley. Whitney, with a definite purpose to serve, seeing Juanito nowhere, joined the old Spaniard.

"It does not take you long to write a letter," said Mentor. "With me, Señor, it is worse than breaking a horse."

"I trust our glass of wine together has made you young again," Whitney answered. "Your clerking is over for the day? And forgotten?"

"Until evening," laughed Olivas. "Then the

muchachos will come in and pay-day begins."

"And of course you pay always in cash. The old way."

"Of course. One estimates what moneys he must disburse; he draws it from the bank—when he is fortunate enough to have the full sum on deposit! He pays out the money and the thing is done. That way one keeps his books straight and bookkeeping becomes simplicity."

"But at times one would be forced to have a rather large sum on his hands in bank notes?"

"I have drawn this time a little over a thousand dollars, Señor," Olivas answered him. "There are the wages; some few bills of the household and Teresa's personally. Odds and ends in these days count up swiftly."

"But surely," Whitney drove straight on to his point, "you don't feel entirely safe with so much in your pocket? It is so easy to drop when a man rides; also, there have been men known who would risk a good bit for the chance of robbing another man of a thousand dollars."

"*Seguro*." Señor Olivas nodded. "But I put it away; I have a place for it inside. A place where I have always kept the expense moneys. The thousand dollars lie there now; the key is turned in the lock; adobe houses do not burn down readily. *Bueno*; it is as in the bank."

Whitney had learned from Mentor's lips what he knew already: Juanito had taken the money, approximately a thousand dollars, for his own purposes and not at his father's command—money which belonged, not to Olivas, but to Teresa Calderon. Well, why not? What did he know of Juanito save that he was like the summer wind, and the summer wind appropriates to itself as a right the sweetest of those treasures which the flowers and woods hold so lightly. If Juanito pilfered would he not commit his crime as lightly as the sunlit air blowing where it listeth across fragrant meadows did its own pillaging? It would be like Juanito to exclaim that he had a right to happiness; that God had made him to sing and dance and love, not to starve for that which other men had in plenty. And yet it was hard, bitter hard, to think of young Juan Olivas as a thief.

When the opportunity arose, conversation dying away, Whitney asked casually:

"Where is Juanito?"

"Riding," laughed Juanito's father. "You have eyes, Señor; my boy grows restless when a certain other man monopolizes in certain quarters. Juanito but a moment ago left me, going to the house for his hat. From his haste I knew. He came out of the house almost running. Somewhere through the woods he rides as youth will always ride when in the heart there is unrest."

"I, too, will be riding a little later," Whitney told him. "Out to the railroad instead of just into Toyon, I think. The trip will not take me long?"

"A couple of hours only, or two and a half. There is a trail through the hills which you cannot miss; it saves you several miles."

"I think I will wait until evening, then. I like riding at night."

For he had a curiosity to see how Juanito carried himself when he returned; and he wanted to be on hand when Señor Olivas went to his table drawer, to pay his men.

"You will have supper with us. Then I myself shall ride a little way with you to put you in the right trail. If you care to return tonight you can be back by midnight. And your room is yours, *mi amigo*, as long as you will."

Impatiently Whitney waited for the afternoon to drag on to a close. There were intervals during which he was tempted toward frank speech with Señor Olivas. And yet it is no simple thing to tell a father that his son is a thief. Then, too, there are always possibilities of satisfactory explanations if one will but be patient. Juanito must have his chance first. Besides all of this, long custom had made of Maxwell Whitney a man who kept his hands off other men's business. It was not likely that circumstances would lead him to maintaining this silence indefinitely; where crimes are committed and witnessed one must stand upon one side or the other. There could be no middle ground; his very refusal to take part aligned him with the criminal. But there appeared no need for haste and certainly Whitney was not the one to rush headlong to Olivas with the thing he knew.

When, in the early dusk and well before Josefa had lighted the lantern on the front porch, Juanito rode a foam-lathered horse back to the house, Whitney was in the yard. He watched the boy narrowly; he noted his every gesture; marked how lightly he dismounted, how his elastic stride was that of youth on winged feet. Juanito's carriage was unaltered, buoyant, graceful, confident.

Of Juanito's expression he could make nothing. It was possible that there was a brighter sparkle in his eyes or that a flush of excitement burned in his cheeks; it was possible, also, that his ride against the wind could have been accountable for both.

"If he's the thief his act brands him," marveled Whitney, "I've never done the boy's character justice. He's as cocksure as any gay young captain of bandits. And he is playing his hand like a seasoned villain."

During the supper hour his eyes were seldom entirely withdrawn from the face of young Juanito Olivas. But still he learned nothing. The boy laughed spontaneously; he frowned more than once, too, at times when Teresa listened to Brooke Sheffield and allowed her eyes to play at the eternal feminine game of hide-and-seek.

True, there was a hint of suppressed excitement at all times, but when was Juanito Olivas the calm, cool-blooded being that other men are? When was the time that he was not singing or sighing, intoxicated with life itself? With him a flush of excitement was only the normal reaction to the electric currents surging through him. . . . No, it did not do to judge by surface appearances. Whitney asked himself fruitlessly if Juanito had the impudence to have the bank notes at this moment upon his person or if he had hidden them somewhere. The boy's bearing gave him no clue.

Sheffield devoted himself to the enjoyment of his meal and to his talk with Teresa. He unburdened himself of many little Spanish phrases in an accent whose atrocity caused Juanito to shudder. Josefa came and went; she loitered about the table; at times into her night black eyes came quick flashes. Whitney, grown watchful of trifles because of the mood governing him, marked something which struck him as odd and which he failed utterly to understand: In some subtle way Sheffield's deportment seemed influenced by Josefa's presence; when the Indian girl stood across the table from him his eyes were lowered; in the midst of a light skirmish with Teresa's wit, during which Josefa entered quietly from the kitchen, the very quality of his voice altered; it became impersonal. Though such a thing struck Whitney as grotesquely incredible, still he sensed that Sheffield took pains to hide from the servant girl his inclination toward her mistress, and that always Sheffield was uncomfortable under the unfathomable Indian eyes.

At first Whitney told himself that he was wrong in such a supposition, that it was sheer nonsense to imagine a condition so utterly absurd. But was it any more incredible than his earlier discovery of the day, that "Soap Bubble Juanito" was a thief?

He studied Josefa interestedly. She was slim and young and graceful; hers was the purely animal prettiness of a half-wild creature; for certain men she would hold a brief but perhaps vital charm. Had Brooke Sheffield's fancies roamed so far afield as to envision a summer idyll in which the girl's shy, lovely eyes played a part?

"*Mi amigo* appears thoughtful today." It was Señor Olivas speaking; Whitney started under the realization that he had been withdrawn from the table talk. "Let us hope that no worldly cares have followed him into our peaceful valley."

Whitney discarded his abstraction and responded lightly. He asked pardon for a wandering mind and swung the conversation into a discussion of ranching matters. Mentor was selecting a cigar. Juanito, his eyes perhaps a trifle more bright than before, pushed back his chair.

"Juanito—" began his father.

"*Un momento*," Juanito pleaded. "There is a strain of music which comes to me all of a sudden."

He half ran out of the room. A door and then

another slammed after him. Then, bursting out abruptly, finding its sweet way through the oaken panels, came the wild, delirious singing of Juanito's violin. Even Sheffield grew silent to listen.

The boy was improvising and there was some tremendous need within his soul to cry out through the sympathetic strings of a beloved instrument. What he played was like some devil's medley, and yet through its fury an angel sang. There was a fierce frenzy of double stops during which it seemed that not one but many violins yearned together; there came a lull, abrupt, emphatic; there followed a pizzicato as light as fairies stepping in a minuet. And then came the long, full, serene note as of one who had gone through uncertainties and grasped full handedly of serene confidence. It aspired, it reached out; briefly it groped, for an instant it faltered toward but a hint of a tremolo. And then again it sang that pure note of an angel, and broke off at the full of its sweetness and power so that the thick walls of earth seemed to vibrate with the resonance.

"Juanito has found himself," said Mentor softly. "Like all of us he has come to a place where the trail forks. Now he knows which way he will travel."

Whitney thought: "What Juanito knows is that his father is going to discover his loss in another minute; that, perhaps, he himself, was to have been sent to the library. He is willing that someone else should make the discovery."

At any rate Señor Olivas, with his cigar going, excused himself and went direct to the library. In the kitchen were voices of men who had just come in and were talking with Josefa and old Uracca, the men coming up for their monthly wage. Whitney, accepting a cigar as Teresa offered him the box, forgot to light it. He was waiting—his eyes had followed Mentor, he was keenly expectant, wondering what sort of look would be in Mentor's eyes when he returned.

Teresa and Sheffield were chatting; he did not realize that Teresa's eyes were on his face, that she must be asking herself for some explanation of his tensely expectant expression. In the kitchen a man slapped another on the back; Josefa was laughing; old Uracca's shrill voice was railing at one of the boys for his pretense of robbing her of a new cake set aside to cool on the window sill for tomorrow. Juanito, in his own room, was playing softly on muted strings. And yet a blow was about to fall! Here, drawn apart from the pulse of the moment, Maxwell Whitney was the one who could briefly look upon a cross section of life. It impressed him as remarkable, rather than the natural condition, that with this blow about to fall these others about him could remain so utterly unconscious of what threatened. To him the very air seemed charged with unendurable menace. . . . He heard a man's heavy voice and Josefa's flippant answer. It struck him that Señor Olivas was gone a long time. . . .

Señor Olivas was returning at last. He came into the room, walking heavily. His brow was puckered, his eyes were distressed. He stopped a moment, looking in a strange, helpless fashion at the three who had not yet moved from the table. He opened his mouth to speak, hesitated, shook his head and crossed the room to the door of the kitchen.

"*Muchachos*," he said, "it has not often happened that I have asked you to wait for your money. I am not ready with it tonight. Tomorrow you shall have it. All right? *Gracias y buenas noches*."

He closed the door softly and returned to his chair at the table. But he did not sit down. He rested a hand on the back of the chair and made his announcement.

"Someone has been in the library. The drawer was unlocked, the money was gone. I—"

"Not stolen!" cried Teresa.

"Stolen," Señor Olivas answered her, looking uncertainly from one to another of the faces turned upon him. "The second theft within so short a time in this house!"

Softly there came to them the strains of Juanito's violin. He was playing his little love song, "*Teresita Mía*."

"Good God," muttered Whitney. He was thinking far less of the thousand dollars than of the sort of

160

man who could sit in there with Teresa's money in his pocket and play as he played, adoringly, a song for Teresa.

He felt Teresa Calderon's eyes upon him. They were dark with trouble. At times when the spirits of men are charged to overflowing, one person not infrequently sees in a vivid flash something of that which is filling the other's thought: She was remembering how she had met him at the library door, how her coming had checked his haste.

Suddenly she rose from her chair and went to the window where she stood with her back to them all, staring out into the night. At that instant Whitney was on the verge of telling bluntly what he knew. But a cool judgment restrained him: The fine pride of Mentor Olivas was too splendid to bring down, besmirched and broken, with a hasty word. A few minutes now would make no difference. Soon he would seek an opportunity to speak with Olivas alone.

"Two thefts," said Señor Olivas ponderously. "It is beyond belief; it surpasses endurance. Juanito must ride for the sheriff—"

"Not yet," said Whitney sharply. "Surely there is no call for a sheriff so soon. Would it not be best, at any rate, to wait a few hours?"

"Perhaps," said Olivas, with whom always procrastination had been one way of dealing with a crisis.

But Teresa, though she said nothing, turned suddenly where she stood at the window and flashed at Whitney a look in which was unveiled scorn. After that look he expected nothing less than open accusation. But she only bit her lip angrily and whirled about, again looking with frowning eyes into the void of the outer darkness.

CHAPTER XV

A STAB IN THE DARK

Whitney considered both Juanito and Juanito's father. The boy was young; he was a likeable chap; it was difficult to imagine him driven by purely criminal dictates. Many motives may lie back of wrong-doing and there are times and conditions when the motive may palliate the offense; the act of a father who steals a loaf of bread for a starving child can be condoned. Hence, to Whitney's mind, Juanito should be heard before he was denounced. There was every likelihood that this was the boy's first offense; that, after all, he had been guiltless of the theft of Tia Tonia's treasure box; that here was but the oft-repeated case of swift temptation made overpowering through circumstance. Perhaps Juanito had slipped this once only, as youth often slips, and if given his chance would henceforth be always on guard against the unwary step which gives to the worn slide down into the abysses.

There was Señor Olivas to think of. It would have been a simpler matter for Whitney to drive an unexpected fist into the old man's face than to strike at all of his high pride, his fond affection, by saying: "Your son is a thief."

Finally there was the further consideration, though a lesser one, which Whitney as a man of practical experience, gave its place in forming his decision: Were he to summon Juanito and say bluntly: "You took that money; I saw you take it," Juanito almost inevitably, prompted by the first instinct of human nature, would assert: "I did not." On one hand there would be the word of Maxwell Whitney, a stranger; on the other, that of Juanito. Whose word would Teresa accept? Where would Mentor's affection lead him to believe the truth lay? . . . In his room Juanito was playing softly; never had gentler, more serene strains invaded a quarter where disaster still spread its black pinions. . . .

Whitney held his tongue.

That Sheffield should grow voluble at such a time surprised no one. He was on his feet on the instant; he was asking questions; he was boiling over with surmise and advice.

"What an insane thing to do!" he exploded as with hands on hips he confronted Señor Olivas.

"To have a sum of money like that—*in cash*—kicking around the house! Olivas, don't you know what a check book is for?"

"My way—" began Olivas stiffly.

"Would be at home in a collection of antiques," cut in Sheffield. "Well, what's done is done. And the money can't have walked off by itself, and it can't have traveled a million miles in this time. Come, let's have a look at your desk."

"It's no use," replied Mentor. "The money is gone."

But Sheffield insisted and dragged him away to the library, still volleying his advice and his questions. He had the air of a master detective come to take charge in a baffling mystery case.

Teresa turned slowly where she stood at the window. Her eyes, dark with questionings, went gravely to Whitney. He met her regard steadily; he guessed something of what her eyes spoke but he waited upon her lips. And all the time he understood instinctively how hard it would be for her to speak. In such Californian hearts as Teresa Calderon's is the sacredness of hospitality held inviolate. He was her guest and she was thinking of that as well as of the other thing. But still he waited for her.

She hesitated to speak and yet there was within her the urge for haste. What she had to say she wanted done with before Brooke Sheffield returned. She lifted her head a little; it was an effort which she was making. But at last her words came as direct in their fashion as her look.

"I think that you know something of this?"

"Yes," he told her. "I do."

Now it was her turn to wait for him. But it was obvious to her that he would volunteer nothing further.

"Then I don't understand—If one knows, in a case like this, I don't understand why he shouldn't tell what he knows. Immediately. Unless—"

"Miss Calderon," he said gravely. "I am hardly more than a stranger to you. You saw me come out of the library. And yet I won't believe that you think I stole from you."

"But it is strange that, knowing at least something of the theft, you can have any reason for refusing to speak of it. For you are refusing?"

He got to his feet and began walking up and down restlessly. Her eyes, frankly perplexed now, followed him. Juanito was still playing; his violin sounded like music faint from a far distance, elfin notes as untroubled as moonbeams. Whitney felt a quick irritation toward the boy. Why the devil didn't he come in and put his own shoulder under his own responsibility? . . . Teresa was waiting. He stopped abruptly, confronting her.

"Look here," he said half angrily. "I'm no thief and you know it. There has happened something which I don't altogether understand. If you were in my boots you'd do just as I'm doing. What I

165

know, I don't want to come to Sheffield's ears—ever. Not to Señor Olivas yet; not yet even to you. Maybe never to any of you. I tell you I don't know yet. I've got to have time; I'll know what to do later—say tomorrow. And, if you can only see it, it will be the right thing for you to do if you'll not mention to anyone that I know any more than the rest of you."

The silence which fell between them might have lasted indefinitely were it not that they heard Sheffield and Olivas returning.

Teresa spoke hastily, lowering her voice.

"You were thinking of riding out to the railroad tonight? You still plan to go?"

The Pajaro Azul rancho, his intended telegram to his lawyers, his thought of anticipating Sheffield—all this had been swept from his mind. All this could wait upon a more vital matter. Of course he would not go. But before he could say as much . . . (Juanito's music was insistent.) . . . a new thought presented itself and he said:

"Yes; I think I'll go. Señor Olivas had promised to put me in the right trail; now, of course, I'll not expect it of him, but Juanito perhaps will help me out."

For thus, and perhaps only thus, could he have his talk with young Olivas.

He saw a swift change in Teresa's eyes. But before he could be sure of what he read there she whirled about and hastened out of the room. She snatched up her white shawl from a table as she went; he saw her go into the kitchen; he heard a door slam after her as she hurried out into the night. She felt the imperative need of open air, of the stars overhead, of a world of which she could be as sure as of a mother about her. She wanted to be alone; in here she was half smothered with uncertainty and suspicion; she could not have borne the further talk which Sheffield would be sure to bring with him.

"It's a mystery," said Sheffield; his manner could have been no more important if he himself had been a manufacturer of mysteries and this his chief product. "But we'll get at the bottom of it yet. You, Whitney; you've been sticking about the house all afternoon; tell us what you know about it."

"Oh, go to blazes," muttered Whitney disgustedly. There is always a limit to restraint and the wonder was that he had not reached his in the case of Brooke Sheffield before now.

Sheffield jerked his head up and stared.

"Eh?" he exclaimed. "What the deuce now? I just asked you a civil question."

"Civil!" Whitney's voice sharpened; the man annoyed him as a persistently obnoxious mosquito might have done; he made a gesture as of brushing him aside. "You attempt to treat the world as though it must waddle up to your door every Saturday afternoon to get its pay and orders for another week's work. Once and for all, Sheffield, I want none of your patronizing."

For a moment Sheffield looked nonplused. But not for long was his supreme equanimity to be disturbed; the self-satisfaction of men of his stamp is like armor plate. He assumed his best professional air of cynicism and sarcasm and said loftily:

"So Mr. Whitney refuses to discuss the matter! Well, well. And why? *I—wonder—why?*"

There was no end of insinuation in the pointed words. He had slapped back with the first weapon suggesting itself to a suspicious brain.

"Gentlemen!" cried Señor Olivas hastily. "We are laboring under excitement. I pray you—"

Just then Juanito came into the room. He entered hastily, no unusual thing with him; he interrupted as though he did not realize that anyone was speaking; he was saying what he had to say almost before he was across the threshold, quite Juanito's impatient way. And yet to Whitney, who had swung about to watch him narrowly, it seemed that Juanito's seemingly spontaneous act was painstakingly premeditated; that it was his intention to get his initial statement placed on record in the minds of those who heard before it could be suspected that he had any knowledge of the theft.

"I am off for a ride," he announced. "I am going into Toyon."

168

"My son—" began Señor Olivas.

But the loquacity of Sheffield forestalled him. He stepped forward; he told of the lost thousand dollars; he began firing his master detective questions at Juanito. Mentor turned away and went to his chair into which he dropped heavily; he appeared to have no interest in what Sheffield might have to say nor in what responses might come from Juanito. He looked like one who had received a blow that staggered him. Fleetingly Whitney marveled at that; surely the mere loss of ten hundred dollars could not so effect a man like Mentor Olivas? But with Juanito to observe keenly, he drew his eyes from Mentor's troubled face to set them searchingly upon the boy.

Juanito bore himself in a fashion which perplexed. There was no hint of that uneasy manner which, under circumstances of this order, might be expected from an amateur thief. He appeared interested, thoughtful; that was all. In the end he even shrugged.

"We know who has been about the house today," he said. "We know that the money has been missing but a few hours. I think we shall have no trouble in getting it back." He addressed his father, repeating his thought lightly. "We'll get it back, papa."

Whitney, merely to see how the boy would accept the suggestion, offered:

"Your father thinks it would be well to have the sheriff in."

Juanito appeared to reflect.

"*Y proque no*? Yes, that is right. Tomorrow we should see what we can do ourselves. Then, if we fail, we should have the sheriff."

There developed within Whitney a certain new respect for an unguessed strength under the frivolous exterior of this youngster. He knew that Juanito was holding himself in check under a tremendous nervous strain; that his muscles must be tense with suppression; that, but for a severe exercise of will, he would now be rushing headlong from the room; that the officiousness of Brooke Sheffield whom always he detested, must have created within him a hot desire to strike the smug face out of his way. But externally nothing of this did Juanito expose.

Juanito's next act gave further cause for amazement. He went to his father and set a hand gently on the slack shoulder.

"This is not a thing to be sad over," he said softly. "God makes things work out all right. Maybe it teaches us a lesson, not to have so much money in the house, not to offer temptation to some poor fellow. Also, I have a thought about all of this. I think I could guess who took it. If I go to that person and say, '*Mira, amigo*, some money is lost and we have a guess who was tempted to take it. Perhaps he did it as a joke. If so it will be returned tomorrow. If not, the sheriff—' And," he added with a shrug and a quick smile, "*mañana* is always soon enough for sorrow!"

Mentor had looked up at him with quick interest. "You know?" he demanded.

"I have a thought," said Juanito. "That is all I will say now." He went across the room to pick up his hat and gloves where he had dropped them upon a little table. "As I have said, I am riding to Toyon. I'll think as I ride."

"I never heard of such nonsense!" cried Sheffield.

And now at last Juanito blazed out at him.

"You, Señor," he cried hotly, "are not concerned. I do not ask of you advice now or ever. On the other hand it is I who advise you, who have visited with us nineteen days, to—"

"My son!" exclaimed Señor Olivas sharply. "Not that!"

For all knew what Juanito's rushing words were leading to; even Sheffield, uninvited guest, must have understood that he was in danger of being told that he was overstaying his welcome. He returned contemptuously:

"It is at the home of Miss Teresa that I am staying."

Juanito under his father's stern eyes kept his peace. But he laughed impudently as he went out. Whitney, taking up his hat, called after him:

"I, too, am riding. I was going out to the railroad

171

tonight. Could I have you show me the right trail?"

"Very gladly, Señor," said Juanito. "*Venga*. It will be growing late."

"A sudden haste of two men to quit the place where a sum of money has been stolen," Sheffield snapped, "has an ugly flavor to it."

Whitney, now at Juanito's side, saw how the boy stiffened, how the hands clenched tight upon his hat and gloves, how for one instant Juanito hung on his heel. Then the impulse was conquered and side by side they went out and to the stable. As they passed through the yard but one remark was made. It was Juanito's saying, less to Whitney than to himself:

"That man is a nasty little bug. It is a miracle of God that I hold my hand back from him."

Whitney looked for Teresa Calderon as they went, hoping to catch sight of her. He was human enough to resent her attitude and yet sane enough to acknowledge that it was natural, almost inevitable. The stars were out, but shadows lay black everywhere through the gardens; at some little distance, under a pear tree, he thought that he caught the glimpse of her white shawl. Well, she wanted to be alone; further, he had nothing to say to her and it was as well if Juanito did not stop to bandy words.

They saddled and brought out the horses. By now, so long away from the brightness of the lighted rooms, one's eyes picked out objects with greater ease. Now he was sure of two things; he had not been mistaken as to the shawl; and its wearer's desire to be alone was emphasized by the way in which she had moved so as to be almost hidden by the pear tree. He judged that there was more than one person on the King of Spain Rancho tonight who wanted a chance to think.

Juanito, about to mount, asked:

"You have tobacco and papers, Señor? Mine are on my table."

"Pipe tobacco only. No papers."

Juanito slipped his horse's reins into Whitney's hand.

"I must smoke," he exclaimed. "Smoke and smoke! Tonight I have nerves that quiver like wires in a storm. You did not guess that! One moment, Señor. I will run."

Run he did. Whitney saw him circle the house to the right. He was going to avoid the room where Mentor and Sheffield were, to come to his room from the front or perhaps to slip in at his window.

Almost at the moment that Juanito disappeared Brooke Sheffield came out at the rear.

Whitney, under the big oak near the stable, watched him idly, indifferently as one, busy with his own thoughts, quite naturally might allow his eyes to be drawn to the only moving thing within their orbit of vision.

Sheffield ran down the steps. He stopped

briefly, standing very still in the shadows. He, too, might have been watching something or listening intently or looking for something. When he moved on it was Whitney's supposition that he had been looking for Teresa and now saw her. For Sheffield went straight to the pear tree.

Whitney was not greatly interested; certainly he had no thought to spy. He was impatiently awaiting Juanito and the explanation which he meant to demand before they had ridden a hundred paces. But his eyes were tricked into attendance upon Sheffield's movements, solely because there alone was motion in a world standing still, and missed nothing of that which happened so swiftly. Sheffield came on to the pear tree, hurrying; the girl—Whitney could see the shawl move toward Sheffield—was so near that he could have touched it. Sheffield was lifting his arms. . . . The girl, as though going to her rightful place, slipped into them. Her head and Sheffield's obscured the light which just now had shone palely between them.

Where Juanito came from Whitney did not know. It was as though he had sprung up from the ground, as though he had materialized from empty space. His cry, choked with jealous rage, cut menacingly through the silence. Between that cry and the blow there was no lost instant of time. Sheffield also cried out; there was a shrill scream; Sheffield fell. Juanito had struck—the

gesture itself, the manner of Sheffield's fall, were
eloquent of it—with a knife. . . .

Whitney dropped the horses' reins and broke
through the shrubbery, running toward the little
group of three which had drawn so close together
and which now drew so widely apart.

"Juanito!" he shouted. "You fool, stop that!
Teresa, run! The boy is mad!"

When he reached the spot he had only Juanito
and Sheffield to deal with; at least a part of his
command had been heeded and she who had been
the cause of a lifted knife fled toward the house
in terror. Sheffield lay where he had fallen, too
severely hurt to rise, or paralyzed with fear. He
lifted an arm over which Teresa's shawl hung,
its meshes caught upon a sleeve button. Juanito,
crouched and tense, stood over him, the knife still
in his hand. Whitney caught him by the shoulder
and hurled him back.

"You fool!" he shouted the second time. "Would
you commit murder?"

"He shall keep his hands off her," said Juanito
huskily. "Yes, I would kill him."

Whitney knelt and found Sheffield's hurt. The
knife point had grazed his neck where it had left
but an ugly scratch though only narrowly had
it missed accomplishing that errand on which a
frenzied will had impelled it; Sheffield must have
whipped back in time; the blade in its downward
sweep had slashed through his coat lapel and the

175

second wound, graver than the first, was a long cut across the pectoral muscle. Blood was flowing freely.

"Come, Sheffield," said Whitney. "Stand up. We've got to get you into the house."

Sheffield stirred weakly and groaned. "Good God! Am I done for, Whitney? Tell me. Tell me the truth."

"I don't think you are even badly hurt, if you'll only let me have a chance to get the blood stopped."

He put his arm about Sheffield and got the man to his feet. They moved slowly toward the house. Juanito, the knife in his hand, did not stir.

For half an hour, Whitney, with Mentor Olivas to aid him, ministered to the wounded man. There was no one else in the house, saving old Uracca who had gone to bed and who, when Mentor went to her door asking for Josefa, told him that the Indian girl was out walking with her "novio," Felipe Moraga.

Teresa did not come in from the gardens; they had not so much as a glimpse of her; Whitney fancied he could picture her as having raced away through the dark to fling herself down in an access of terror not untouched with horror at her own part in what had happened; she must have known of Juanito's love and of Juanito's jealousy. Now she would see so many things clearly!

176

The two men got Sheffield to bed. Mentor's face as he did what he could, quietly obeying Whitney's commands, standing like a steady old rock when he was not needed, was carven into an image of heartbreaking distress. He did not speak his son's name; he made no excuses; he kept his heavy silence.

Sheffield, lying flat, his wounds bandaged, a generous draught of old brandy stimulating him, looked into the two faces above him curiously. He was shaken; he was in some pain; the fear had not yet all gone out of him. Whitney thought, trying to read Sheffield's look, that he was asking himself if even now he was out of danger from an attack; if Juanito would come in for a moment to finish what he had begun; if he was safe in the hands of Juanito's father. His eyes roved away to the corner of his room where his pump-gun lay.

"Put that where I can reach it," he told Whitney.

Mentor himself, though he winced, went for the shot gun and set it against the bed.

"You have that right, Señor," he said brokenly. "But you have my word that you have nothing further to fear. And you see in me a man so anguished, so humiliated, that I would to God I had died before tonight."

Sheffield, not of the fortunate ones of the earth who have understanding, sneered. And then, his eyes vengeful, he muttered:

"If I do nothing else in this life, by God, I'll

177

put that young villain in the penitentiary for the rest of your days, old man."

When Señor Olivas turned and went out of the room Whitney followed him, closing Sheffield's door after him. The old man stood with his hands clasped behind his back, a terrible look in the eyes which he turned on his companion.

"My Juanito did that," he said heavily. "My little Juanito! You saw it, Señor!"

He shook his head; a gusty sigh expanded his chest; a bright glitter as of a fever dimmed his eyes which softened and grew misty.

"My son—in the penitentiary!"

Whitney was at a loss for anything to say. There was nothing to stay the old man's grief; there was nothing to bolster up the ancient pride which the heedless hands of a beloved son were tearing down. Mentor began pacing up and down, the monotony of fatigue in his steps. At last he confronted Whitney again; he even shrugged his shoulders in an elaborate pretense of being resigned to the inevitable.

"The will of God must ever prevail, Señor," he said. "It is a great sorrow to me that you, whose respect I have craved, must think so ill of us. And now—I must go to Juanito."

"Señor," returned Whitney, "let us be glad that matters are not so bad as they might be. Sheffield is in no danger. And as for his threat of prison—

well, it is to be expected in the first shock of the thing, before the first anger cools. If Sheffield were minded to do so, I suppose he could make trouble. But not every quarrel between two men means penitentiary, and when Sheffield has had time for cool thought—"

Olivas shook his head.

"There is bitterness between them; it has come lately, as you see, to actual hatred. Señor Sheffield will do all that a man can—and remember he is a lawyer who will know how—to make trouble for Juanito. I am frank with you, Señor Maxwell. You are like an old friend. *Bueno.* I know the type of man this Sheffield is; with him everything is money; if I had money to pay him, he would be willing to forget what has happened."

He threw out his hands widely in a gesture of hopelessness.

"But I have not the money, Señor. Even this loss of a thousand dollars today looms like disaster. You see I am confidential, Señor!"

They heard Sheffield call. Mentor went in answer. Through the still house their voices came to Whitney.

"Shut my window, will you?" Sheffield asked. "And lock it. There is somebody out there. Pull the shade down."

"*Sí, Señor*," agreed Olivas colorlessly. Whitney heard the window close, the shade unroll. "But, Señor Sheffield, I pledge my honor—"

"I wouldn't pledge too much, Olivas," said Sheffield irritably. "And listen: About that stolen money. Juanito was in there with you, he knew where you put it—"

"Señor!" Mentor's voice burst out thunderously; one might know from the very sound of it how the white head was lifted, how his eyes blazed. "My son, enraged, may strike at the man who has angered him; I do not excuse him though that I may understand. But steal? My son a thief? In my presence, Señor, you will not breathe such a thing."

He returned to the room in which Whitney waited, walking vigorously, carrying himself with something of his natural pride. In the code of the Olivas there might come times when one man killed another; stoop to theft, theft of mere money, never! That was unthinkable.

Quick shifting thoughts playing on the strings of varying emotions created confusion in Whitney's consciousness. But out of chaos grew one tall perfect blossom, that of deep compassion for Mentor Olivas.

"Señor Olivas," he said abruptly, "I am going to ask something of you. I trust you will grant it. Let me go out to Juanito first. And you wait until he comes to you."

"That is a strange request, is it not, my friend?"

"There lies a reason back of it. A sound reason.

180

I know something which you do not know. I am, what you have called me, a friend."

Olivas regarded him fixedly. Then he bowed, making the courtly old-fashioned bow reserved for great moments.

"It is as you wish, Señor. But you will understand that I am impatient?"

Whitney, hurrying away, was already shaping his plan, a plan bred from Mentor's own unconscious suggestion.

CHAPTER XVI

THE WILDNESS OF YOUNG OLIVAS

Whitney found Juanito with the horses under the oak. By now the boy was a bundle of nerves aquiver; the horses, sensitive as are all of their kind, especially the highbred, had caught something of their master's unrest, and fidgeted at the ends of taut reins. Juanito demanded sharply:

"He is dead then?"

"No. Not even badly hurt." He looked curiously at the face which though so near his own, was masked by the dark. "A lucky thing for you, though, that another inch wasn't added to that knife blade!"

"Lucky for me? Or for him?" Juanito assayed mocking laughter but it failed miserably to ring

181

true. He began to roll a cigarette; his fingers tore the thin white paper and spilled the tobacco.

"For you," repeated Whitney sternly. "As it is the man swears he will send you to prison for attempted murder."

"Prison?" Whitney knew from the odd inflection that here was a thought which Juanito had not entertained. The boy tensed and thereafter a shiver ran through his body. "Prison for me, Juan Olivas! *Pero, Señor*—" He broke off impatiently and this time his reckless young laughter, contemptuous and defiant, rang true. "He but spews threats like any coward. When he is well I shall slap his face, and with my boot drive him from the rancho."

"You still count on riding to Toyon? What has happened makes no change in your plans?"

"Why should it? Yes, I ride to Toyon. It is important."

As they were mounting they saw Mentor Olivas step out on the back porch.

"Your father naturally wants to talk with you," said Whitney. "But he has consented to wait until you and I can have had a word together. I think it would be best if you told him now not to wait up for our return; that you and he can talk in the morning."

"Yes," answered the other absently. "I am late now." And as they approached the house, to turn into the road to the lower valley, Juanito reined in by the porch. Whitney, holding back, heard the father and son speak briefly and saw how at the end Mentor put out his two hands and clasped Juanito's gloved fingers. "*Hasta la mañana,*" Juanito said softly. "It will be all right then. *Buenas noches, papá.*"

Mentor called good night to Whitney and the two rode away. Juanito stooped suddenly in the saddle, touched his horse with the spurs and shot ahead. Whitney raced after him, calling to him to stop. What he had to say he did not care to have jolted out of him at breakneck speed. Juanito, though plainly his mood called for wild riding, tightened his reins and the horses drew down into a restive walk.

"First of all," began Whitney, "I have business which carries me out to the railroad. I am depending on you to show me the trail."

"There are two ways to go," answered Juanito. "One is through Toyon where I am going; from there by stage road. The other, though shorter, runs back of our house here, over the pine ridges; you would not be able to find it alone at night."

"What if you ride with me? Your visit to Toyon can wait?"

"No!" cried Juanito ringingly. "It is vital that I go now. There is a man who waits— There is no business so urgent as mine, Señor, since even my honor is at stake!"

The honor of this mad youngster! In just what

did it consist? Whitney was quite unconscious of his own involuntary grunt by way of comment; in general he was given to distrusting the man who dwelt verbally on the sacredness of his honor and tonight, in particular, he had little faith to pin to any word of Juanito Olivas. He answered sharply; he himself, with no tangible obligation laid upon him, was riding tonight seeking to save at least a semblance of repute to the son of Mentor Olivas and he had no sympathy to waste upon high-sounding talk.

"There is something else at stake and you ought to be able to see it. Your own personal freedom and, what is of more importance in my eyes, your father's peace of mind. Let us understand each other, Juanito, for we have precious little time to get done what must be done. I am going far out of my way to try to save you from your own foolhardiness; for your part you are going to turn back here with me and ride with me the shortest way to the railroad."

"Señor!" The boy's words came like burning flashes of a hot spirit seething within and ever ready to stab, lightning-swift, at the first sign of outside interference. "Such words to me are not to be understood! Mind you, I do what I do, and when I am as I am tonight, the world itself must stand aside."

Extravagant as always, more turbulent than ever before, his impulses churned into a froth that blinded his truer vision, Juanito believing himself a masterful, dominant ego was yielding to every cross wind which stormed through his uncertain soul. Tonight he would quarrel with any hand seeking to draw him forth from drowning. Something of this Whitney glimpsed. But he himself was not the most patient of men, he himself had the blood of youth and not the slow tides of age pulsing through him. He put a sudden hand on Juanito's reins and with a jerk brought both horses down to a halt.

"Listen to me," he commanded sternly, "and use your brain instead of letting that wild heart of yours drive you. You have come near killing a man tonight and he is minded to make you pay for it. If anyone can save you from the mess you've made of things, I can. All I ask in return is that you ride with me."

"I ask no man's aid," said Juanito hotly. "And I ride where I please."

"Listen until I finish. There is one thing which you must not forget: That is the loss of your father's thousand dollars."

"Well?" The exclamation burst from a startled Juanito.

"It happens," Whitney told him bluntly, "that I saw you take it."

"You saw?" Juanito did not so much as think of denying. But he drew himself up, straight and tense in the saddle, and spat out the words

185

accusingly, contemptuously from an exalted and disdainful insolence: "You spy!"

For a moment that he held his tongue Whitney had to fight with himself to hold his anger in check. But in the end he held his mind to the main issue, not Juanito himself but Juanito's father.

"I have told no one as yet," he said. "Think of others a while, Juanito, rather than solely of your dramatic self! What would Señor Olivas say?"

Still Juanito sought to hold himself rigid, stiffening his figure that so, also, he might stiffen the purpose within him. But gradually his slim body began to droop.

"Just now," ran on Whitney hastily, "Sheffield, lying in there on his bed, filled with hate for you, eager to give you a bad name, had the rage-inspired thought to call to Señor Olivas that that theft would be like your work. You might guess how your father would answer a thing like that? I heard him silence Sheffield; I heard him say that a son of his, though he might kill a man, would never soil Olivas hands with theft. Theft of money."

"You do not understand!" Here abruptly was another Juanito, one of almost a timid woman's weakness. "My God, how I have been driven!"

"We can talk about that as we ride. Provided you ride with me as I ask."

Juanito, as though now everything depended upon the passage of time, peered at his watch. It was so dark that he lighted a match; in the sudden glare Whitney saw the glisten of tears on his cheeks.

"Come!" cried the boy excitedly. "I ride with you. We have horses under us to carry king's messengers! They will wait for me in Toyon for they know that, having promised, I will come. As I shall lead you we are going to come to your destination in two hours, no more. A little over two hours after that will put me in Toyon."

"But remember, you and I have some talking to do—"

"When we hit the wagon road, then, where we can ride abreast. On the trail I lead you now a man can converse only with his own soul."

He wheeled his horse and shot away, retracing the steps which had brought them from the house, racing across the outer yard, passing the barn, heading straight for the wooded ridges. They passed through a gate which Juanito opened, stooping from his horse, and which they did not tarry to close; they came into a trail which the flying hoofs found but which a man might not see half a dozen yards in advance; they began penetrating an ever thickening forestland. After a half hour, during which a rider must be ever on his guard lest some branch across the way sweep him from his saddle, they came out into the open road. Just ahead was a steep hill; Juanito slackened his speed, mindful of his horse which he patted lovingly upon the shoulder. Whitney drew up at his side.

Juanito began rapid speech. He had forgotten his earlier resentment; he was concerned only with his own tumultuous emotions. And Whitney, listening, was given a glimpse of a soul running a fiery gamut.

"Who would have thought that of Teresita, Teresita whom I have adored since we were babies together? What is a woman, Señor? A terrible thing, a curse, a creature who shears the strength of a sleeping Samson, who pours poison into the wine of life, who conducts a man into paradise in order that her pretty eyes may watch as he slips on down into purgatory! My little Teresa in the foul arms of that man! My God! Teresita doing that!" His voice broke. But before Whitney, thinking he had ended, could speak, he found fresh utterance, declaiming harshly: "Love—Do you know what it is? You others, you think you understand. But only we Spanish know! God made us like that. And we too know what hate is. Hate is love turned to poison. That Señorita Calderon now, do I love her?" His attempt at jeering laughter was pitiful. "I hate her! *Sí, Señor*; it comes like that. Will I give her her pleasure where she seeks it? Will I go about singing songs with my eyes shut while she goes to that low-bred beast? Ah, you do not know me yet; you do not understand my people. What shall I do when I see her tomorrow

188

morning, when we sit at table together—as we have sat since I have known what it is to live? I shall smile into her eyes, Señor; I shall smile straight into her eyes. And *she* will understand for she, too, is Spanish; and she will feel cold at her heart, Señor; and she will shiver.

"Listen, Señor! I know that you have words to say but what of them now? What of money taken? What of a man feeling a knife? Bah. Money is of the importance of the dust our horses pound up from the road; a knife in a man's shoulder is as important as a burr that I brush out of my horse's mane. There is love; there is hate; there is honor. Love, Señor, with us of Spanish blood, is the tree of life. Hate, Señor, is the bitter fruit that grows on that tree. And honor, Señor, is the rich soil into which the crooked roots thrust themselves. You do not understand? But I, with clear eyes, I see and I know all about it. Love I spurn; it is detestable. Hate I chew in my mouth. And my honor? Where would it be if I allowed her, whom I have loved, to lie in the arms of a man like that? . . . Oh, when I look straight into her eyes tomorrow, *she* will know!

"*Tomorrow!* Look, my friend, see what life is! One day it swells to bursting with joy; the next it is in a shroud, all black."

He sank into a profound meditation, steeping his soul in romantic melancholy. Suddenly he cried out sharply; from the very tone of his voice even before the words grew significant, Whitney knew that the emotional nature had bounded to another sort of pattern upon the mosaic of his psychological experiences, like a rubber ball struck sharply.

"A thought strikes me, my friend. No, not a thought—an inspiration! Shall one condemn without hearing? Does not one misjudge, when he trusts alone his senses and crushes his heart? Did she go willingly into his arms? Did she, perhaps, feel a sudden dizziness, a vertigo in which, falling, he caught her? Or, if not that, did Teresita, just a young girl, Señor, fail to understand what it was that she did? Did she but play? Did she but seek to tease one who, she knew, adored her? *Mira*: I have known her always, I have shared her most secret thought. Tell me, is one who has ever been the sweetest, the most pure and innocent and angelic of women, to become in an instant a vile thing? God! Have I wronged her? Have I, Juanito Olivas, thought evil of a pure angel? We are hot-blooded, those of my race. We are at times unjust; oh, I know that. And is it fair to judge by appearances? Why, look you; today you have seen me take another's money and what have you done, what would the world do? Call Juanito Olivas a thief! And I am so innocent, Señor!"

Whitney remarked drily:

"And, as I understand the matter, the money is really Miss Calderon's!"

"To be sure, Señor, and—" Then only there broke in upon the boy's understanding all that lay under the words. His voice fell away and he seemed to have ceased breathing. Then again, more torrentially than before, he began speaking excitedly. Whitney, following the incoherent words only with extreme difficulty, was amazed when he understood to what foreign conclusions the boy was rushing. The dejected Juanito was gone in a flash; he who had exuded gloom and breathed despair now radiated optimism. And by the strangest of mental processes did he progress. Himself, he was sure that he was expounding logical reason firmly based on analogy while what he was doing was nail a triumphant hope among the stars and then seek props to keep it there. He exclaimed,

"It is God Himself who sends you to me tonight! To save me from doing cruel injustice, to keep the sun in the sky and happiness in the heart. It is like this: Within me a voice shouts, 'Judge not lest you shall be judged!' The Voice says, 'What worth are appearances? She seemed to be a light woman, unworthy of your love? Well, and yourself, Juanito, my boy? What have you seemed to others? To your friend Maxwell? You have seemed one who could steal, steal mere money, steal the money of Teresita!' "

Never was Juanito so dramatic, never so intense, so eager, so athrill to the moment; his spirit that had gloomed and sought dark caverns now stood a-tiptoe, aspiring the light-smitten crests of things. After his own thorough-going fashion he had swept through his orbit, done with the nadir, on fire to scale the zenith. In a word he achieved simply that which he ordinarily accomplished; he succeeded in believing that which he wished to believe. Doubts might flock again, doubtless would. But for the present he was a young summer sun that had burst through storm clouds.

"I have been mad, Señor," he cried vibrantly. "But who shall say without cause? You saw me in the library? Well, that is one thing. You saw me strike that man down; another thing. But you do not know how near I came to striking down yet another man! You do not know what this day has been for me. No one but myself can know." He struck his breast heavily. "In here there has been hell, Señor, raging. But now, at the end of the day, what have we?" He swept off his hat with a flourish and lifted his face to the stars; there was light enough for Whitney to guess at the smile which, so long absent, had returned. "I take off my hat to the stars, to the open sky, to the universe, to God behind it all! In my heart I kneel, pouring out thanks. For life, Señor, is glad and golden; love is eternal; a man has the right to his happiness and— Oh, you will see!—all will be well! There will be an explanation; Teresita herself with tears in her eyes will make it. But I will not listen to it; I shall demand, 'What is faith, if it require explanations from the beloved one?' Rather I shall go down on my knees to her and plead that I be forgiven for having been cruelly unjust to her in my heart. Or in my mad brain, rather, for always in my heart I knew that Teresita Mía was not the one to forget herself like that!"

For a while, as they rode on side by side, Whitney could find nothing to say. The wind, which Teresita had called Juanito, blew from so many quarters of the compass that for a man who sought to talk with him it was hard to know what course to steer. For Juanito's part, though he fell musingly silent, sustained silence was impossible. He broke out now and again in exclamations, fragments of sentences, vehement always. Whitney began to ask himself if he himself were but dropping into the commonest of human errors, seeking to intrude into that which were better alone without him. To reason with this wild heart was like striving with a thunder storm. Juanito had named himself mad today; on what day was he sufficiently like normal men to be called what normal men name themselves, sane? Yet in the end, and despite all this, there were two bleak and sordid facts to stand on and Whitney, with them in mind, said curtly,

"Juanito, do you want your father to know that you took that money? And do you want Teresa Calderon to know?"

193

Juanito jerked about in the saddle.

"Señor," he cried, "you will not speak? Have I not called you my friend? You will keep my secret!"

"And," continued Whitney sternly, angered by a bearing which he failed utterly to understand, "do you want to face Sheffield's accusation? Forget your fine sentiments a moment and think of what will happen. You will be arrested; he will swear that you attacked him with intent to kill; that the assault was unprovoked; I will be called as a witness; what he says I will be obliged to corroborate. There will be the disgrace to your name; there will be your father's sorrow; there will be Miss Calderon's name used in an ugly way. And, on top of all this, there will be conviction."

"But," muttered Juanito, "that is terrible! If the man dared—"

"Of course he'll dare, as you call it. He'll be glad of the chance; you realize, don't you, that he'd be quite as content with you out of his way? In short, you've got yourself into a nasty mess on two counts. . . . Why do you suppose I am making this trip tonight?"

"I had not thought—I have been—"

"If there is a way to shut Sheffield's mouth I think I have found it; if the job can be done I mean to know it tonight. Tomorrow, if he is left alone, he'll send for the sheriff. That's why I am riding."

"My friend—!"

"Never mind that," Whitney cut in. "If I can do the thing I hope to do, if in downright talk I can save your bacon—"

"Then, Señor, you will know that I am grateful! That there is nothing I would not do for you." His hand was on his youthful heart. "Were it to die for you—"

"Hold on! There's no talk of dying yet. If tonight I succeed, it will be quite another thing which I shall ask."

"Granted, Señor." There was a wide gesture against the stars. "No matter what it is."

"You will tell me what the devil you meant by taking that money—and you will put it into my hands so that I can return it to the library table drawer."

Now that a swift response was to be expected, Juanito instead of making it sank deep into thoughtful silence. The horses went forward at the swinging, tireless gallop to which they were trained; their hoof-beats rang out rhythmically, little puffs of dust from a road already dry from two weeks of fine weather rose and vanished like uncertain ghosts. Whitney, certain that in the end Juanito's answer must be an assent, no matter how reluctant, waited for the slow-coming decision. He saw Juanito making a cigarette; his hands were steady now for with his horse at full gallop he achieved the difficult task, his reins dropped to the saddle horn. He even got a light from one of his sulphur block matches. The spark, glowing as he drew deeply at his cigarette, was like a little captive star which he had made his own to lead him aright through a dark labyrinth. . . . At last, in a new voice, one of great serene calm, came Juanito's answer, prefaced by a question:

"There is a God, Señor? One Who sees when the sparrow falls, when the little birds build nests for their eggs, when a child is hurt? A God of an infinitely sweet and compassionate heart?"

Whitney's eyes were on the stars above an ebon-black mass of pines; the night was a perfect California springtime night; a flush of promise above the eastern horizon bespoke the moonrise. From some sleepy nook far off came the subdued tinkle of a bell as a drowsing cow stirred and was still again. Peace rose from the quiet earth and met peace descending from the stars.

"You see, Señor," continued Juanito, speaking as simply as a child of ten, "one knows that in the end everything comes out right. We make so large a fuss over money, and God laughs at us. Does He want money? Does He say, 'Hands off! That is mine!' " Juanito laughed as he held that God laughed. "You do not see everything in my heart, Señor, for my heart is a mystery. But you do know me for a man of honor, whose word is sacred. Thus, then, I make you my promise on my oath as an Olivas and a gentleman. We shall ride together; you shall do what you plan to do; you shall tell me, Juanito, I have the power to become your savior at this crisis.' And in return, I shall put into your hands, before breakfast time tomorrow, the money to return to its place."

And with that must Whitney be content. In fact he was content; the boy's tone carried conviction that he would keep his promise. Now, when they gave over talking and hastened on, Juanito, with never a care in the wide world, his responsibilities placed confidently in the higher hands and in those of his friend Maxwell Whitney, sang softly his beloved little song.

CHAPTER XVII

THE DICE ROLL AT TOYON

Arrived at the railway station they rode first to the stables. The horses were to be cared for, there was further riding to be done tonight and Juanito insisted that no stupid and careless stable attendant should come near the two overheated red bays. Personally he would give them their water, he would rub them down, he would allot them their rations. Whitney hastened away to the telephone office.

There he was busy for upward of an hour, in prolonged, earnest conversation with his attorney in Los Angeles. The lawyer listened to his inquiries, assured him that considerably more than had been expected had been salvaged from his business collapse, and undertook to secure for him an option on the Pajaro Azul rancho. In addition—what to Whitney seemed almost the best news of all, he relayed the information that Brooke Sheffield was in ill repute with the state bar association, so much so that he was threatened with disbarment proceedings and had been made to feel that it would be decidedly to his advantage to stay away from San Francisco.

With these stimulating bits of information added to the night's work, Whitney was somewhat jarred to find—though, he reflected, he might have suspected it—that Juanito had not waited for him, but had taken to the road half an hour before he emerged from the telephone office.

The lad had left word for his friend that he would see him before breakfast next morning at the ranch house.

When Whitney's horse was brought out to be saddled, it became doubly clear that Juanito had planned all along for a little time to himself. For, while he had rested his own horse, Juanito had busied himself putting a delay in the way of any hasty pursuit. The cinch of the saddle had been taken off and tossed behind a box; the latigo removed from its ring; the bridle, wherever there was a buckle in head stall or reins, taken apart. Several minutes were required, the stable man and Whitney both working, to reassemble the various bits of the accouterment. The attendant, sensing a practical joke, and in no wise affected by it himself, laughed appreciatively.

"Always full of fun, that Olivas kid," he remarked.

"Full of the devil," grunted Whitney.

And as at last he rode out of the stable he asked himself what on earth Juanito counted on getting done before he could come up with him?

When but a few miles on the Toyon road Whitney was briefly misled by his eager desire into thinking that he had overhauled Juanito, naturally supposing that some little mishap had delayed the over-impatient boy. For already the night was late and the road, save for himself and young Olivas, should have been deserted. But by the roadside was a small camp fire burning; a man sat brooding over it at an hour when country folk should be in bed and asleep or at the very least making what haste they could to get themselves home. Whitney reined in; when he got the light of the flickering blaze on the man's face he saw that he had to do with a specimen of a very definite class; here was one of the tramp species, the bindlestiff, in the vernacular; grizzled, unkempt as to hair and beard, no doubt red-rimmed as to eyelids, as grimy as the ancient blanket-roll beside him. The man did not give over scratching himself while he turned his eyes up at the horseman.

"Hello," said Whitney. "I thought you were someone else." Then, about to ride on, impressed by the oddity of a man sitting up at a fire at this hour, he added, "Not in any kind of trouble, are you?"

"No," came the querulous voice in answer. "Couldn't sleep, that's all. Got to thinkin' and thinkin'."

"How long since somebody passed you, on horseback?" asked Whitney.

"Who was he?" The tramp got up stiff-jointedly and came to set his claw of a hand in the horse's mane. "He was ridin' a Calderon horse, wasn't he?" The bleary eyes made a swift examination of the red bay which Whitney rode and which, snorting its mistrust of the hand upon its mane, jerked back. "So're you."

"So you're not a newcomer here?"

The old man grunted and spat and answered pridefully:

"Newcomer? Say, Bo, I been hittin' the King o' Spain Valley regular for thirty year. Ask anybody. Jenkins, the name is; Captain Jenkins, by title. Late, this year; been sick and in the hospital in the next county. That was the Olivas kid, wasn't it?"

"Yes. I wanted to overtake him. How far ahead is he?"

The old fellow chuckled mirthfully.

"Overtake *him?* Guess you're the newcomer, Bo! It can't be did, not when that kid's in a hurry like tonight. . . . Say, what are *you* doin' in this country? Ain't livin' here, are you?"

"No, I'm camping up toward the Santa Lucias. But tell me; how far—"

The voice interrupting him sharpened and, in Whitney's ear, seemed to ring suspiciously.

"What are you campin' there for? What did you come for? What in hell do you expect to find up there?"

"I'm in a hurry," muttered Whitney, his patience gone. "Will you tell me how much of a lead Juanito has on me?"

"You answer me first and then—"

Whitney whirled his horse back into the road and, with the thin old voice lifted in a whining curse after him, pressed on. Just now he had no time to squander upon any such queer bird as this flea-bitten bindlestiff. At least Juanito had passed this way and was to be found in Toyon. If only he could be overhauled in time, before he had committed himself to the third idiocy of the day and let the money pass out of his possession! The fact that Juanito had failed to wait at the livery stable but had rushed back to Toyon, caused Whitney no little uneasiness. Though repeatedly he told himself that the whole affair was none of his business, still he could not shrug his shoulders free of a certain responsibility. Either he should have ignored sentimental considerations at the jump and have informed Señor Olivas of what he knew, or in lieu of that he should have seen that Juanito was denied any opportunity of eluding him.

He had not looked at his watch once tonight but knew it must be long after midnight when he rode into Toyon. The little town was as still as a country graveyard and smothered in darkness. Here and there an old adobe wall shone palely under the stars. He passed along the street, looking about him to right and left, hoping to see somewhere a lighted window. But the darkness was unbroken.

With no knowledge of Juanito's plans and small enough suspicion, he none the less fancied that the boy's errand would in some way have to do with Asa Vogel. If Juanito had, as he had claimed, urgent business in Toyon, with whom but Vogel could it possibly be concerned? Especially since into this urgent business the thousand dollars must enter in one way or another. To think of Vogel was to think of money: now, conversely, to think of money suggested Vogel.

A dog rushed out from the Dominguez hotel and set up a furious barking. Whitney, had the opportunity been given him, could have choked the animal into silence. Juanito, warned, would no doubt elude him again. He dismounted, tied his horse to the roadside fence and called softly to the dog. It was a typical Toyon shepherd, vastly more given to friendliness than to evil suspicions, and came up without hesitation to lick at the hand extended. Whitney patted its head, smiled at his own now vanished animosity toward the dog, and walked swiftly toward the store and post office.

The front of the building was pitch dark; no ray of light filtered out at door or window. He peered about the corner, all dark, steeped in quiet. Quietly he stepped to the other corner. Now he saw that at the back of the house there was a lighted room; the rays of a lamp poured out at an open window. But still the house was as silent as the outer night.

He remained motionless, pondering swiftly. A light would not be burning in Vogel's house at this time of night unless Vogel was up. Vogel would not be up unless he had company or expected someone. Whitney stooped and again patted the dog which had followed him. It was not difficult, he fancied, to hit upon the explanation of the silence enwrapping the building. Whatever was going forward in Vogel's place was not meant to be subject to any interruption from him; inside they would have heard the dog bark, they would be listening for the sound of his horse's hoofs. Again he was conscious of his own feeling of responsibility for the acts of Juanito tonight. Juanito with upward of a thousand dollars of another's money—Vogel with his crafty eyes and covetous soul—it went without saying that Maxwell Whitney was not without his right to learn what he could learn and see what he could see.

Consequently, determined that he could remain stone-still as long as Vogel and Juanito, he stood without moving hand or foot. And soon he was rewarded by the sound of low voices, Juanito's first, since Juanito was ever the impatient one, then Vogel's, then another man's.

Still keeping the dog silent by stooping now and then to pat the friendly head, Whitney moved on into the yard, drawing opposite the window but keeping at a little distance and in the shadows. The window was low and wide open; it had been Juanito's command that had opened it since the foul air of Vogel's dirty shack sickened his fastidious nostrils. Without obstruction Whitney could look in.

"I tell you," he heard Juanito cry sharply, "we've got to get this over with! It's dragging like a lame horse. My friend Whitney will be here at any minute and then there'll be the devil to pay."

Beside Juanito and Vogel in the room were three others. One of these was Vogel's boy, Henry, watching excitedly that which went forward; one, unknown as yet to Whitney, a sluggardly looking giant known about the neighborhood as Nig Chorro; the third, cheaply yet flashily dressed, with eyes as hard as agate and a bleak, cadaverous face, was, as Whitney came soon to realize, that type of gambler that still infests the West, with his regular beat across a number of counties, a bird of prey ever as quick to sweep down upon the thoughtless possessor of a thousand dollars as is a turkey buzzard to drop from the void of the sky when a horse dies. This man, when Juanito had done, spoke sharply.

"What's eating you, Olivas? You've had the devil's luck tonight; what more do you want?"

Juanito looked sweepingly across the table; there were no chips, tonight they played for and with real money. There was some little silver, a number of bank notes. Until just now the four men had been playing; Nig Chorro, with a look at Vogel such as a dog may give its master, had drawn back, his money gone. In front of Vogel's tapping fingers were some bills, not a great many. Much more money was represented in the bits of paper in front of the man who had just spoken. And, surprising Maxwell Whitney no little, there were even heavier winnings in front of Juanito.

"What do I want?" Juanito cried. "You ask that, Kelvin? I want action, I want speed, I want this cursed thing over with! Shall we play all night for a miserable sum?" Whitney knew that just as sure as there was more than one thousand dollars on the table, there was twice that sum, and yet Juanito termed it a miserable amount! The boy wore the look of one inspired with an abandon of recklessness. "Don't I tell you that soon we are going to have an interruption? You demand that tonight I pay or play; well, I come and play. But have I a thousand years?"

205

"We've been playing less than an hour," snapped Kelvin. "Go on, Olivas. Your deal."

"That's right," said Vogel, still tapping, looking to be in the grip of a nervous ague, his eyes never lifting from the table. "Your deal."

"I tell you—" broke in Juanito.

"And I tell you," said Kelvin sternly, "that you came asking for speedy play and we gave it to you. You've got a game with a stripped deck and the joker wild. What more do you want?"

Vogel could not contain himself; he was as white as a sheet with the fear upon him that something might go wrong. He began to curse, in a voice as shrill as a nervous woman's, shouting out:

"You, Olivas, deal! I am telling you to hurry and don't forget what I tell you to do you must do. I've got you where—"

Juanito sprang to his feet, defiant. He caught up the cards and hurled them across the room so that they flew in all directions.

"Who here shall dictate to me?" he demanded arrogantly. "Remember, storekeeper, that a Vogel does not dictate to an Olivas! And I am sick of this dragging game; I win, you win, Kelvin wins, even for a little that Chorro there won—nobody wins! The dice, Kelvin, the dice! And, for the love of God, quick, man! Before my friend Whitney comes."

But his friend Whitney held where he was, though restlessly. If he broke in now, what good

206

would it do? Juanito would still play, in the end they would fleece him—and what part was Whitney's in this game? He could threaten to denounce Juanito, to say where the thousand came from which he staked on the table before him; but was there a man there who did not know already?

"No dice this time," Kelvin was saying stubbornly. "Cards."

Juanito jeered at him with impudent laughter.

"You call yourself a gambler and you are afraid of a chance taken while the dice roll!" he cried ringingly. "Vogel there shivers like a man in the cold. You are two of a kind, Señores. I would rather be like Chorro there." Chorro's heavy face grew uglier with its ponderous scowl than Whitney had thought a human face could. "But look, I will tempt the two of you. You say I have the devil's luck tonight? You do not know what luck I have, or from where it comes. I know; and I know I will win whether it be in one second or all night. But look; this way will I make you play!"

With them all watching, completely puzzled, he counted the bank notes in front of him, dropping them to the table.

"When I came I put into play one thousand dollars," he ran on then. "The amount which I owe you, Vogel—or which *you* say I owe Kelvin! It's all one to me. And now I have four hundred and thirty dollars more than I put into the game; one thousand four hundred and thirty dollars. *Bueno.*

You hold papers which I have signed, altogether worth one thousand dollars. I give you odds, fourteen hundred and thirty against ten hundred! Now will you give me the dice, Kelvin? Now will you give me the dice, Chorro? Now will you let it be dice, Vogel?"

"Mad as a March hare," muttered Whitney under his breath.

And mad the others as plainly held him. Vogel's squinting ferret eyes at last came up from the table: they probed at Juanito; they flitted away to Kelvin's bleak face; they traveled back to Juanito, via the table route. Vogel began wetting his lips, working one over the other, showing the tip of his tongue. Vogel's boy drew nearer; there were red spots in his pasty cheeks.

"You're the great little sport, Olivas." It was Kelvin's voice and though it was cold and steady, like his basilisk eyes, it carried with it a jeer meant to sting the boy into a fine frenzy of recklessness. "What else have you to offer in the way of odds? We're all listening!"

"What you please," retorted Juanito hotly. "Tonight I win, damn the odds. Let's have the dice."

The lean pale hand of Kelvin brought forth from his pocket five ivory cubes. They were spilled to the table; they in their turn caught and held Vogel's agitated stare. Juanito swept them up lightly.

"You ask for odds and more odds, do you?"

Juanito's eyes were on fire with what he meant to do and gleamed feverishly. "Then I tell you, Señores all, what you will not understand—that the hand of God is in this! Either it is meant that I win or that I lose and what is meant will be." There was utter conviction in his voice which now, for the first time, was tremulous with the import of his dictum. He shoved to the table's center his own stake and winnings. "Put there the papers I have signed. And you, Kelvin, name for me what odds you want!"

Kelvin nodded to Vogel; Vogel, like a man in a dream, reluctant to move and yet impelled on, obeyed the nod and the papers were added to Juanito's money. Kelvin, all this time, was musing and watching Juanito and trying to read the boy to his last thought. Now, straightening in his chair, he said quietly:

"All of us have lost money to you tonight, Olivas; Vogel and Chorro and myself. All of us, then, have an interest in that money. What say you that each of us takes one die, that each makes his throw, that the high man wins everything?"

Whitney, seeing that already had Juanito given odds of one and a half to one, and was now invited to a fresh hazard of three to one, fully expected to hear the boy break out in angry rejection of so absurd an offer. But Juanito did not so much as appear surprised at Kelvin's suggestion. He shrugged elaborately; he drew his slender body up to the last millimeter of his stature and said confidently:

"It is all one; if I win, I win. If I lose—" He shrugged again.

Now there sprang up in Maxwell Whitney's heart, despite all he knew of Juanito Olivas and against him, a sudden admiration for the boy. And now, though he felt that he should interrupt, he had no impulse to do so. If the boy lost—as he must—and carried himself like a man, then did Maxwell Whitney vow to go down into his own pocket to see him clear of the mess he was making of things.

"Let each man take a die," said Kelvin quickly, putting out his hand.

But now Juanito laughed at him.

"They are your dice, Señor," he said meaningly, "and if anyone could select wisely the owner should, eh? *Venga*, Henry," he called. And when Vogel's boy dragged his heavy shoes forward, Juanito gave him the five dice. "Shake them in a hat," he ordered. "Then, without looking, put in your hand. One to Vogel, one to Chorro, one to Kelvin, one to me."

"One tie, all tie?" demanded Vogel, clearing his throat before he could work the words out.

Again Juanito laughed.

"There will be no tie," he responded. "Ace high, deuce low, one throw for everything."

Twice, before Vogel could make his throw, the

die jumped out of his hand; he had to go down on his hands and knees and grope after it under the table. Even the sluggishness of the great-bulked Nig Chorro was not impervious to the zest of the moment, though doubtless his own share, did he win, would be negligible.

Henry brought a cup which all were to use. Vogel, having insisted on being first, hesitated so long to make his throw, that finally Kelvin gave the first sign of his own nerves, in cursing him and commanding him to hurry. Vogel still hesitated; he seemed powerless to act toward having the thing over with. Kelvin snatched the cup from him and threw his own die so that it rolled half across the table.

"A five," he announced colorlessly. "Not so bad, friend Olivas."

Nig Chorro followed. The die rolled, balanced on an edge, settled.

"A four," he grunted.

"Rather little for a big man," snapped Kelvin. "Now, Vogel. You or Olivas. Who's next?"

Vogel caught up the cup; the die began rattling before he voluntarily shook it; he moved jerkily, half risen from his chair, half crouching over the table, and cast.

"A six!" He fairly shrieked it out. The blood rushed into his face and he shouted over and over. "A six! A six! I win! It is mine!"

"Looks like it," muttered Kelvin. "Or rather,

you and I win; don't forget that, Vogel. But we'd better give the kid a chance. Spill it out, Olivas."

Juanito's face was set; it was suddenly pale. Into the boy's eyes came the look of one who prayed with all his soul. He made his throw. And Vogel, straining forward, jerked back as from a blow in the face.

"The ace!" he gasped. "The ace! My God—He has tricked us!"

He threw himself forward face down on the table, clutching. But Juanito had been the quicker, perhaps Juanito had more than half expected something of this sort. At any rate his hand, a half inch before Vogel's, caught up the banknotes and signed papers. Juanito sprang back and thrust everything higgledy-piggledy into his coat pocket. The blood swept back into his drawn face, his eyes were bright with triumph.

"It is not I who win," he cried out at them. "You said it, Vogel: It is God! Señores all, *buenas noches*!"

He clapped on his hat, made them an ironic bow and turned toward the door. Thus he did not see what Whitney saw so well; the look that came into Vogel's straining eyes; the expression in the eyes of Kelvin, the gambler; the look which passed between them. . . . Juanito was going out at the rear door; Whitney ran around that way to warn him.

Already Juanito had run down the back steps

212

and was in the yard going to his horse beyond the fence. It was the big man, Nig Chorro, whom they sent first after him. Whitney, coming to the back steps, saw Chorro catch up a stick of wood, an oak limb thrown aside as too long for the kitchen stove fire-box. Chorro ran with a nimbleness which one would not expect to encounter in one of his tremendous bulk. In the dark he mistook Whitney for Juanito; he lifted the oak club to strike. But it was Whitney who struck first. He drove a fist into the heavy face, and Nig Chorro, with a grunt, was jolted backward. The club in his hand was lowered as, for a brief instant, the big man was dazed. Whitney caught at it, jerked it away with a sudden wrench, lifted it and struck the second time. Chorro, had he been the ox he looked, must have staggered at the impact of the hard wood. He sagged in the knees and stumbled and fell.

Behind Chorro came Kelvin, whipping out something from his pocket.

"Olivas!" he called. "Stop or I'll drop you. I—"

"What's that?" Juanito called from the fence. "What's happening?"

"I want a word with you," said Kelvin. "And I mean to have it."

He had not seen Whitney in the shadows; he had perhaps supposed that it had been Juanito who had put Nig Chorro where he must stumble over him. But Whitney, having him against the light, saw what it was that he had in his hand. He threw up Chorro's club, stepped in close to Kelvin, and brought the oak bludgeon down across the gambler's hand. There was a cry of pain from Kelvin and the gun fell to the ground. Whitney caught it up and said almost into the ear of the astonished gambler:

"Back you go into the house, Mr. Kelvin. And step lively!"

There was an ominous sound in the voice of this unexpected stranger; the gun barrel was not six inches from Kelvin's face. The gambler drew back, back another pace, caught his heel against the bottom step and began a slow retreat up to the porch. By now Vogel and Henry were staring out into the dark from the door.

"That is you, *amigo*?" It was Juanito's voice calling. "You here!"

But Whitney had no time to answer him. Nig Chorro, on his feet again, was wiping a big hand across his eyes and was muttering in his thick throat.

"Back you go, too, Chorro," he commanded. "As lively as you know the way."

Chorro came a step nearer, lifting his thick arms like a bear. But now he saw what it was that Whitney thrust forward to meet him, for the light from the kitchen fell across it, and he stopped and began drawing back. Juanito in the meantime, leaping down from the fence, came swiftly to Whitney's side.

"The murderous dogs," he cried hotly. "Robbers!"

"Back you go, Chorro," Whitney kept on saying. "Hunt your hole, you fat grizzly."

"I go," said Chorro thickly. "With my hands I fight you, *cabrone*. I no like gun-fightin'."

Whitney stood where he was until at last the ponderous Chorro stood beside Kelvin at the top of the steps. Behind them the strained faces of Vogel and Vogel's boy stared. Then, with Juanito following him step by step, still facing the four men at the house, Whitney began slowly withdrawing.

"*Amigo mío*!" Juanito was saying excitedly. "You save the life in me tonight. That life, from now on, is yours. For you—"

"My horse is tied in front of the hotel," Whitney whispered to him. "Get yours and wait for me."

Juanito nodded and slipped away. Whitney circled the house, hurried out into the road, came to his horse and swung up into the saddle. From the storekeeper's house rose a mumble of voices, Vogel's rising hysterically through the other undertones. Whitney leaned forward in the saddle; the red bay leaped under him; he was away to join Juanito for whom he began to feel he was developing a decidedly strong liking. The boy should be brought up with a round turn; he was the sort to make much mischief; but—for

215

a' that and a' that, Juanito Olivas had faced in a manner smacking of the heroic that adverse wind which his own recklessness had whistled up and had played his lone hand with a fine if misguided courage.

"We are friends, you and I!" Juanito awaiting him in the road, put out an eager hand. "In after days it shall be said of Maxwell Whitney and Juan Olivas, that they were Damon and Pythias reborn. Is it not so, *amigo*?"

And Whitney, accepting the hand and the heart which impulsively accompanied it, answered without restraint:

"Friends, Juanito."

CHAPTER XVIII

AN ULTIMATUM

Their horses were tired, the night's work was done, and they rode slowly up the King of Spain Valley. Thus they were upon the road a full two hours during which time the effervescent Juanito knew scarcely ten consecutive seconds of silence. More than ever was he the wind which Teresa Calderon had named him, blowing every way at once. He was visited by moments of his own peculiar religious fervor; he swept off his hat again and adored the Master commanding alike

216

the cycling of heavenly orbs and the fall of a die on a gambler's table; at such moments his voice was the voice of a priest sunk into a calm monotone. Then came periods of exhilaration like wine in his turbulent veins when his altered voice made gay music of his words and his extravagance worked the words themselves into little songs of joyous acclamation: the world was so fine a place!

Between him and his *amigo* Maxwell there were no secrets tonight! From his pocket came those papers bearing his signature which Vogel had held menacingly over him. Incoherently he told his tale while his quick fingers tore the papers into shreds, flinging them to the awakening breeze. He had made mistakes in his life, oh, *seguro*! For why? Because, as Maxwell would so readily comprehend, he was a gentleman and not a bookkeeper. Vogel had tempted him, for which might Vogel be damned in due time. Vogel, too, had brought about other games; Juanito had played with fine scorn of mere dollars; he had lost, not the once only, but every time. Yes, Kelvin was always there; Nig Chorro often. Vogel had not played until tonight that Juanito demanded it and Kelvin nodded yes, as much as to say, "No matter. It is I who will win the money and between you and me there is understanding."

"Kelvin," said Juanito coolly, "is a cardsharp. He cheats; I know. He and Vogel split between them what moneys Vogel leads him to. Nig Chorro, he is but Vogel's dog; he barks for Vogel, lies down for him, shows his belly upward at the lifting of Vogel's boot.

"Ah, this Vogel!" he explained, gone sober-thoughted again. "But he is the evil genius of the valley, *amigo*. He's got his claws into its fair throat. To look at, he is nothing; less than nothing; a pinch of dirt, no more. But never mind that; he throws a bigger, blacker shadow than the old Santa Lucia mountains. He is dictator; he is an ignorant and cruel despot. He has no mercy and much craft. Before now he has driven families out, gobbling up their holdings as a gopher-snake chokes down a baby squirrel. Despot Vogel! Now, when you look at him, that seems strange, no? But it is true."

Again he chuckled.

"And tonight he is a despot purple in the face with rage! I fancy across the miles I can hear him sputter. I have slipped out of his grip; with me I have taken a handful of money, money his or counted his! He'll be angry enough to chew nails."

"Having slipped out of his grip, as you term it," said Whitney drily, "I hope you are going to have brains enough to keep in the clear."

"Oh, sure," said Juanito confidently. "I'm not a fool, *amigo mío*."

After two o'clock and a light burning in the King of Spain ranch house! They saw it a mile away and

218

after that rode for the most part in silent haste. It might be only that Mentor Olivas sat up, waiting for his son, sleepless because of the hand that son had lifted in anger against Brooke Sheffield. But also it might mean that Sheffield's wound had been more serious than Whitney had estimated it—At any rate the two men left their horses in the yard, not stopping to unsaddle and hurried into the house. Both Señor Olivas and Teresa Calderon, on their feet at the sound of horses' hoofs, met them in the big living room. And in the eyes of both excitement mounted high.

"You are back," cried the girl. "Thank God!"

Whitney stood looking at her with something of pure wonder. Had he once, if though only for so brief a time, regarded this superb creature impersonally? Why, every curve of her splendid body, every glance of her flashing eyes, every tone of her low voice, were but so many gauntlets cast down in defiance of any man's aloof regard. And now, as that fervent "Thank God!" burst from her lips, though her eyes might have been for either Juanito or himself coming abreast through the wide door, he knew within him that she had been fearing that Juanito would return alone; that it was for his return that she was grateful. He knew, as a man at moments may know much that is passing through a mind in tune with his own, that she had fought against the suspicion which he had created in her; that she must have said, "If he is guiltless, he will return soon. And everything will be clear."

But still the look of excitement remained. Juanito saw it and was quick to demand:

"What is it? Something has happened! Is it— Has Sheffield—"

"Señor Sheffield," his father told him in a troubled voice, "does not appear to be any worse; things are bad enough, my son, as they are."

Juanito went quickly to his side and set his hands upon his father's shoulders.

"Forgive me, papa, for what I did," he said softly. "But you know what anger does to us of Olivas blood." He sent a flashing look, full of question and pleading, toward Teresa. "You know what love is and how hot jealousy burns in the brain."

"Of this we will talk later, Juan," said Mentor gravely. "You and I."

"But then there is something else?" persisted the boy. "Something happening while Maxwell and I are riding?"

"Yes," Mentor answered him, looking puzzled. "I do not know what has come over us here at the King of Spain." His eyes went to Whitney's; they seemed half apologetic and something akin to apology entered his tone as he continued: "First, Tia Tonia's box is stolen; then there is the theft of my moneys; then—then," he hurried on, "a man stabbed. And now another attempted robbery."

"Come," said Teresa nervously. "I will show you."

She led the way to her room; on through to the room which once had been her father's, where the King of Spain painting hung.

"Look!" she exclaimed. "There. And there."

To begin with the iron grill over the north window had been wrenched away; at a glance it became obvious that no trust should have been put into the thing for years. The iron bars were let into thick slabs of hard wood, seasoned oak from the neighborhood; the oak itself, to stand against attack of saw or ax had been protected by riveted strips of iron. But for many years, in a house whose inmates loved the free, fresh air, this window had been left open far more than shut; the rains had washed in; the wood had rotted where the rivet-holes allowed access to moisture. When a determined hand had pried at the oak slabs they had offered scarcely so much resistance that a child might not have laughed at them.

But that was not all, and the other mischief done showed something of the intent of the nocturnal intruder. Teresa was pointing to the King of Spain painting. Of the stout oak pegs holding it to the wall, two, the lower ones, had been drawn out; they lay discarded on the floor. One of the others had known the feel of the thieving hands; it was half way out of its socket so that the picture hung insecurely.

"It was half an hour after you left," Teresa explained. "Señor Mentor and I were talking in the dining room. Señor Sheffield had asked that we sit up a little; he was not sure that his hurt was not worse than we thought. I don't know what made me go to my room; just restlessness, or—I don't know. Nor do I know why, once in my room, I was prompted to come in here. Señor Mentor thinks I must have heard something." But she shook her head. "I think I must have known, I don't understand how, that a hand was lifted against the painting. I found the door fastened. I called out; Señor Mentor came with me; we ran outside, Señor Mentor carrying a rifle. When we came to the window we found it like that."

"And no one here?" demanded Juanito. "But of course he had gone!"

"No one." Señor Olivas spoke heavily. "But—"

He hesitated. Juanito swung upon him, urging:

"Go on! But what?"

It was Teresa who answered.

"Outside we came upon Josefa. We thought, both of us, that she acted strangely, that she sought to avoid being seen, that she knew."

"Josefa again," muttered Juanito. "Remember that she was in the closet that other night. She must be made to speak!"

A wintry smile touched the lips of Señor Olivas. He shrugged.

"A woman will talk when she will," he said.

"Not when a man bids her. You may think to own a woman body and soul—her tongue is always her own."

It was Whitney who again made the grill across the window as secure as it might be done tonight. Thereafter he closed and locked the window.

"Shall we take down the painting and put it in a safer place?" asked Juanito.

But Teresa answered quickly, saying with the firmness of an old determination:

"Where my father placed it it shall remain. I shall sleep lightly and the door to my room will be left open."

They returned to the living room. Juanito was nervously restive. Perhaps from the knowledge that the eyes of his father and of Señorita Calderon watched him curiously; perhaps, thought Whitney, because there was in his pocket a sum of money which should be elsewhere.

"Who's there?" It was Brooke Sheffield's voice, querulous from his bed chamber. "That you, Whitney?"

Whitney excused himself quickly, his eyes conveying to Señor Olivas a certain assurance which at once mystified and yet, so calm was it, carried comfort.

"I'll go to him," he said quietly. "I'll be back in a moment."

For he hoped with new impatient eagerness for

a few words with Teresa Calderon before good night was said. As he left the room he heard Juanito saying: "I'll go out and stable the horses." Juanito, too, was impatient, and Whitney guessed something of the boy's intent; to slip around outside to another door, to steal soft-footedly to the library table and place the money back in its drawer.

Whitney found Sheffield lying upon his back, his right hand pressed against the bandage of the wounded, left shoulder. The man's brows were drawn, his eyes looked wild, he seemed to be in considerable pain.

"Shut the door after you," he growled. "Is that young savage in there? God, I've had a close shave. . . . Give me a glass of water, old man."

Whitney brought the water. Then he stood over Sheffield, waiting for him to drink. Sheffield groaned as he was forced to move slightly to get the glass to his lips; he drank thirstily; he sank back with another groan.

"You've got no idea how infernally sore it is," he muttered. "It near kills a man to move. Now, I suppose, I'll be laid up here, flat on my back, for a month. Curse that black-hearted fool."

"You'll be about in two shakes," grunted Whitney. "Of course it will be sore for a few days, but not more so than enough to remind you that you ought to thank your stars you are alive. Now, Sheffield, what's in your mind regarding the boy? Are you going to make a fuss over this thing?"

Sheffield's eyes flew wide open.

"Am I going to make a fuss?" he exclaimed. "Take me for the sort of man to say 'Thank you' for a knife cut? You're damned right, there'll be a fuss, as you call it, such as was never raised in this valley. Johnny Olivas is going to jail down a greased slide and, if I know any of the short cuts of law methods, he's going to slide right on into the penitentiary! I'll show him—"

"Ease up," commanded Whitney curtly. "Let's talk sense. You come here a guest; you are treated like the salt of the earth by both Miss Calderon and Señor Olivas, despite the fact that you invited yourself. Juanito's father is already distressed over what has happened. Naturally Miss Calderon, too, is terribly worried. You owe them something, Sheffield; you've got the chance to show them you are a square shooter."

Sheffield laughed contemptuously.

"I don't owe old Olivas anything," he retorted. "As for Miss Calderon, it would suit me just as well if that mooning idiot Johnny Olivas were out of the way. You are barking up the wrong tree, old man. Besides it is none of your damned business. And thirdly, I've made up my mind. Everything I know how to do to hound Stabbing Johnny into jail, and I guess I happen to know just about all there is, I am going to use. Now suppose—"

"I want you to go slow—"

"Drop it!" snapped Sheffield. "I'll trouble you to keep your sop and sugar doctrines to yourself. And your paws off my affairs."

Whitney looked at him steadily.

"Rather," he went on coolly, "I'll come at it from another angle. I'll ask you a question and I don't care whether you answer or not: What made you decide all of a sudden to leave San Francisco?"

Sheffield's look sharpened.

"I'll not go any deeper into your affairs than becomes necessary," continued Whitney. "Frankly, I don't enjoy the sort of odor which arises from the disturbance of sleeping facts of your sort of a career. But I'll ask a second question: Do you wish to have stirred up and aired all of the circumstances which put into your head the notion to come visiting in the country?"

Narrower and narrower grew the eyes of the man on the bed.

"If you mean anything, say it!"

"I mean rather a good deal. You can hound Juanito Olivas if you like. He will be ably defended; your wound will be healed and won't amount to a snap of the fingers; the boy's youth will be taken into consideration as, also, will be your character as it is pretty well known in San Francisco. I have the idea that some of the biggest attorneys in that city, for the pure joy of thwarting you, would handle the case without asking a two-bit retainer. You'd lose out. And, in the meantime, all of the nasty facts which have threatened you with an act of disbarment will come to light."

When he said the word "Disbarment," Sheffield winced visibly. In those three syllables he had his answer.

"Who the hell are you?" he demanded suspiciously. "Some nice little gumshoe artist sent down on the job, eh?"

"Never mind who I am—"

"But I do mind!" He surged up on his elbow; his face reddened with rage. "And let me tell you something, my fine friend! You come to me with threats; you work your damnedest to keep me back from instigating an act of mere justice; you thus become an accessory after the fact, if not before. And that nice little club you think you hold over me, know what they call that sort of thing? It's blackmail, pure and simple! And if you don't keep your coattails out of this, I'll put you in the jug, too!"

Whitney laughed at him and turned away.

"Suit yourself," he said bluntly. "Weigh matters; consider what you stand to lose, what you have a slim chance of winning. That's all."

He went to the door. Sheffield lay motionless, watching him go. But when the knob turned under Whitney's fingers, Sheffield called sharply.

"You're a pretty wise guy," he sneered as Whitney returned. "All right, let's talk. If I keep my hands off Johnny Olivas, then what?"

"I keep my hands off you."

"For good?"

"I suppose so. Certainly at least as long as you refrain from interfering with my friends or myself."

"Old High-and-Mighty!" said Sheffield, already yielding and yet not the man to do so without his show of scorn.

"It's a take-it or leave-it proposition." In his heart, however, he was not absolutely convinced; he held one more trump, that of his option in the Pajaro Azul ranch matter—a card which, for reasons no longer utterly formless, he did not wish to play.

"What are you getting out of this?" Still was Sheffield suspicious; if a man took a decided stand, anywhere on the way, he must have his own interests to consider; which was an essential bit of the Sheffieldian philosophy.

Whitney ignored him, merely waiting for a decision.

"You can go tell your friend Johnny," Sheffield exploded, "that so long as he keeps his hands off me I'll let him go this time. And remember—you are to keep your mouth shut."

"As long as you behave yourself, yes." This time Whitney went out.

• • •

He found Teresa Calderon alone in the living room. She turned at the sound of his steps.

"Señor Mentor has followed Juanito out to the stable," she said quickly. She came closer; her voice was lowered and he marked the anxious note in it. "There is so much happening that I do not understand! And, in at least some of these happenings, I am the one most concerned. Does it seem to you unreasonable, Señor Maxwell, that I should ask again that you tell me what you know?"

"You mean about the money that disappeared? No; certainly not unreasonable. Such, I am afraid, must seem my refusal to answer. And yet I am going to ask if you will let the answer go for the present. If tomorrow the money is not returned, I will tell you all I know of it."

She pondered his answer, looking at him steadily. In the end she sighed and shook her head.

"For an instant," he went on equably, "you suspected me. You remembered how you had seen me coming out through the library door, and even at the time you remarked on my rushing along like a man catching a train; you recalled, further, that you had seen me shove something into my pocket."

When it was plain that he awaited her answer, she gave it.

"Yes. I did suspect you."

229

"You don't any longer?"

"No." She was perfectly candid, her level glance hid nothing. "I do not believe that you are a thief."

He inclined his head, thanking her with his eyes. That she should refuse to give credence to such evidence, knowing as little of him as she did, was a tribute which he accepted for its full value.

"There are other reasons than guilt, though," she went on, "which would make a man like you hold his silence."

"Yes. There are other reasons."

"Is friendship one of them?"

But now it was Whitney who shook his head, saying thoughtfully:

"Believe me, it will do us no good to discuss this. Were you in my place, I know you would do as I am doing."

"While Señor Mentor is away, there is another thing." She paused and then continued with grave slowness. "You will remember that it is in the Calderon home that these things happen; that the Calderon name means very much to me; that my father left it a clean name for me to keep clean. It must not be cheapened by dirty rumors. Tonight Juanito, who has been to me like a brother since we were babies, has stabbed a man who is my guest. In return, my guest threatens to hound Juanito to jail. And I—"

"I have just had a talk with Sheffield," he

230

interrupted. "He has agreed not to make trouble for Juanito."

Obviously the information amazed her.

"But—Are you *sure?* He and Juanito have never liked each other." He saw a flush, defying her will and rising into her cheeks. She hurried on: "Won't he change his mind?"

"No." He was positive and his voice carried conviction. "Juanito will leave him alone in the future and Sheffield, for his part, will not take any action against him."

She looked at him queerly.

"You appear to know more of my guest and of Juanito than I know myself!" And when he made no reply, she added: "What happened? What caused Juanito to do a thing like that—to stab Señor Sheffield and nearly kill him?"

It was Whitney's time for astonishment.

"Surely, you do not need to ask *that!*"

Again Teresa's face reddened. But her eyes held steady and she answered:

"I mean something definite must have happened to precipitate violence of that sort."

"Good Heavens!" exclaimed Whitney. "Wasn't the cause sufficient? Surely—" But he stopped there. And still her eyes were candid as she insisted:

"Tell me. You must remember I knew nothing until it was all over; until I returned to the house and found you and Juanito gone, Señor

Sheffield wounded in his room. What was—"

"You mean," he muttered, "that you didn't see? That you weren't out there with Sheffield?"

"Maxwell Whitney!" She was aghast at what he implied. She came closer to him, she put an impulsive hand on his arm, commanding breathlessly: "Tell me. Tell me everything!"

Had he told her everything just then, beginning at the beginning of what lay uppermost in his mind, he would have caught her hand and cried out: "When you touch me like that you set my blood on fire. When you look at me with those Spanish eyes of yours there is nothing else for me in the world. I want you!" . . . He stood silent, looking at her.

"What is it? What makes you look like that? I asked you what happened—"

The whole scene of an earlier hour in the garden flashed into his mind in vivid detail, Sheffield hurrying as to a tryst, a girl standing by the pear tree, Teresa's white shawl gleaming through the dark—

"Your shawl," he said sharply. "When you left me, going out, I saw you snatch it up. You went out through the kitchen. *Did you wear your shawl into the garden?*"

Before she answered—for her reply came only after a long silence during which, puzzled by his words, she sought to remember a trifle making one of the minor details of a night of tense nerves—

Maxwell Whitney's mind leaped to the truth. He remembered Josefa, the strangeness of her bearing, the look in the black eyes which always followed Sheffield.

"No." At last Teresa was answering. "I felt like one smothering. As I went through the kitchen I threw it off. I expect we shall find it there now, on a chair or slipped to the floor—"

"I am glad of that," he exclaimed fervently.

"But you don't explain anything! You yourself appear to understand everything. I understand nothing!"

"Then I can tell you this in a word: Juanito thought that he saw you in Brooke Sheffield's arms. There was someone; there was your shawl; Juanito is the kind to strike first and ask questions afterward. And—"

"Someone in Brooke Sheffield's arms!" Dazedly she repeated the words after him. "My shawl—" Her eyes were blazing now; her slim body stiffened. "You saw, you thought that it was Teresa Calderon!"

Her eyes baffled him. He had no key to what lay deep in them. And before either spoke again they heard Mentor Olivas coming alone into the house.

"I can't find Juanito," he said. "The horses are in the barn but he is not there."

The mystery-filled Spanish eyes had never left Whitney's face.

"Perhaps Señor Whitney knows where he is,"

she said serenely. "He seems to know everything!"

Whitney fancied that he did know. But he contented himself with saying:

"I'd imagine that he came back to the house by another door. Suppose we see if he is not in his room?"

Mentor went swiftly to the door and called:

"Juanito!"

Juanito's voice, careless and unconcerned, called back:

"Coming, papa. I was just getting my slippers on; my boots hurt my feet."

The Spanish eyes were inscrutable now.

"You see," said Teresa with a little shrug, "Señor Whitney does know everything!"

Mentor came hurrying to them, his eyes shining.

"Look!" he exclaimed, and showed them all the money he had in his hands. "Something made me go back to the desk and look again; I couldn't believe, even after all this time, that such a thing had really happened. Look!"

"Oh!" cried Teresa. "Then our money was not stolen at all? And we were ready to blame everybody!"

"It is a miracle, Señorita," said Olivas. "It was in the same drawer that I put it, just shoved far back. And the true miracle is this: All the money came back—and it brought about five hundred extra dollars with it!"

CHAPTER XIX

DAYS IN CAMP

Maxwell Whitney returned to the wilderness, as so many a man has done before him, as so many will come to do in the fullness of time, richly content to be alone with the forests. Here one got a proper perspective; here one might tramp all day through the shady woods or might lie on his back staring up at the blue California skies and judge the true values. Such a man does not grow lonely; companionable thoughts troop through the hours; he lives to the limit of his possibilities in past, present and future. He comes to suspect that a half loaf of brown bread is better than a pound of minted gold. He communes with the verities.

Though always hitherto a doer of deeds rather than a dreamer of dreams, now he found a certain satisfaction in introspection. He was in love with life as he found it, as it came ready made. He was solaced and moved by the old-age quiet and peace of the valley whose influences seemed to pervade the solitudes about his camp.

He would have said that the adventure of coming here had served to purge him of earlier ambitions—mean and sordid ambitions, as he saw them through the leafy green of the immense roof above him. Where was he getting in the city? Toward wealth, presumably, until the smash-up came. When he got his wealth, what then? Why, then he had always promised himself just such an idling experience as he was now enjoying! He would have stuck his money away into a bank or into "safe investments"—and would have gone camping! What in the name of folly had been the use of the wealth in the first place? He shook his head with a tolerant smile at the old Benjamin M. Whitney whom, by the way, he now deemed extinct.

Thus other days drifted by. The season changed; almost over night the springtime was gone and the full summer shone unclouded. The various promises of rain had failed of fulfillment; the grass was turning a paler tone, would soon grow yellow, then the shade of bleached straw. It was to be a windy summer, they said down in the valley, shaking their heads. For at times the unwelcome north wind had a fashion of finding its way from the more open Salinas Valley into the sheltered King of Spain. It, more than anything else, hastened the departure of the gentler spring; it whipped the moisture out of the ground and seared the spears of grass and grain. The days already were growing hot.

Hot out in the open spaces; delightfully balmy in the forests. The upper tributaries of the valley river still ran ice-cold through the half-gloom of the narrow cañons. Here the days, for one who would idle, were perfect. And now, in this environment, Maxwell Whitney began to formulate a theory of the ideal life utterly at variance with all of his earlier doctrines and, though not yet did he understand this, equally foreign to his own essential character. It was that of standing aloof from the traffic centers of frenzied endeavor; of sitting and watching and letting the stream go by.

He had blocked Brooke Sheffield's game in the matter of the Pajaro Azul; he had done all that he had set out to do and there the thing ended. He had no further interest. He would instruct his attorney to keep Judge Belden's former manager at the place; to let things go as they were. He himself would continue to cook his meals over a rude rock fireplace; to catch a trout when his appetite suggested it; to bathe naked of a hot day in the cool pools; to tramp to mountain tops. He had a little money left, after all; he didn't need to worry about getting back into the treadmill. One of these days, when he had made up his mind very, very definitely, he'd ride down to the valley ranch house again; would seek a talk with Teresa Calderon, would then either return, saying nothing, to his camp or would set about making her marry him. Was he in love with her? He fully intended to be quite cool-thoughtedly satisfied on this point before he committed himself to any final line of action.

And all of this, had Maxwell Whitney known himself half as well as he thought he did, would have caused him high amusement. He meant to play the part of a wise old philosopher with the approaching chill in his veins while essentially he was as young as a boisterous spring morning. Young, hardy, lusty and, above all, eager; eager for what he might be confronting him with the opening of any new door; eager to come to grips with destiny, being borne along with the flood of a triumphant optimism, the inheritance of a long line of ancestors who had striven and fallen and arisen, but who had always broken through barriers and forged ahead, let the end be what it might; glad because hale youth is glad. In short the blood of Maxwell Whitney was what the blood of Young California is: mixed, turbulent, onrushing; red rather than blue.

And yet, in no wise was Whitney's brief sojourn in the wilderness a loss of time. He came to have at least a bowing acquaintance with his Other Self. That was worth something, even though that Self might soon bow himself on out of sight, to be glimpsed from a distance but rarely in days to come. He came to have a much more intimate friendship with the world of outdoors. He marked small, near-invisible details in the yellowing grass; he caught the larger massed mountain groupings; he made a great and trusting friend of the chipmunk whom he had named the Senator;

he whistled to the birds and had them answer; he imitated the dove's call and brought a pair of the quick graceful wings into his camp, cutting the air audibly. He came to know individually each of the winds that blew. The summer wind, lazy, languid, scented; if you shut your eyes and listened and felt the hot sunshine on you and let your mind be led hither and thither by the faintest suggestion, it was no time until you fancied you drowsed on a white beach with a creaming surf rolling ceaselessly—palms, blue sky, a scent of magnolia blossoms.

Then there was the belated spring wind which had gotten itself lost among the woods; that was fresh and fragrant; that ruffled the pools and the air and the blood; that whispered of wild roses in a hidden tangle. And the north wind, a harsh, ill-humored old fellow, blowing all your feathers the wrong way, putting your nerves on end, rustling the dry grass, parching throat and world, a thief of moisture. A wind among the pines; a strange new quality here. You do not know whence it comes, whither it goes.

Were you out in the open valley you would mark the mad dance of the fallen leaves, not so mad, by the way, that they do not all run in the same direction; the drift of chimney smoke in the distance tells whether it be a rain wind or quite another sort; there are so many. But up here, among the pines, there is nothing to answer the question the wind itself, like another Johan Bojer, is always asking: "Whence and whither?" The trees toss their arms, but in a hundred different directions; there is a soughing all about; a moaning, a playing upon ten thousand thousand stringed instruments in a tremendous symphony in which, while vibrant strings pulse and ring out in triumphant crescendos, others sink, lulled to the tenderest of diapasons. A whirlwind on the valley floor, dancing to its own tunes, as light, as inconsequential a thing as Juanito himself, playing with leaves, tossing them about, forgetting them to race on to gather up other finer ones because they are a little farther on. The dawn wind; the gentle breathing of the wind at nightfall.

So Maxwell Whitney camped and tramped and relaxed utterly in a genuine vacation. And meantime the Great Mother, working busily rearing up and tearing down, in her proper, jealously guarded demesne about him, the mother of moods who is at once merciful and merciless, tender and cruel, adopted him as one of her great brood and got her busy fingers into his individual pie. He grew as hard as nails; the golden tint of his healthy skin was deepened, made more golden, more healthy; new vigor awoke with him in the still dawns, pulsed through him through the days and nights. He was overflowing with well-being; with energy; he began to grow restless. He took longer walks; he found the narrow, hazardous trail across the ridges to the Coast; he looked far out, far down, and saw the fogs of the Pacific; he got the smell of the salt sea in his nostrils. His Other Self, making a valiant stand before beating a headlong retreat, asked him what the devil he meant by getting restless? What did he want? What did he want to do? Hadn't he decided to let the stream go by? Well, it was going, wasn't it, leaving him alone as he desired to be? What was the matter with him?

The matter was two-fold. He had been idle just exactly as long as it was possible for this particular Maxwell Whitney to be; that was one thing. And the other—He'd gotten into the habit of dreaming every night of Teresa Calderon.

Though he did not even faintly glimpse the fact, that day his vacation was over.

The first thing he did was instruct his attorney in Los Angeles to buy the Pajaro Azul.

CHAPTER XX

VOGEL'S GRIP TIGHTENS

Pleasant days had blossomed for the Calderon heiress. She went about the house singing; about the gardens dreaming when the soft loveliness of starshine and moonlight bathed the valley and it chanced there were no callers. For the dry harsh summer, burning up her lands, had little meaning for her. She did not do without the little things she liked; she sent her bills to Señor Mentor and what he did with them did not concern her. She knew very, very little of ranching and its problems, she had grown up as the daughters of the Calderons had done for centuries. Their men-folk shouldered the burdens of life or refused to shoulder them; these were not matters upon which a girl, raised as had been Teresa Calderon, was accustomed to dwell. Mentor was consciously a barrier to shield her. Was that not what he was for?

But Maxwell Whitney, through whom the old restlessness was surging as yet in no definite direction, came swiftly to understand a great deal that was going on. He noted how slowly the barns filled; how inferior was the crop; how the grazing cattle were already forsaking stubble fields for the hills and pushing always farther into the mountains for forage; how they were losing their sleek, fat look. He saw the haunted look in the eyes of the small farmers whom he had come to know; he heard much of their talk on mail days in Toyon; he saw and came to understand the sharp glances they shot at A. Vogel. He observed how Vogel looked more content every day. Whitney began to have it borne in upon him that all was not well here in the peaceful valley.

Frequently, more and more frequently as time

passed, he rode across the Pajaro Azul, his own ranch now. There were some few cattle and horses there, his own stock. One day he noted that they, too, were taking on that pinched look; that feed was short and scarce. At first he thought little of it, accepting a condition as he found it, and merely realizing that he would have to see that hay was bought before long; of course hay would be high. He noted that a few of the orchard trees were dead. This ride brought a sober look to his face before it was done. Vaguely—only vaguely at first—he felt that the Pajaro Azul was looking less picturesque than down at the heel.

That day, riding along the hills at the base of the Santa Lucias, he came upon a man digging. He drew up, wondering who the fellow was and what on earth he sought to find there on the bank of a dry gulch. Beyond him, half seen in the woods, was an old cabin used by Felipe Moraga when he chopped wood up here or mended fences.

The man looked up. He was a tattered, disreputable individual, close to sixty, from the look of him, grizzled, unkempt, dirty. The eyes were bright and quick, however, like those of a man in fever, and the light in them was one of suspicion. This man might have been builded around suspicion for a back-bone. Before he spoke Whitney recognized him; he was the tramp whom he had seen on the Toyon road that night he sought to overtake Juanito Olivas.

"What do you want here?" demanded the tramp. He straightened up, wiping the black soil from his short-handled pick. "Follerin' me again, be you?"

Whitney laughed.

"Of course I am not," he said good-naturedly. "And I wasn't following you that other time, either. You mean when I came by you on the road by your camp-fire?"

"Well," said the old man, mollified, but still eyeing Whitney keenly, "I got a right to potter around, ain't I? Long as Mentor says so, anyways."

"Go to it," answered Whitney heartily. "Prospecting a bit? Think there's gold in these hills?"

"What I think, I think an' what I know, I know," muttered the tramp. By now the name which he had called himself came back to Whitney; this was Jenkins, *Captain* Jenkins, by title. And *Captain* Jenkins, done now with talk, spat on his hands, lifted his pick to dig, thought better of it and walked off into the woods, muttering to himself.

"Queer old duffer," thought Whitney. And, for the second time, rode on and thought no more about him.

Before the long dry summer ended, matters stood thus in the King of Spain Valley: The Calderon ranch was confronting another year fraught with peril; Vogel was offering to take a mortgage; five separate mortgages on smaller ranches had been foreclosed. The valley seethed with hatred of Vogel, despair for the future. Vogel was the uncrowned king.

CHAPTER XXI

A BLOW AT THE PAJARO AZUL

From a purely passive and altogether superficial interest in the tramp, Jenkins, Whitney came abruptly to take a keenly active one. This was within ten days of encountering him in the hills.

A busy ten days they were, teeming with plans and the beginnings of endeavor. For the present Whitney said nothing to Teresa in criticism of ranch methods or in suggestion; he did not refer to these matters to Mentor Olivas, knowing well that the old Spaniard would be even more set in tradition, more aghast at the idea of new-fangled ways than was Teresa. What he would do was mind his own business for the present; his hands would be full that way; and from the work he accomplished they would read all that he meant, when time was ripe, to have out with them.

So he formally took over the Pajaro Azul and its fortunes, assuming personal management. He got his coat off, his sleeves rolled up and went to work. He hired men from among the local farmers or their idle helpers and began what he meant to continue into a gigantic clean-up. The gardens were cleared of weeds; the roads were scraped; the fences were mended and every post *plumbed*. Men of Toyon shook their heads at that; who ever heard of lining up fence posts to a dead level? But he surprised them all along the line he meant to travel; posts were not only plumbed but painted or whitewashed.

A gate that had sagged, been mended and sagged again, came down, was broken into stove wood and a new, freshly painted gate on strong hinges went up. The house was painted; the roof was gone over, to make sure that it was watertight. The barns were cleaned up, filled with hay, a portion of which came from the Pajaro Azul itself, a portion being hauled in from the railroad. The orchard could not be plowed to advantage now, but men were set to work in it, clearing and working about the trees. The corral was torn down and a new, sturdy enclosure went up in its place. And then, the day the smaller barn was filled, came the fire.

Vogel's handiwork or Sheffield's—of that Whitney was never for one second in doubt. For, positive he was that here was no accidental conflagration and to whom else, beyond these two, could he look for such a thing? Sheffield, he knew, was consumed with rage, now that it was common news in the valley that the man who had beaten the lawyer to the acquisition of the Pajaro Azul was Maxwell Whitney; Juanito had teased all of the complacency out of his hated rival one day in Toyon, with half a dozen men to hear, and Sheffield's face had gone first scarlet, then white. Vogel, still holding a ten thousand dollar mortgage on the Pajaro Azul, covetous of the rich acres, feeling that the purchaser was pressed for money or would not have let the mortgage run on—the interest was high—was not above seeking to further cripple the man over whom he now held, as he must believe, the whip hand.

By now Whitney, having had the house thoroughly scrubbed and scoured and freshened, was living here alone in a sort of camp-continuation; the men taking his wage made the trip daily from their homes, one coming as far as five miles. Because of the soft warm nights he slept at the rear of the house on the porch; here it was always coolest. At an hour of night late for country folk, he was awakened by a strange light playing in his eyes. He jumped out of bed; the barns, both of them, were on fire. And both were filled with hay as dry as gun-powder.

Not for an instant did he have the fond hope of saving the barns. They and their contents were doomed; some sheds and farming machinery would go too. That much was inevitable. But the house he did save, unaided, working furiously

247

throughout the rest of the night. There was a well in the back yard; he drew up water, filled all the buckets he could find, got a ladder up, went up on the roof. He wet sacks and fought with them. Where a far-flung spark lighted on the dry redwood or cedar shingles or seasoned pine, there would have been swift answering combustion had Whitney chanced that night to be away from home. Home! That was what it was. And, after he had fought grimly for it that night, he loved it the more.

His business methods stood him in some stead now. Everything was insured, despite the high rates, house, barns, contents. This, something which perhaps Sheffield or Vogel would not have counted on since there are in the world no more careless men in the matter of fire insurance than farmers, would temper the financial loss. That he could stand without worrying about it. If only the fire stopped with the barns; if only it let his fields and forests alone! For Maxwell Whitney, in his own way, was the man to be as proud of his monster oaks and aspiring pines as any Calderon who ever owned an acre of land.

Fortunately for him, his men had already been several days cleaning the yards and grounds; they had made war on the dry grass always to be feared as a fire-duct in summer; due to that fact and to Whitney's own watchfulness tonight, the fires did not spread into either hill or valley.

Black, smoldering, smoking heaps were his barns by morning; like scotched snakes they were still to be watched, lest a gust of wind carry sparks afield.

Whitney made his breakfast at four o'clock that morning. Then he sat on guard until his men came to work. And only then, having spoken his suspicions to no one, he went for a little ride.

A shoulder of the King of Spain ridge came down just back of the house, pine-timbered to within a couple of hundred yards of the barns. It was in Whitney's mind that the man who had set the fires would have come that way, would have returned by the shortest line to the woods, a line however which would have kept him at all times with the barns between him and the house. There was little likelihood, Whitney knew, that in riding a cold trail thus he would come up with any information. And yet he did but the natural thing. And so chanced, he believed, on a new angle and perhaps the heart of the matter.

That which startled him out of his musings now was a rifle shot. He heard the explosion and the ping of a bullet singing just over his head.

"Say, you! What the devil are you doing?"

Only when there was a second shot, as wild as the first, followed by the sound of a horse breaking through the bushes, racing away somewhere deeper among the timber, did he grasp that he was being shot at. His first emotion was a sudden flare of anger; on his own place, some idiot was shooting at him! His second was that that someone, having sought to pot-shot him from ambush, was now running for it. And then came the sudden certainty that if he overhauled that man he would get a look at the fellow who had fired his barns for him. He dipped his spurs, crouched a little in the saddle, and gave chase.

Though the fugitive was some distance away from him, higher up on the ridge, and urging his horse on wildly, as one knew from the ripping and tearing of brush, Whitney never for an instant doubted that he could overtake him. For Whitney was riding the first horse he had owned since a boy when he had dreamed of fine horses, a red bay bought a few days ago from Señor Olivas. And he knew, that unless the rifleman himself rode a mount from the Calderon stud, there could be but the one end to the race.

Nor did any thought of the other man turning to fire again deter him; if the fellow couldn't make any better shots than he had while sitting a still horse, any bullet pumped from his gun now that he was off like a shot himself was not to be considered.

Whitney caught no sight of his quarry until after he had crested the King of Spain ridge and started down on the far side. Now and then he still heard flying hoofs ahead. And a moment later he saw his would-be killer dash across a bit of open space.

Even at the distance Whitney knew him. The man turned his head over his shoulder; it was the hairy face of Jenkins. Captain Jenkins by title. But both hands were grasping his reins quite as frantically as both heels dug into his horse's ribs; he carried no gun—

"Threw it away, as an ugly bit of evidence," Whitney understood. "Well, we'll find it somewhere along the way later. And now for a chat with Captain Jenkins if I follow him all day."

A little more than a mile farther on, down open, gentle slopes where he could let the red bay's reins slacken, Whitney came up with Jenkins. Jenkins, seeing himself caught, jerked in his panting horse and sat staring at Whitney with queer, blood-shot eyes. For the first time Whitney saw that the man looked emaciated, sick, a bundle of crazed nerves.

"Now," said Whitney, looking at him wonderingly. "Suppose we have our little talk."

Jenkins stared back at him sullenly and fell to plucking at his ragged beard.

"I got no talk with you," he muttered. Then, suddenly a look of guile lighted up the bleared eyes. "What for did you take a shot at me?" demanded Jenkins with a ridiculous, eleventh hour assumption of dignity. "I could have the law on you for it."

Whitney remembered how, even that first night when he had seen the tramp on the Toyon road, the tramp's air had exuded suspicion; how, when the other day he had come upon Jenkins digging near Moraga's cabin, there had been the same suspicion, distrust, a shadowy ill will. Yet it puzzled him to imagine what could possibly have set this poor derelict against him. He looked at Jenkins narrowly and saw in him a miserable, half-mad, half-starved wretch hardly to be held accountable for what he did.

"Look here, friend Jenkins," he said suddenly. "Who set you to firing my barns? Vogel or Sheffield?"

Jenkins blinked at him and finally said gruffly:

"What do you mean?"

"I mean, who paid you for trying to burn me out and shoot me into the bargain?"

Jenkins laughed scornfully; quick fires flickered in the red-rimmed eyes.

"Paid, paid *me?*" He broke into cackling mirth. Then again he drew himself up with that grotesque dignity. "There ain't no one got money enough to pay me," he muttered in his beard in such a fashion that Whitney could scarcely catch all the words. "Me, I'll be doin' the payin' first thing you know! Me, I'll have my own share; I'll fill my two hands—"

But the look of cunning came back in his eyes and his voice trailed away into inarticulate mutterings and he fell silent.

"Going to strike gold, are you?" Whitney, growing to believe that the man should be shut up in an asylum, forsook his former line of enquiry, thinking now only to seek to gauge his sanity.

"Gold? Who told you I was lookin' for gold or what I was lookin' for? By God, young feller, a man told me a thing or two about you, if you want to know! And I ain't to be fooled with; you know that, don't you?"

"What did they tell you of me?"

The old man flared out wrathfully, clenching his fists.

"That you ain't the kind that minds his own business; that you're trailin' along after me, watchin' what I'm doin'; that when I get what belongs to me, there'll be you, hornin' in."

"Sheffield told you that? Or Vogel? Which one? Look here, Jenkins, I'll forget that you tried to burn me out and tried to pot me into the bargain, and on top of that I'll give you a hundred dollars, if you'll tell me who has been filling you hide-full of lies about me! Vogel or Sheffield; come, now; which one?"

Jenkins' mind had gotten no further than the money Whitney mentioned.

"Pooh!" he scoffed. "Hundred dollars. Why, man, most any time now I'm goin' to be worth—" But again came discretion; again the old mouth clamped tight and though through the ragged beard the lips could be seen moving, no words came.

Whitney turned to ride back to his ranch.

"Just a last word, Captain Jenkins," he said sternly. "I'm going to look up your case. In the meantime, leave me and my place alone. If you don't, I give you fair warning, or if I hear of any more funny business of any kind, I'm going to put you into the insane asylum."

The old man started back as though a whiplash had cut across his face; a look of wild fear sprang up into his eyes. And then, the final touch of incongruity in him, the tears gathered in his eyes and spilled unchecked down upon the leathery, grimy cheeks, weaving in and out among the grizzled beard. Whitney saw the sunlight glint upon them. After that Whitney had nothing to say; the tears of a man, an old man, were not for him to sit and stare at. He whirled his horse and rode off.

CHAPTER XXII

TERESITA HAD FORGOTTEN!

The sixteenth of September still remains a day of feast and festivity in certain portions of California; in those rural communities in which the population is largely of a blood sprinkled with the spice of Old Mexico. Explain it who may, the fact is that these dark-skinned folk, though throughout the year they like to term themselves Spanish, on this one red day of the calendar to the last mother's son and daughter of them, they are all Mexican. They recall that this is the anniversary of beloved Mexico's independence from Spain; they awake with a sonorous "*Viva Mexico*!" on their lips and for a good twenty-four hours out of the round of eight thousand seven hundred and sixty they are very intensely if somewhat vaguely patriotic.

There is the barbecue, be times good or bad; the long pits ready beforehand, the fires set burning by old Jesus Chavez at an hour when customarily that skillful old rascal is innocently asleep, the willow rods cut and peeled and laid at hand, the beef slaughtered, the *frijoles* cooked, benches and tables in order where the shade is thickest down by the river. And this year, though until almost the eve of the glorious Sixteenth there had been little heart for merry-making in the environs of the King of Spain Valley, the old joys revivified and the oft-repeated "*Vivas*!" were as ready and as spontaneous as of yore.

Last year the celebration was at San Miguel; this year it returned to Toyon. To the old spot in the grove at the edge of the Garcia place where were the scars of many a roasting-pit from other years, came trooping the valley folk in the best of their variegated finery. Men came on horseback from miles in every direction, wearing their newest hats decked out with their flashiest hat-bands of rattlesnake hide, of red or black leather, with shining buckles and often with a rose or a geranium flower stuck through; if they had new boots, they squeezed their toes into them today; new overalls were turned up with precision at the bottom of the leg to show the breeches underneath; they rode with a dash, they dismounted with a flourish, they walked about the picnic grounds with that inimitable grace of a tight-booted Mexican; they called rollicking *"Haychiboys!"* to all new arrivals; they were ready with laughter and prank and practical joke. Along the roads from valley and mountain came whole families rattling along merrily in dry and creaking old wagons many of which, with weaving wheels, left in the dust a track easily to be distinguished from other tracks by knowing eyes; these vehicles passed one another; men drove by clucking at their horses; the brightest of their women-folk's scarves and veils and ribbons trailed behind; they beat up clouds of dust; they brought along the grandmothers and the nursing babies and were followed by the dogs.

In the King of Spain Valley this was always the one great day of the year. Moraga and Nig Chorro and Nuñez would be there; Teresa Calderon and Señor Olivas and Juanito would come; Vogel and Henry, Josefa and Uracca, everybody. There would be a "crowd" from San Miguel; they would come from two or three of the nearest of the railroad towns; some even in Salinas would remember and heed the call and make the long trip by train and by wagon. There would be many strangers when the thing all began; there would be none by the time the big dinner was ready; they would be all *"amigos"* before the afternoon brought the first notes from Celestino's orchestra of violin, guitar and banjo inviting to the *"baille."* And the dance would whirl on all afternoon, all evening, all night and would be at its mad-merriest when the sun that had gone down upon it arose once more like a guest who had feasted with them, succumbed briefly to the heavy sleep of a full stomach and now returned, flushed and eager, for the conclusion.

When Maxwell Whitney rode down from the Pajaro Azul it was to find the benches at the long tables all filled, the big chunks of barbecued beef being carried on the long green sticks to the feasters and dropped to their platters generously to augment the general condition of abundance of *frijoles*, *chile con carne*, cakes and pies and countless savory dishes of Mexico. He found this day that even a cask of wine was not wanting; everyone had his glass and all eyes went gratefully to the little group at the head of one of the tables. For always, on the Sixteenth of September, some bit of graciousness was to be looked for to *la gente* from the old Calderon home.

Whitney saw Teresa Calderon—and a blur of faces. The blur did not matter; Teresa did. He had never seen her sparkle as she sparkled now; she was all youth and laughter today; the carnival spirit had set her quick blood to running; her cheeks were wild pink roses, her eyes were bright with a light that danced. . . . Teresa had seen him, was making a place for him at her side. No; the others did not matter. For the moment he took no stock of Juanito at her other side or of Mentor Olivas who, seeing Teresa's spontaneous gesture, drew aside to permit his *amigo* Whitney a place between himself and Teresa.

"You have almost missed the wine," Teresa laughed at him. "See, it has all been poured. But you may have a little from mine; you look so hot, Señor Max."

He drank from her glass and as he did so his eyes never left hers. Teresa, full of fun, always ready to dare, made a little face at him and at that which his eyes ardently said for him. And still Whitney was not concerned with the "blur," not even with that portion of it which was the face of Juanito. Only a second ago Juanito had been so boyishly gay. . . .

When the bountiful meal, worthy of Roman capacity, was but a pleasant memory and an easeful feeling, preparations were made by those remaining alert for the games. All the old traditions were maintained; the greased pig dodged and grunted, slipped and squealed and afforded yells and shrieks of delight; the greased pole was attempted and officials watched that the boys did not sand their overalls; sack races, egg-in-spoon races, one-legged races, fat men's, fat ladies', girls', boys', old folk's races made much excitement and satisfaction; bets were made, haggled over, won and lost.

Once, during the dance, Vogel sought out Whitney; he wanted to talk of the mortgage he held over the Pajaro Azul, to ferret out all that he could of Whitney's affairs with a special eye toward financial matters.

Across the platform Whitney saw Teresa; her amused eyes caught his. Also he saw Sheffield leaving a knot of men, strolling toward her.

During the afternoon Whitney had a word with Sheffield.

"My barns that burned were insured to the limit, together with contents," he said, looking Sheffield straight in the eye. "I needed new buildings anyway, so not a great deal of harm was done. Just the same, if you're a wise man, you will call your dog off."

"I don't know what you mean," said Sheffield.

"That's a lie, Sheffield." Whitney's blood was hot despite his attempt to be cool. "Jenkins is half crazy; you have found the way to get it into his head that he ought to burn me out or pop me off with a rifle. Among my papers I have set down an account of what has happened, together with your name. Your reputation is none too good as it is; better let bad enough alone and call off your dog."

Sheffield laughed at him. But none the less, as Whitney turned away, in the eyes following him there was much thoughtfulness.

The "Grand Baille" began in the barn-like hall in Toyon as soon as it was dark. Brooke Sheffield was among those thronging the door when the music struck up. But while men were taking partners for the first dance, Sheffield with a look about the room which appeared to be checking off certain faces, drew back, and hurried away to where his horse stood saddled. He rode down the deserted road in the direction of the railroad, got beyond the last of the straggling houses, turned into a field and made a wide half circle which brought him into the road leading back toward the King of Spain Ranch. No one missed him; his precautions seemed unnecessary; tonight no one would mark the going or coming of Brooke Sheffield. Unless it be Josefa.

Celestino's "Stringed Orchestra" had but warmed up during the afternoon. Celestino with his guitar was in the mood to make music that defied anyone's two feet to remain passive. That guitar of Celestino! One knew of it for many miles; how, always after a dance, Celestino "stepped across the street" and they played cards, how always Celestino lost. First went the money which he had earned by the day's dance music; then went the guitar, put in "hock" to make Celestino's bets good. It would be held until the time of the next dance; then when they asked him to play they knew just how he would open his blue eyes at them—Celestino was really Spanish and had the really blue eyes of Castile—and lift his big shoulders and say,

"You go get me back my guitar and I play. Sure."

A collection was taken up; the guitar was redeemed and set into Celestino's skilled hands; he caressed it, turned it this way and that to make sure that all of the little scratches were of his own engraving. And then, to hear him playing was to know that he was renewing an old love.

If here was one tradition in the valley, there was another which everyone knew. Since Juanito had been a little boy and Teresita a little girl, these two had always had the first dance together. No one sought to seek for that dance of Juanito's. And just so, lulled into security through the years of habit, Juanito did not take the precaution of asking Teresa in advance. But Whitney, knowing nothing of all this, had bespoken the first dance and the last and many others, while in the pits the loaded spits were still turning.

Now Juanito, all eagerness, laughing, patting friends on the shoulder as he sought to pass among them, made his way toward his adored Teresita. He saw her where she sat across the room; saw her rise and turn her laughing face up toward the face of his *amigo* Maxwell. Juanito came to a sudden halt, a look of consternation in his eyes. Whitney's arm was about Teresita, her hand lay on his shoulder. They were dancing—dancing Juanito's dance!

"She does that to tease me!" cried Juanito within his convulsed soul.

That would have been bad enough. But it was worse than that, a great deal worse, and Juanito as he stood, unconscious of the couples bumping into him, was not unconscious of the fact that Teresita was not even thinking of him. He saw her eyes as she swept by him, whirling in Whitney's arms; he knew that her eyes did not see him, that the flush in her cheeks was none of his doing. Not only had she given away his dance—she was not even remembering him.

Slowly Juanito drew back, at last realizing that he was in the way of the dancers. At last he stood with his back to the wall watching them. The quick contraction about his eyes might have been in unison with a sudden spasm of the heart. His lips twitched and his face, with all of his laughter wiped clean, looked haggard. Still Teresa did not look; his friend Maxwell did not look. They were not teasing him—they had forgotten—

Juanito turned and went to the door and outside. Already the soft summer night was glorious with its stars, stars behind which before now Juanito had seen God. He went for his horse, unlike Sheffield not caring who saw. Juanito might know that there would be remarks; that some would laugh as fools are ever so ready to do at that which is beyond them. But he did not think of this. His gay young heart, so ready always to be lifted into his singing throat through very joyousness or to be dashed down, now lay in the dust of despair. Juanito's one most cherished privilege, one that he would not have yielded for a king's crown, had been ignored.

Teresita had forgotten—

CHAPTER XXIII

AN UNEXPECTED ENCOUNTER

Juanito Olivas, as a hurt child may run to its mother, the wild flutter within him gradually soothed by ten miles under the stars but his sadness deepened, had the one thought only of going to his violin. That alone of all created things understood him and sympathized with him; an ancient master with a soul not unlike Juanito's must have made it; kindred souls had expressed themselves through it when deeply touched with the varying emotions which lodge restlessly in the bosoms of the artistic; the rich wood of the instrument had life within it; it had drunk through many generations of fine hearts of their finer qualities. . . .

Juanito dreamed of himself dead; of his passive body buried far out in the woodlands; of a tree whose roots reached down and touched him, sleeping, and drew the very essence of his mortal self into its own vigor; of the sap pulsing up joyously; of the tree singing across the forests through storms and springtime breezes; and then, finally, of another violin made from the wood of this tree. How that violin would thrill through the world! . . .

The Calderon home should have been tenantless upon this night save for old Uracca who had returned in the afternoon with one of the men who did not care to dance. Old Uracca would be asleep. The quiet world would be Juanito's own.

He stabled his horse and came to the house. There was a light in the living room; old Uracca had forgotten it, perhaps. The shades were down; country folk do not draw their shades to shut out the night, but the boy had no mind for trifles. Already were new, yearning strains stirring within him. He threw open the door, went in— and confronted Brooke Sheffield with the lamp in his hands.

Clearly Sheffield had just lighted it; the burnt match lay on the table where he had carelessly dropped it and where it had scorched the table top. He was just leaving the room, going toward Teresa's room. He jerked about, looking blankly bewildered at the first shock of Juanito's unexpected coming. But his surprise was as nothing to Juanito's.

The two stared at each other and for a moment found nothing to say.

"What do you want?" Juanito blurted out finally. "There is no one here."

Sheffield's agile mind, given the necessary few seconds in which to banish confusion, was ready now with the answer.

"Some things of mine were left here when I moved into Toyon. I needed a certain paper; it is in my suitcase."

"One does not enter another person's house at night, like this," muttered Juanito, "without a by-your-leave. I don't like the look of this, Señor Sheffield!"

Sheffield came back to the table and set down his lamp. From his cigarette case he drew a cigarette which he lighted before he spoke. And all the time his keen eyes were on the boy's face. Less perspicacity than that of Brooke Sheffield would have marked Juanito's agitation.

"You don't take me for a thief, do you?" he demanded coolly.

"Since you ask me, Yes!" cried Juanito. "If there were something worth while to be stolen and if there was small likelihood of being caught."

Sheffield assumed an air of contemptuous amusement.

"A whole lot there is left to the whole raft of you worth a man's riding ten miles to steal!" he laughed. "Personally, I'd as soon think of robbing an asylum for beggars."

Juanito flushed and bit his lip. His look darkened.

"I would suggest, Señor," he said stiffly, "that you get your papers and go. I will go with you for the suitcase," he added significantly. "And, by the way," and he jerked about suspiciously, "your suitcase is not in Señorita Calderon's room. You know that it is in the closet in the library! What did you want in there?"

"I was going to the library." Again he caught up the lamp, and this time, with Juanito at his heels, turned toward the room where his suitcase was. What his emotions were his rigid features did not disclose. He jerked the suitcase from its place; for an instant appeared about to carry it away with him; altered that intention suddenly and threw the thing open. He withdrew a paper—to Juanito it seemed merely an old envelope; the suitcase was practically empty—thrust it into his pocket, tossed the suitcase back into the closet and, once more carrying the lamp, returned to the living room.

"While you are at it, better take the suitcase with you," Juanito said bluntly.

But Sheffield ignored the suggestion save for a

curt, "I believe this is Miss Calderon's home and I have her permission to leave it here."

Sheffield's hat was already on and he was going to the door, when a fresh thought suggested itself and he gave it jeering voice:

"You didn't care to stick at the dance, I notice! Somebody smiling sweetly in the direction of that four-flushing Whitney?"

"Shut your mouth!" cried Juanito hotly.

Sheffield laughed. But also he moved swiftly to the outside door and held it open. The jeer went out of his eyes to give place to a look of shrewd speculation.

"I am out of the running, Johnny," he said with a semblance of frankness. "Your Teresita wasn't my type of girl, after all. She'd have fallen for you, I'm damned if she wouldn't, if Whitney hadn't butted in. He's an adventurer, that chap; he's all for gobbling up her lands. If I were you, I'd put a spoke in his wheel. The girl was yours, by rights. There's a chance yet; a girl that isn't worth a fight—"

Juanito took a sudden step toward him, hands clenched. "You go!" he said harshly. "It is not for you—Go, I tell you!"

Sheffield went.

Juanito stood uncertain. Slowly Brooke Sheffield, as a minor consideration, faded from his thoughts. The former look of pain crept back into his eyes.

He went softly through the still house and to his own room. He took the old violin out of its case and lifted it to his shoulder. But before a single string had known the touch of the bow, Juanito's desire for expression in yearning notes had passed. He clutched the violin in both arms, hugging it to his breast and let the tears run unchecked down his face.

CHAPTER XXIV

THE OCCURRENCE AT
THE OLD CABIN

What business Brooke Sheffield had that night with the tramp Jenkins never became apparent. Whether he had taken alarm from Whitney's blunt warning and meant to call his dog off, or whether it was his plan to incite the warped brain of Jenkins to further attacks, must remain a matter of conjecture. For Sheffield stumbled upon a discovery which drove all thought of Whitney from his mind. But at any rate, on leaving the King of Spain ranch house, instead of turning back toward Toyon he rode purposefully toward the upper end of the valley, going straight to the old cabin, recently deserted by Felipe Moraga.

A bad night for Brooke Sheffield. Whitney's attitude, whose straight-line methods disturbed the circuitous paths through which the lawyer's actions progressed, had unsettled and irritated him. Just how much the unexpected coming of Juanito had meant to him, he alone knew. But now his fine complacency was ruffled; he urged his horse forward mercilessly, cursing aloud the fine-spirited animal which was doing gallantly more than a horse should be called on for. The second ten miles of the ride, over the rutty road and finally the uneven trail extending between the house and the old cabin, were flung off in less than an hour.

He tied his horse to a young pine and went swiftly to the door. With his hand lifted to the old-fashioned, clumsy latch, he paused, uncertain. There was a light within, shining through the chinks, and he heard a voice. Someone with Jenkins? Who, then? Sheffield was moved to ever ready caution; after Whitney's words today, it would be something better than just as well if he were not seen here with Jenkins. But who the devil would have thought that Jenkins would be entertaining company at this time of night?

Sheffield tip-toed away from the door and began circling the cabin, seeking for a crevice in the old log wall through which he might look in. Though the light filtered out in many places it was difficult for him to find a crack which gave him a view of what he wanted to see. The two windows were curtained with sacks, painstakingly arranged.

"Secretive old cuss," muttered Sheffield. "Crazy enough to be always scared to death somebody is going to pop him off, I imagine."

He paused again and listened. He began to believe that, after all, Jenkins was alone; that the old fool was talking with himself. For certainly it was only Jenkins' voice that he heard, though variously intoned; it muttered, it rose and sank away, it exclaimed. Sheffield moved on, still seeking, bent on finding his spy-hole. And at last he found it at the rear of the cabin, so placed that he commanded a sweeping view of the interior and had even the added fortune to see Jenkins faced squarely toward him.

Jenkins' red-rimmed eyes, in the light of the three candle ends he had stuck along the edge of the old table, glittered with a feverish excitement. For at last, no longer ago than a late hour of the afternoon, Captain Jenkins had found that for which he had sought during twenty years. It lay on the table before him, under his raking fingers. At first Sheffield thought that he was sitting; but Jenkins crouched, his attitude grotesquely that of an excited old hen seeking to hover a new and unduly large brood.

Sheffield had difficulty in making out what it was that the old man gloated over. There was an old box, dirt-encrusted, fallen into a dozen pieces;

there were small objects, clutched by the nervous fingers, dropped for others. But at last Sheffield saw and his own body stiffened, his own fingers were rigid.

"The tramp has beat me to it! Before Juanito came, he was there!"

That was the thought taking full possession of his brain, bounding at once to the supreme place in exclusion of aught else. Jenkins had been before him; the dirty tramp had succeeded where he had failed—had robbed him!

Sheffield crept back to the door. But here with his hand lifted he paused the second time. Jenkins would have it fastened, would have a bar dropped into place or a bed shoved against it. He did not want to call out. He meant to come upon the man with all the shock of surprise, to frighten him, to browbeat him while still confused into relinquishing that which by right belonged to Brooke Sheffield. He went to the nearest window. Long ago had the glass gone; there was only the sack across the opening. A man could go through here in a flash.

Sheffield began working with the sack, freeing it at the bottom. He was now at Jenkins' back; he made no sound; Jenkins, muttering again, was absorbed in his own money-mad thoughts. Sheffield got the sack loose along its lower edge, moved it an inch, another, and looked in. Still Jenkins had heard nothing, had not turned.

Sheffield put his head in, drew himself into a knot, got one leg through—

Then it was that Jenkins heard him and jerked around and saw him. For the instant only came that stupefaction of surprise which Sheffield had counted on; before Jenkins' open mouth could shape the first word or the old stiffened body straighten, Sheffield was through the window confronting him ominously.

"It's you!" gasped Jenkins. "It never was that man Whitney. You lied to me all along. It's you that's been spyin' on me. . . ."

He stood between the intruder and the table; he sought to spread out his thin old body to hide what lay behind him gleaming in the candlelight.

"Look here, old man," said Sheffield, "you're a thief. Thieves go to jail. You—"

"You lie!" shouted Jenkins. "It's mine! I found it! It's mine, I tell you!"

"Shall I tell you when you *found* it and where? Tonight, while all the household were at the dance. In the Calderon home. That's burglary."

"You lie!" cried Jenkins again. He was trembling from head to foot now. "It was not in anybody's house. It was out in the woods, where I knew it was; where I've been lookin' for it for twenty year! *That's* not burglary and that's not stealin'. It's findin'. And, by God, it's mine; all mine. You're the burglar, breakin' in here—"

"Say what you please about where you found
272

it; I know. It came from the Calderon home. I've known where it was for a long time; I've been waiting for a chance—"

He himself was excited; suddenly he realized it. He, the shrewd lawyer, having to deal with a stupid know-nothing like the old tramp, must keep cool, very cool. He must dominate Jenkins, frighten him, and himself make no useless admissions. Also, he'd have to shut Jenkins' mouth for him; there would be only one way to do that. Jenkins must have his share, his very meager share, just enough to make him a *partis criminis* and force his silence.

"I'll play square with you, Jenkins," he said. "You've run a risk in getting it; you've brought it here. You'll get your share; I am willing to allow you that. Enough to pay you gloriously for a big day's work, old chap." Sheffield's eyes, filled with the wink and shine of such of the hoard as the tramp failed to hide with his body, might have been reflecting the fires burning in Jenkins' eyes. "What say you, go to jail for burglary or get a hundred dollars for your work?"

Jenkins, by way of inarticulate answer, shrilled with gibbering rage. If only Sheffield had not mentioned that hundred dollars! To be sure that was but the beginning of his bartering, as he planned he would come up another fifty, and another. But this Jenkins could neither know nor care. For twenty years, lured on by one of those same golden rumors which Juanito so loved to repeat, he had lived for this hour. Trudging along weary roads, when a racing automobile swept by him, honking him out of the way, covering him with dust, Jenkins had muttered stubbornly to himself that the time was comin' when he'd show them a thing or two; yes, him, Jenkins, Captain Jenkins by title. He'd be riding in a finer car than that; he'd roll across the world behind plate glass like a king. The word "king" came to him often; King of Spain; unlimited wealth; King of the World! And now a man standing across the small bare room from him, sneering at him, said: "A hundred dollars for you!"

Sheffield saw the changing look in the old man's eyes just before he plunged to one side. There, propped against the wall, stood Jenkins' rifle; the one with which he had shot at Whitney, which he had hurled away from him, which he had retrieved so that, when the glorious hour dawned, he would have that to protect himself with—himself and his treasure.

Sheffield saw and stood petrified with fear. He knew now what that look in Jenkins' eyes meant. The man was going to kill him. Jenkins wasn't just "queer." He was crazy. He meant murder.

Sheffield was galvanized into action, momentary paralysis having given place to nervous swiftness. His brain, not unused to situations arising during the years of his legal training when quick, sure

274

thinking was demanded, was clear. He wanted to flee but knew there was no time for that. The door was fastened; if he tried to undo the clumsy bar or scramble through the window, Jenkins would shoot him. He imagined the feel of a bullet gouging a great hole between his shoulder blades. There was but one thing to do; cold as he was with fear, he launched himself toward Jenkins.

The shaking old hands were at the rifle when Sheffield struck with his fist, since there had been no time to snatch up a weapon. But he was young and vigorous and Jenkins was old and frail. Further, that inordinate bodily power which is at times produced from mental crises, was his now. Jenkins, whipping up his old rifle, received Sheffield's fist full in the mouth; he was lifted off his feet and hurled backward. He fell, his head striking against the stove in the corner.

Sheffield snatched up the rifle and stood over him, his heart pounding wildly, his face suffused with blood, his eyes wide with panic. When Jenkins should rise—he was trying to think just how he should act. It would serve the old fool right to have his brains blown out. No; that would be murder. Sheffield shuddered; he knew what was done with murderers.

But Jenkins did not rise. Sheffield had struck hard; Jenkins, falling, had struck his head hard against the stove.

Stunned! Here then was Sheffield's chance. He

could have laughed; how simple a thing it was to get an old starveling like this out of the way for a few minutes; knock him unconscious, get done what was to be done, be away before the old man crawled to his feet. Sheffield set down the rifle, caught up a barley sack which had served Jenkins as a bag to bring provisions from Toyon, and began dropping into it the articles on the table. All the time, hurrying, he kept one eye on old Jenkins. If the old fool sought to play possum and tried any tricks, it was only the act of a second to catch the rifle up again.

"Gold," Sheffield was muttering. "No doubt of it. Bullion, too, by God. As old as the hills from the look of it; lucky thing gold doesn't rust!" A parcel about which Jenkins had wrapped a greasy newspaper burst open. Sheffield's pulses hammered afresh. There were other lights added to the dull yellow gleam, red and green and the dancing, shifting hues from the heart of a diamond. Sheffield tumbled everything into his bag, hurrying, hurrying.

"I would have left him two or three hundred dollars; now he gets nothing."

He started toward the door but came back and, carrying the heavy bag in one hand, picked up the gun. He could drop it outside, somewhere in the bushes.

Jenkins' eyes were open now, wide open. And yet the man did not seem to have his wits about him; it was a vacant stare that he turned up at the ceiling.

"Dazed yet. He'll be on the rampage in another shake."

With the gun, Sheffield went again to the door. He undid the hook which held the bar against the lift of the latch from the outside, threw open the door and stepped out. Once more he turned to eye Jenkins suspiciously.

But Jenkins had not stirred. He appeared concerned only with the smoke-grimed ceiling straight above him and with that only after an oddly aloof manner. His expression struck Sheffield as idiotic; his mouth sagged open—

Something drew Sheffield back into the cabin. The one impulse standing highest in his conscious mind was to run. An intangible fear was on him; a nervous tremor shook him; he wanted to get away from this place, to get on his horse's back, to run for the open fields. And yet, slowly, his steps dragging, he returned.

The candles shone on the upturned face. It was dead white. There was a bit of color only at one temple, that which had struck the stove. A little cut showed, a little, a very little blood had run out. Jenkins had the look of not having a great deal of blood in him. His eyes were glassy. His hands did not move; his breast did not stir.

A shudder shook Sheffield from head to foot. But he had to know! He had to call upon his will now; his hand seemed animated by a will of its own; it did not want to touch the tramp. Sheffield forced it on. He touched the hand on the floor; he touched the white face. Cold; colder than it seemed possible flesh could have grown so suddenly.

Then all of the horror of the thing burst upon Brooke Sheffield and he stood quaking as with an ague. He had not meant to kill; it had been an accident. . . . He saw himself standing up in his own defense: "Why, Gentlemen of the Jury . . ." Self-defense and accidental death; that was it. "Your Honor . . ." Jenkins had come at him with a rifle; Jenkins was crazy; there was Maxwell Whitney to testify that Jenkins had burned his barns, had shot at him from the woods!

Horror of the dead, then terror of results. Justice miscarried so. If someone came now! Brooke Sheffield standing over the dead man, clutching the dead man's rifle, the dead man's gold—

He threw down the gun and, with the sweat breaking out through every pore of his body, broke into a run. He must get back to Toyon; he must have his alibi ready.

CHAPTER XXV

THE DEVIL DRIVES

Sheffield's horse whipped back at his onrush as he fled from the cabin. He came to a dead halt; the animal might break loose, leaving him on foot up here among the hills. He got himself in hand; he gentled the frightened horse with his voice, approached more quietly and breathed a sigh of relief as he got into the saddle.

He turned for a last look at the cabin. The door was wide open; the light of the three candles shone out serenely. Sheffield heard a sound somewhere in the bushes; it sounded like a footfall; like somebody moving guardedly. He sat motionless, his heart pumping. The woods were quiet now. After all, that sound could have been made by a bird, a rabbit, a squirrel. His nerves were upset. They would play him tricks if he let them. This was a horrible thing for a man to go through. Again he exerted his will and quieted his overwrought emotions.

"Not Guilty!" That would be his plea, firmly and confidently made. No one had seen; Jenkins could not talk. Jenkins was dead. He had himself in hand now; he was thinking coolly, logically. The one fact was that of death. And, regarded as now Brooke Sheffield regarded it, it suddenly lost its honor. Rather it brought relief, it promised security. For Jenkins, the only one to accuse him, was beyond accusing anybody!

Suddenly he realized that he was senselessly remaining on the spot, actually holding taut reins. He gave his horse its head, raking the flanks with his spurs. He shot out into the trail, hastening back toward the road in the valley. Why, there need be no plea of any kind! Jenkins was still; no one else had seen. Then who would even think of Brooke Sheffield in connection with this unfortunate circumstance? It would look as though the old man had fallen, striking his head— he was old and tottery, anyway. And there was no one interested in him, no one to stir up a lot of enquiry.

Sheffield's brain, as he rode on furiously toward that alibi he meant to establish, was like a screen upon which some drunken operator casts all sorts of pictures at all sorts of speeds. He saw time passing, two or three days, several weeks, before anyone found the dead man. He saw animals come in at the door, sniffing. He had left the door open—he wished that he had shut it. He saw the discovery made by Juanito, recoiling. By Whitney. By the man Moraga. He saw the room as he had just left it; three candle stubs burning. Burning ever closer to the table top! One, he recalled now, was stuck in its own grease in an old tin-top. The others, he could not remember. Were they placed directly on the table? He saw one of them roll to the floor, still burning; he saw another, burnt down, its wick flickering, drooping over. The dry wood of the table, the dry wood of the floor, caught. The flames stood higher. The cabin was burning! . . . He jerked his head back, looking over his shoulder, half expecting to see a sheet of flame. . . . Involuntarily his grip tightened on his reins. What if he left *nothing* to chance? If he went back and made a little pile of dry wood on the floor at Jenkins' feet, setting the candle to it?

He was torn two ways; it was dangerous to return, it was dangerous not to make sure. And meanwhile his horse, snorting with pain under the raking spurs, bore him on.

The farther he rode the more did Sheffield curse himself for a fool for not having returned to fire the cabin. It would have burned to the ground; the dry grass would have caught; there would have been a forest fire. That would have wiped everything clean; it would have licked up any chance trace. For he had begun to think of the unlikely; had he dropped anything from his pocket? A knife, an envelope, a handkerchief? Had a fingerprint on a rifle barrel remained to damn him in days to come? Perhaps he should go back yet. . . .

A mile down in the valley he turned widely out of the road, pushing into the scattered trees. He had seen something moving—a horse which, he fancied, carried a man. It had been riderless but Sheffield did not know. For now he was of those to whom each bush is a menace. After that he kept away from the road. Thus did his Fate, toying with the man, make the first play.

So lightning-swift did his mental silver-sheet image one after another of the countless scenes which the happening of the night had given birth, that it was only when several miles on his way that Sheffield made what he must have considered an amazing discovery. He had held from the first glimpse of what lay on the table before Jenkins that the tramp had robbed the Calderon home, having in some way hit upon Teresa's father's secret, the family treasure chest.

All of a sudden it dawned upon him now that it was a strange thing that there should have been so much jewelry, so many rings, that diamond pendant, the bracelets and necklaces. Even the conception that they were ornaments which Teresa's mother had worn and loved and which her sentimental husband had hidden away during the years, failed to convince. There were too many of them, they were of too many kinds. It was as though they had been worn by a score of different women. . . .

He could still hear the old man's voice, declaring that he had not been in the house, that he had found these things in the woods, that they belonged to no one. *The legacy of the old-time bandit, Joaquin Murietta!* It came over him in a flash. The tales of Juanito, the golden stories of the wealth of Murietta, things at which Brooke Sheffield, the skeptical, had laughed, were true then! Jenkins, after twenty years of seeking, led on by some clue dropped in his hearing long ago, had at last come upon that which he sought. No evil chance, but high fortune, had led Sheffield to him tonight. For Jenkins was dead; no one knew; no one had seen; and the loot of Joaquin Murietta belonged to him who held it.

Sheffield clutched the bag tighter.

A second time he thought that he saw something down in the road. By now he was not abnormally fanciful. But he saw reason in playing safe. One could never tell who might be riding on the Sixteenth of September. He put a greater distance between himself and the road. Thus, instead of passing in front of the Calderon house, he would ride through the timbered hills at its rear.

At last the house itself loomed up ahead of him. He stopped his horse in the dark under an oak tree. The house was dark, pitch black. Juanito would be in bed by now, fast asleep. The others would still be dancing, they would dance for hours yet. He doubted if it were even now after eleven o'clock; certainly it was not midnight. He had left Toyon early; he had ridden hard; he had tarried nowhere. Even the episode of the cabin, now that he estimated, had been over in ten minutes.

He was about to ride on when he heard voices, a man's voice and a woman's. Whitney and Teresa had just returned, was his first thought. They were at the house, on the back porch. The man struck a match; he lifted it to his cigarette. The woman said something, laughingly. They were Felipe Moraga and Josefa.

Sheffield sat still and waited.

Presently Moraga, with the horses, went to the barn. Josefa entered the house. There was a light. She had a lamp burning in the kitchen. Sheffield watched for Moraga. The man came out of the barn and went to the men's quarters. Sheffield heard his door slam; saw his lamp light stream out. Within that brief time required by one like Moraga to undress and tumble into bed, the second lamp was extinguished.

Moraga in bed, Juanito asleep, Josefa alone awake in the house!

Here then was a new chance to be taken, if a man had the nerve for it. Once successfully taken, then good-by King of Spain Valley, for a while if not forever, at least until men ceased talking about Jenkins, until a certain other matter was ironed out by time. And this chance, if let slip now, when would it come again? Only Josefa to count with . . .

A chance to take? The thing was simplicity itself. He had called earlier, had he not, for a paper left in his suitcase? In his haste, he would say, he had taken the wrong one. Only when he had ridden back to Toyon had he discovered his error. This time he'd take the other and, while he was at it, his suitcase.

He made a circle to come to the house from the front; he rode slowly, keeping his jaded horse at a walk, that Moraga and the sleeping Juanito might not hear. And he left the horse a hundred yards from the building.

The barley sack he sought to hide. He put it at the base of the tree; there was nothing to throw over it. The grass was dry and short-cropped. He moved the sack to another place. He turned toward the house, hesitated, looked back. It seemed to him that the thing would be seen by anyone who chanced to pass. Someone, a farm hand returning from the dance, might first see the horse, ride up, see the sack. Sheffield went back for it. He rolled it into as compact a bundle as possible, tucked it under his coat and hurried to the house. Once he got the thing in his suitcase he could breathe deeply again.

He moved silently, keeping close to the adobe wall, coming cautiously to the rear. He heard Josefa moving about; she had a fire in the kitchen stove; he could see her bending over it. She was alone. He tiptoed up the steps and to the open door. Josefa, straightening up, turned and saw him. She uttered a little smothered exclamation of surprise.

"Sh!" he commanded. "Needn't wake anyone."

Josefa stood looking at him with wide, wondering eyes. A little flush ran up through the dusk of her skin.

"Señor Brooke!" she whispered.

Sheffield came to her and put one arm about her. Josefa's face was lifted; he stooped and kissed her swiftly. Her cheeks flamed, her eyes were burning.

"Listen, Josefa," he said hurriedly. "I am going to see you tomorrow. We will have a long talk; we will make everything right. You will meet me at the same place, the same hour, Josefa."

Josefa stood looking at him queerly. Her two slim brown hands had risen to his shoulders.

"With you an' me, will it always be *mañana*?" she asked.

"No," Sheffield assured her. "Of course not. Tonight, though, my dear, I'm in a tremendous hurry. Business, you know; a deal to get closed up. I came a while ago for a paper; I got the wrong one. It's in my suitcase."

That look in the Indian girl's eyes did not alter. There was trouble in it, profound misdoubting. Josefa was not listening to his explanations.

"You said once we would marry," said Josefa softly. "That night when I saw and did not tell others what I saw. Are you marrying me, Señor Brooke? Or do you play? Am I a little fool? Do white men fool Indian girls all the time?"

"Before God, no!" muttered Sheffield impatiently. "Of this we are going to talk when you meet me tomorrow. Tonight I am in a hurry. That's a good girl—"

Slowly Josefa's two hands dropped to her sides; slowly at last the look in her eyes changed. Sheffield could not read their meaning; they were Indian eyes hiding an Indian's thoughts. Vaguely they made him uncomfortable. Josefa looked at her kitchen fire; at the coffee-pot she had set to boil, trifles at a time when in Sheffield's consciousness there was no room for trifles. Josefa might have spoken; perhaps for an instant she was about to speak. But in the end her red mouth hardened and remained silent.

"I'll get the suitcase, Josefa," said Sheffield. "Oh, I know the way. And, while I'm doing that, you'll bring up a bottle of wine for me, won't you? I'm as dry as summer."

"*Bueno*," responded the girl colorlessly.

Sheffield knew that she would have to go outside, down the steps and so to the wine cellar. He waited for her to go and then hastened about what he had to do. He went into the library, got the suitcase, threw his barley sack into it, and came back into the living room. Josefa was not in sight; still in search of the wine he liked. Sheffield, his heart in his throat, startled by every board creaking underfoot, afraid of waking Juanito went swiftly into Teresa's room, closed the door—

While Brooke Sheffield at a moment large with destiny thought to keep his mind shrewdly upon only the *big things,* he neglected utterly the really biggest; he had failed to mark any significance in Josefa's upturned face. He might have guessed that which he did not know; he might have seen that, in the clutch of circumstance, it would pay him to be sincere with Josefa.

He had sworn that he would marry her—and at last Josefa knew that he lied. He had played with her from the first—to keep her mouth shut. Josefa went outside, knowing he would watch; then she ran back along the wall and peeped in at the living room window. She saw him go to the library; she saw him return with the suitcase; she saw the expression stamping his sharpened features.

She watched him go to Teresa's room.

CHAPTER XXVI

A VOW TO THE GHOST OF TIA TONIA

For an Indian girl to be married to such as Brooke Sheffield—that would have been a fine thing! To be tricked, be fooled, used as a tool, ah, that was something else! Josefa ran out into the yard, looking into the dark toward Toyon, listening. The night was very silent. And yet she and Felipe had not ridden fast—She turned again to the window. The door through which Sheffield had gone was still closed. She ran about the house to the barred window of the King of Spain room. The shades were down, but a pale light outlined them. He was in there—

She drew back into the garden and scurried through flower beds to Juanito's window. She was just opening her lips to call softly "Señorito!" when at last from the valley road came the sound of hoofs. The others were returning as they had told her they would, "by the time she had coffee ready." Teresa and Whitney had had the one waltz only after Josefa left and now, loitering under the stars, were coming.

Josefa ran with flying footsteps to meet them.

She called when she dared, when she judged that they would hear and Sheffield would not.

Whitney shouted back to her. There was a note in Josefa's voice which made them hurry. Their horses' hoofs pounded noisily; Josefa feared Sheffield would hear and make his escape.

"What is it?" demanded Whitney.

"Señor Sheffield is in the house," said Josefa sharply. "He has come to steal something."

"Josefa!" chided Teresa.

"Oh, I know! He took Tia Tonia's box that time. I saw."

Whitney, putting nothing beyond Sheffield, was already racing on to the house. Teresa hung back for a word with the Indian girl, then followed.

"They make so much noise, he will have heard," muttered Josefa. "But anyway, they will trap him in the house. And I, I will laugh at him!"

And now was Josefa bound that she would not lose this opportunity for her laughter. She saw Whitney dismount hastily at the kitchen door; she saw Teresa riding after him. She knew that Brooke Sheffield, if he sought to break and run for it, would have them to do with first—unless he thought to escape from the house through a window. With this in mind Josefa, too, was running now. He had gone through Teresa's room; it would do him no good to seek escape through a window in the King of Spain room, since the iron grilles were again in place. It was clear to her, and no doubt would be clear to Sheffield when he heard the racing hoofs, that he would be cut off unless he slipped out through one of the windows in Teresa's room.

"If he does that," Josefa was crying within her bitter heart, "it will be in a new fashion that he feels Josefa's arms about him!"

As it was she came to the window first. Sheffield had heard. She saw him standing uncertain, his head jerked up, alarm shining in his eyes. Plainly he had just come from the King of Spain room as the lamp was still in there. He stood with something in each hand; his suitcase in one, in the other a barley sack, bulging and heavy. The suitcase was empty, its lid dragging on the floor.

Whitney's spurred boots, striking the floor of the back porch, sounded loud through the quiet house. Sheffield started and sprang to the open window. Josefa heard him cursing; she saw his agitated face. He was about to pass through. And then he saw her, barring the way.

"Josefa!" he cried softly. Again quickened hope sprang up in his heart; Josefa had been his tool so long.

Josefa could not hold back all of her laughter until the final moment. It jeered at him now. Her arms were extended to right and left. But the man must have known from her mocking tone, from her attitude, what was the new fashion in which the Indian girl meant to embrace him.

"Josefa!" he pleaded.

By way of answer came Josefa's shrill call:

"Felipe! Felipe Moraga! Hurry, if you love me!"

Moraga heard and shouted back wonderingly; already he was on the floor, drawing on his overalls, plunging toward the door.

Had Sheffield needed further sign to tell him which way the wind of a woman's fancy blew, he had it in Josefa's call to Moraga: "If you love me!"

"Damn you, you double-dealing squaw," he muttered.

Whitney was calling: "Sheffield! Sheffield, I say! Where are you?"

Sheffield jerked down the window shade. Josefa ran to the other window but he was before her here. Down came window and shade there. Save for the thin lines of light shining at the edges Josefa was given no glimpse of what went on within. Just the same, she was assured, Moraga would be here in a moment, Whitney would come on through the house, and Señor Brooke who made love lightly to an Indian girl and then sought to have done with her, was trapped.

Whitney, running into the kitchen, then into the dining room, found the house dark. He struck a match, lighted the lamp bracketed against the wall and went on toward Teresa's room. For he heard Josefa's voice calling from that direction, heard Moraga answering her. Though they were just outside their voices sounded as though in the house. So he hurried on. By now Teresa was with him; they came to her door, flung it open and on the threshold were confronted by Sheffield.

In his hand he carried a suitcase, his own which both remembered he had left here when he moved into Toyon. He had in his lips a cigarette freshly lighted. Though there was a flush in his cheeks and bright excitement in his eyes, he forced himself to appear quite at ease.

"What the devil do you mean by this?" said Whitney sharply. "What are you up to now, Sheffield?"

Sheffield, after a swift insolent glance, ignored him. Turning to Teresa, he said smoothly:

"I must ask your pardon, Miss Calderon—I had meant to do so tomorrow, in any case, so why not now?—for having entered your home uninvited and while you were away. I had left certain papers here which I required suddenly. They were in the suitcase."

"But the suitcase," Teresa said pointedly, "was never in my room. And you knew that, Señor Sheffield!"

"Certainly," he admitted. "Naturally it must appear strange that I am in this part of the house. I can explain, however. Shall we go back to the living room? And then will you let me clear myself of your very unjust suspicions?"

He assumed an air of injured dignity.

"First," cut in Whitney, "I am going to have a look at things. You will remember, Teresa, that one night when only you, Señor Olivas and Sheffield were in the house, an attempt was made to steal the King of Spain painting."

Sheffield managed a contemptuous laugh.

"You may also remember," he retorted, "that I was in bed, half dead from a stab from young Olivas! That I could not have moved——"

"Rot," snapped Whitney. "Your wound did not amount to the snap of a man's finger. Unless," he added, "it afforded you a certain opportunity."

Whitney stepped by Sheffield and to the door of the adjoining room. Since now the lamp was in Sheffield's hand, since also Whitney all the time was determined not to lose sight of Sheffield, it is not remarkable that he did not see more than he saw. He counted that there was nothing of value here to be stolen except the painting; he made out in the half light that the picture was in its place; he returned with the very strong opinion that Sheffield had a second time attempted to steal the canvas but had been interrupted before he could do so.

"By your leave, however," he said, "we'll have a look inside your suitcase."

Just now they were aware, for the first time, of Juanito's presence. The boy had not slept; had not gone to bed as Sheffield had imagined, but had been walking restlessly down by the Mission ruin. Only Josefa's cries and the sound of horses running had brought him down to earth and back to the house. The fear had sprung into his lover's heart that something had happened to Teresa. Now he stood silently regarding her; he had no eyes at first for the others; what did it matter to him if Maxwell Whitney and Brooke Sheffield quarreled over a suitcase or fought or died? Other considerations haunted him; he looked at Teresa as from a remote distance and his eyes were full of the reproach which surged up from his heart.

Sheffield was shrugging. He threw open his suitcase with an air. It was quite empty. He put a hand to his pocket and drew out a few papers.

"These are what I came for," he said coolly.

"You have never explained what you were doing in this part of the house," Whitney reminded him.

"Nor have you, my busy friend, ever given me a chance to do so!"

Tonight, after the first few dances, Teresa had missed Juanito. And she had understood how she had hurt him and was sorry. Of this was made the one little cloud over the happy ride homeward with Señor Max. She would make what amends she could, she would be kind to Juanito. But she had not been able to foresee any such situation as now had arisen. Now she was making bad matters much worse by forgetting all about Juanito again, even while his eyes were fixed upon her face. As they returned to the living room it was to Whitney that she looked to represent her in any discussion with Sheffield. And it was Whitney who quite unconsciously took upon himself the part of one who had the right to speak for Teresa Calderon.

In the kitchen, looking in on them, were Josefa and Moraga. Josefa was whispering in Moraga's ear; his swart face was the brick red of anger and he shifted about restlessly, his eyes glued on Sheffield's face.

Sheffield made his explanation. Juanito was not listening. He had at last turned away from Teresa. Josefa caught his eye, beckoned to him, and in a strange automatic fashion Juanito went to her.

"It was just a moment ago," Sheffield was saying. "I had gotten my suitcase. I was thirsty; Josefa was getting me a glass of wine. She had gone out for it. I was in here, waiting, looking over my papers, making sure that I had the one I wanted. The house was very quiet. Then I heard a noise as of someone walking softly. I wondered who would be creeping about at this time of night. I, too, remembered that someone had tried to steal the picture. I took up the lamp and went to see. Just then you came. That was all."

Whitney grunted; a lying explanation, he was downright certain. But it appeared that it would serve Sheffield's purpose as well as any.

Meanwhile Josefa had been talking swiftly to Juanito.

"That night Tia Tonia died, it was Señor Sheffield who stole the little box. I saw! Tonight he came again to steal. I know. He had with him something he hid under his coat. Where is it now? I saw him through the window; I was watching all the time. He went quickly to Señorita Teresa's room carrying the lamp. He did not stop there; I saw the light in the next room. He was there all the time—"

Ever was Juanito's that "southern soul" which makes its quest through dreams of love and dreams of gold. Now, if one thing in all of the wide world could tend toward withdrawing Juanito's moody thought from his slighted love it was this suggestion borne to him through the Indian girl's words. *Tia Tonia's box!* So it *had* been Sheffield! Sheffield had twice entered the house tonight. Twice had he shown his intent to go toward Teresa's room, toward the room beyond! He had had a bundle hidden under his coat; so Josefa swore. Where was it now? He did not have it with him; it was not in his suitcase—

A sudden little cry broke from Juanito; a sudden inspiration visited him. He broke away from Josefa and ran through the room, going toward Teresa's room. They heard a door slam after him.

Juanito's blood was all atingle. Always, since imaginative childhood, he had been the one to proclaim that some fine day it would be he, Juanito Olivas and none other, who would discover the long lost treasure! This had been one of his two dreams; he had held to it consistently. And now, he felt sure, the golden moment had dawned.

Now, at the end of the dry summer when the King of Spain Rancho was in dire need of money, it would be Juanito Olivas who cried:

"*Venga*! Come with me! Look! I show it to you!" A wide flourish. "There is the gold, gold for Teresita; it is hers!"

In the King of Spain room Juanito saw all that Maxwell Whitney had seen—but clearer. He had lighted a match, had caught up the lamp from Teresa's table, had carried it with him straight to the King of Spain painting.

It was in its place, each peg firmly inserted through each corner. Yet Sheffield had been hasty in replacing it. Juanito's triumph set his wild heart throbbing to wilder measures.

The picture was upside down!

Juanito had it away from the wall in a flash. There, where always the painting had hung, hiding it, was a large rectangular opening; a man's body could have gone through without difficulty. Juanito ran for a chair, stood upon it, leaned through the opening, holding the lamp before him. The treasure room! For a room it was, as large as any closet in the house, made in a corner of the three feet thick adobe walls. He held his lamp lower. There, on the floor, was the very bundle Sheffield had sought to rob them of! Juanito was sure of that! That was the thing a Sheffield would do. And then, when he heard others coming, what was left for him but to throw everything back? Juanito could have laughed. He looked further and saw an old chest, its lid hiding its content. Full of gold, Juanito fancied. He started to crawl through. Then he remembered; this was Teresita's. He turned to run and call to her.

No one, saving Sheffield and possibly Josefa, had given any serious thought to Juanito's actions. As for Sheffield, there was nothing to be done; he had replaced the picture and endeavored to assure himself that there was no reason why Juanito or anyone else should guess what he had been up to. True, he would like to have tarried until Juanito came back. But no excuse was offered him, and beside Whitney, getting his permission from Teresa's eyes, nodded toward the door.

"You've got what you came for, Sheffield," he said curtly. "You will note that no one is asking you to tarry here."

Sheffield went jauntily to the door. He did not like the look he saw in Josefa's eyes; he was vaguely afraid of something which he failed to read entirely in Felipe Moraga's look. He began to be anxious to get away; to have his horse under him; to be riding back to Toyon. The scene in the cabin in the woods flashed back across his mind; he felt a wild urge to get that as far behind him as he could. He said a short "Good night" and ran down the back steps.

Moraga followed. Josefa's eyes gloated. Neither Whitney nor Teresa noted. They turned toward each other.

There came a sharp cry from Sheffield. Josefa sprang to the outside door, shut it, ran through the kitchen into the dining room, slamming the second door after her. Sheffield's cry was followed by the sound of a scuffle and a blow; by another cry.

"They are fighting!" cried Teresa, catching at Whitney's arm. "It is Felipe. He—"

Josefa's eyes burned like coals of fire.

"Señorita," she said harshly, "let them be. Listen: That man is bad; he made love to me all the time. He—"

There came to them the sound of regular blows now, one after the other, like clockwork. Whitney sprang toward the door.

"Moraga will kill him."

"Wait!" Josefa stood with her back to the shut door. She caught at Teresa and pulled her close. "Listen, Señorita. He lied to me. I thought he would marry me. That is why I did not tell of Tia Tonia's box. And, little fool that I am—" She began whispering into Teresa's ear. Her own face was a fiery red now, she was shaking like a reed in a gust of wind.

Sheffield's cries rose into shrieks of fear and pain, and wails for help. Whitney caught Josefa by the shoulder and thrust her aside. Be Sheffield what he might, Moraga must not be left free to murder him.

But now it was Teresa who detained him. She caught his hand and held him back.

"Felipe has a whip," she said, and he marveled at the strange new quality of sternness in her voice. "He is whipping him as the man deserves. Josefa has told me something."

Whitney got the door open and went on through the kitchen; Teresa was at his side, her hand was still in his. At the moment neither was aware of the fact. With Josefa at their heels they came out upon the porch.

They saw Sheffield and Moraga, not a dozen steps away. Moraga had at last come to grips with the man he hated and with even better cause than he himself fully understood. Sheffield, whom he had caught and held and whipped, he had now hurled away from him. But not yet had he done with him. In Moraga's hand was a merciless bull-whip. While he had held Sheffield it had been necessary to keep the whip doubled, so long was it. But now as Sheffield reeled backward and fell and gropingly rose, Moraga flung out the entire length so that the whip hissed and writhed through the air like an angry snake, so that the lash cut through Sheffield's clothing like a knife and drew the blood. Shriek after shriek burst from Sheffield; he sought to run. Moraga plunged after him and again and again the whip writhed and hissed and fell.

"It is terrible!" Teresa was shuddering; her hand tightened spasmodically upon Whitney's. "But it is just. He—"

But at last even Felipe Moraga was satisfied. They saw him drop his whip, rub his hands together as though he were cleansing them and turn back to the house and Josefa.

The light from the kitchen streamed across those on the porch. Juanito came running, his lips open to the gladdest of tidings.

"Teresita!" he cried.

She and Whitney turned together. Only now did their lingering hands fall apart. But Juanito had seen and all joy died in his eyes.

"What is it?" asked Teresa. "Something has happened to make you look like that, Juanito!"

"Tonight it would seem that much happens," answered Juanito. His voice altered; it was cold and lifeless. He turned abruptly before their wondering eyes and went back through the house. He walked hurriedly as a man does inspired with a sudden determination. So, she must hold Maxwell Whitney's hand with them all to see, must she? Thus he, Juanito Olivas, no longer counted. He was as nothing. All of his old insane jealousy seethed in his heart. He went to Teresa's room; closed the door after him; hurried into the King of Spain room. With hasty hands he put the picture back into place, securing it with its pegs. He stood looking at it with a white set face.

"Tia Tonia," he muttered, as though the spirit of the dead woman were at his side and he saw her and spoke to her, "you kept your secret well. Through many years you knew and said nothing. That was because in your heart there had been for a time only love; because thereafter there was only hate. Because of love and hate I am like you, Tia Tonia."

He extinguished his light and, without saying good night to anyone, went to his room.

CHAPTER XXVII

THE VISION AND THE SHADOW

Maxwell Whitney had discovered that the true lode star of the universe, that one bright star about which circled the stately worlds extending into infinity, was a girl. One certain, particular girl with Spanish eyes. And Teresa, for her part, was not far behind him in making her own amazing discovery. But a shadow lay over the two.

Whitney was striving full handedly with life. He had found his niche; he had set his foot in the one path which it was best that he should find. He had weighed great and paltry considerations; he had looked into his heart; he had gleaned a lot of wheat and thrown a lot of chaff to the winds.

In his heart was a vision; he loved it. Further, his was the rare good fortune of seeing the way to make of his vision something concrete, something worth while. An old impulse returned, remained, became an actuating, driving power: He wanted to create. He wanted to serve. To build. He was done with money juggling.

"I am a rancher," he said when he spoke of himself. Nor did he look forward to a time when he could say: "I am a retired millionaire." What he looked forward to was just to continue being a rancher.

He was as happy as a man must be who is deep in congenial work and love. And yet there was the proverbial fly in the ointment. He was so full of his work that he wanted to talk of it, wanted most of all to talk of it with Teresa Calderon. And she would not let him.

"You have changed," she would say, a little sadly he thought. "You liked us as we were when you came. You saw the beauty of our King of Spain acres as God made them, as my father won them, as we have kept them. Now you are for making them all over. Build your dams, if you must; make your hideous irrigation ditches on the Pajaro Azul; turn the wild into the tame. Make it make money for you! But let us not talk of it."

Whitney, profoundly convinced that Teresa's own interests lay in that readjustment which he was determined to bring about, sought in many ways to break down the barrier of her stubborn adherence to the old traditions. One day when they were riding together he brought her unexpectedly upon one of his dam sites. To him the thing breathed mighty epic drama; for he looked through work going forward and saw the completed Vision at the end. But before he could begin his swift explanations he saw a look on Teresa's face which checked him. He had succeeded only in shocking her, in hurting her. She had been happy, laughing; hers a mood expanding to the beauty of the forest lands. That which he showed her now struck her as a blight, a menace, a desecration.

On the ride home he, too, was stubborn. He told her of the great Marshall project, that gigantic undertaking which is still but a dream in California and yet which one day will be one of the proudest facts of which the western state can boast.

"A Marshall once discovered gold in California," he cried warmly. "His day's work made history. Now comes another Marshall, Colonel Bob, as they call him, with a promise of such golden days for California as the man of '48 never dreamed of. The name is one to conjure with in this state of ours!"

He told her how during many months of many years there are large regions of California lying parched and dry, suffering that acutest of all agonies, the thirst agony. How lands of rich, deep soils were next door to worthless, depending on the vagaries of the relentless Great Mother. How in northern California there were the great rivers pouring their priceless gift unchecked through deep river chasms into the salt ocean. How Marshall would have men construct monster dams, high up above Sacramento and the big valley, thrown across the gorges of the American, dams which would impound water for millions of acres of lands; how his irrigation ditches would run lengthwise of the state; how the water power would be harnessed.

"We would but use what God gave us and meant us to use! We would have no bad years; we would have no crop failures. Men would not be mortgaged to such as Vogel; they would not suffer from dry years; their stock would not die on their hands and their grain fields would not burn up in the long summers."

What the Marshall project would do for California, Whitney's work would do for the King of Spain Valley. He meant, on a small scale, to develop power; he would bring in tractors for the big fields; he would have a telephone line, electric lights.

Teresa saw only that he would make of her beloved holding a hideous farm, commercialized; that he would drive out the poetry of life. The old order of things was a part of her; it had entered into her being with her mother's milk; it had its own sort of sacredness. She could not or would not get his viewpoint. Today, for instance, at his dam site: She saw in a blinding flash that there was a small grove of oaks which were doomed. To cut down an oak in the King of Spain Valley was desecration. Yet she had said only, and without looking at him:

"You are going to have those trees cut down?"

"Look here, Teresa," he had expostulated, "I am no vandal; I hate like the mischief to murder an old oak. But, can't you see, they stand in the way. In the way of progress."

After the ride, at the house, a little constraint fell over them. It was the oaks, if any one definite thing. Teresa had twice been on the point of demanding:

"Will you spare them? If I ask it?"

Had she asked it, he would have had but the one answer to make. She could ask him for nothing within his power that he would not grant. But something, a bit of old Spanish pride, perhaps, restrained her. She felt that he knew her wish; that he should grant it unasked. And for his part he told himself that if she did not care enough for the oaks to come to him and ask him frankly to keep his hand back from them, they were not worth the work and expense of other surveys and more difficult dams.

Another day he and she rode up to the crest of the King of Spain ridge. They sat under their favorite tree and looked down across her valley lands. This day he had sought to banter her upon her clinging to old-fashioned ideas.

"You are Ancient Spain!" he told her.

"You are Young America!" Her answer came with unexpected heat. "And Young America commercializes everything. You would take the valley of the King's Ranch and coin it into dollars and cents!"

"Not by a jugful," he laughed at her. "No nickel-shooting for us, Ancient Spain! No coins less than twenty-dollar gold pieces admitted as legal tender in our big deal." But his smile faded and he studied her seriously. "To go back to that commercializing idea," he said quietly. "That is just talk, you know. What did your distinguished ancestor want with all these acres? You hold some forty-five thousand and that's just a fragment of the ancestral estate, isn't it? There were originally two hundred thousand acres, weren't there? Why did he want all that? Just to look at? Just for the beauty of the scenery?"

"He wanted a home," said Teresa, stiff and on the defensive. "He wanted—"

"Half the earth, with Indians to work it for him! Herds roaming everywhere so that he could live on the fat of the land and have his pockets stuffed with money to throw at the blackbirds. He indulged in trade; he had his caravans trailing from here to Santa Barbara, Los Angeles, San

Francisco. He dealt in hides and tallow and was as rich as adobe mud. In his elegant fashion, my dear Ancient Spain, he commercialized for further orders."

She stirred restlessly.

"But—"

"Why did your grandfather come out here in the first place?"

She shrugged.

"The spirit of adventure, the desire to do big, sweeping things."

"Or was he lured by tales of gold to be had?"

"You'd make greed the inspiration for everything," she objected indignantly.

"I said nothing about greed. No one ever named the Calderons misers! I am talking about human nature."

"Sometimes I wish," said Teresa, "that it wasn't quite so human."

After a little silence, Teresa said abruptly:

"You are still going ahead with your big dam?"

"Of course," he said. And then, "Why not?"

She made no answer. Yesterday Juanito had said to her:

"That Whitney, whom once I called *amigo*, is a gringo vandal like the rest. He murders forests; he cares nothing what we others think, we who have lived always in the valley."

Teresa had said nothing to Juanito; she had not appeared interested. But she, too, had thought that

309

if Whitney cared, he should know how she felt and he should observe her wishes, though unspoken. Now she rose and went to her horse.

Whitney *knew* that he was right; if a man's hand stood in the way of a man's health and perhaps life, the hand should come off and that was all there was to it. And he knew that one day Teresa would see that what he was doing was right. Further, he waited for her to come straight to him with any request she had to make. All of which, as they both knew somewhere within their hearts, was but rocking the boat.

It was permitted Juanito, a changed, moody Juanito with distorted vision, to upset the canoe. He brought in word:

"Tomorrow that money-grabber sets his men cutting down the trees."

Teresa, with a sudden impulse and striking a compromise, said swiftly:

"Juanito, do something for me, like a good boy. Ride to Mr. Whitney; say that I make a first request of him. It is that he will not cut those oaks. Tell him that once my father had a camp there. That I ask him as a favor."

Juanito stared at her curiously. He went for his horse. And then he flared out in bitter anger, anger embracing three people, not sparing Teresa, not forgetting Whitney, but striking straightest at Juanito's own self for being a fool.

"If he would ruin the King of Spain Valley, if he

would take my Teresita away from me, am I to aid him? And what are oak trees set over against the love of Teresa?"

So, instead of carrying his message, he rode into Toyon and demanded of Vogel that Kelvin be sent for a game. He did not return to the house that night. Before Teresa saw him again she had had word from Felipe Moraga that the trees were being cut.

Juanito came in late that evening; you knew before he entered a room that his old reckless mood was upon him. He went by Teresa in a sort of devil's dance; he stopped for no one. He went to his room and for an hour thereafter the old violin sang in a dozen varying passionate moods to the sleeping valley and the stars above. At last he put away the beloved instrument and went into the living room. His father had gone off to bed; Teresa was sitting at a window, staring out into the night.

"Life is a stupid thing," said Juanito. "The world is broken to pieces and is dead and of no use. Look you; strangers come into our valley and there is the end of happiness. A year ago life with us was glad and golden. I—My God, Teresita! Sometimes I think I must kill myself!"

"I remember that Juanito's birthday comes in a week," said Teresa. "It is sad to hear you talk like this at such a time. And I, sitting here, have been asking myself: What can I give Juanito this year?"

"Then you had not forgotten that, too?" He was very bitter. "These are days of forgetting things." His voice caught; he hesitated, then burst out vehemently: "What shall you give me! You, who know that there is, on earth or above or below, but one thing that I want—"

Teresa said slowly, barely for him to hear, like one in a dream:

"I know, Juanito. And—if I gave you that?"

"Then, by God!" shouted the boy, "I am King of the World! Teresita Mia—"

"For your birthday present?" said Teresa.

Juanito went down on his knees at her side; her hand was caught against his hot lips.

CHAPTER XXVIII

THE VISION—AND LOVE

"You shall not do this mad thing!" said Maxwell Whitney sternly.

It was the evening before Juanito's birthday. And tomorrow the priest was coming.

Teresa lifted her eyebrows at him.

"Shall I not?" she asked serenely. She laughed then. "Señor Maxwell Whitney, modern farmer of the Pajaro Azul rancho, forbids!" she mocked him.

Whitney's face was white, stern like his voice.

"You know I love you," he said hotly. "And I know that you love me. Teresa Calderon——"

"Love is a strong word, Señor," she said lightly. "You and I have had pleasant hours together, *no*? We have perhaps—yes, flirted a little. We shall not spoil a nice friendship by growing serious over play, shall we?"

Why she spoke like that she did not in the least know. She looked cool and demure and serene. But within her breast her heart was beating like mad; her eyes looked at him as clear as summer pools and yet in her brain it seemed that a mist was creeping.

"If you talk like that——"

"How else should I speak, Señor Max?" She could not refrain from using the familiar name; she even spoke it with a hint of mocking tenderness, and there was a strange flutter of triumph and pain in her heart as she saw how she was hurting him. "You see, Señor, we are of different peoples, you and I. Perhaps we have never understood each other quite? And, of course, you could not guess how a little country girl grows so lonely that she is glad of the company of strangers who come and go. Have I seemed gladder than I was?"

"Are you just a flirt?" he demanded angrily.

If her soft laugh was any answer, she was.

"I think," said Teresa, and her eyes were sparkling, "that we of Spanish blood love music

313

better than groaning, and play better than stupid humdrum. You would forgive me if—"

Whitney strode across the room for his hat.

"Good night," he said bluntly. "At least you will not ask me to the wedding. I'll be very busy tomorrow."

"Of course," said Teresa, with a great assumption of carelessness. "You will want to get a lot of wood chopped this year."

Juanito had come into the room and waited for them to finish. He looked like a sick man.

"Juanito!" Teresa started up, alarmed.

"Let me talk!" cried Juanito. His hands were clenched, his eyes seemed enormous with all of the shining agony in them. "I am a robber, a thief, a liar. I am worse than Brooke Sheffield who, men say, killed the tramp. I am worse than Vogel, who opens letters in his post office and burns down his house for insurance moneys! I am more contemptible than that man! I hear that Sheffield is afraid that every stranger is an officer; that he will hang for a man killed. I am more criminal than Brooke Sheffield.—Teresa! . . . Teresita Mia . . . Forgive me!"

With no key to his meaning they could but stare at him. They thought that he had gone mad. His eyes gleamed at them wildly through unshed tears.

"Teresita, I have loved you so! Everything begins there, ends there. But, never mind; that excuses nothing. I have betrayed you; I have been traitor to my friend Maxwell. In what? In everything. Your word to Maxwell about the oak trees—I did not carry it! And then, in something else—Oh, I have been worse than the devil himself! Come with me!"

He almost ran from the room, shouting to them to follow. Poor Juanito, perhaps he distrusted himself, perhaps he wanted this done swiftly for fear that, if he delayed, the old insane jealousy would again distort his vision and make him play the pitiful part of a Tia Tonia. They followed, wondering. He led them to the King of Spain painting. Though Teresa cried out, he jerked out the pegs and removed it from its place. He showed them the opening, he caught up a lamp and held it to shine within.

"Everything there has been gathered and put into a bag," he said hurriedly. "You will take it out, Teresa. It is yours. And I have known of it since that night we found Brooke Sheffield trying to take it."

"But, Juanito—"

"It is I who talk tonight!" he interrupted wildly. "This is nothing, weighed against the other thing. This is only gold." He struck his breast and cried: "You two whom I love, what have I done for you? Tried to make you unhappy, that is it! And now, thank the good God, it is I who give you back happiness. Tomorrow, when the priest comes, Teresa will not marry me. For it is you whom she loves, *mí amigo*. And I—I—"

But at last words failed and the tears came.

Teresa came to Juanito and put her two arms about him and held him tight, tears in her own eyes now.

"My poor Juanito," she whispered. "Oh, I do love you."

Juanito patted her hair, murmuring:

"Yes. Of course you love me—like that. And I am proud, more proud than a king! But listen again; you must not cry, Teresita. You must not be too sorry for me. And for why? Because had I held back the truth, never in all my life could I have laughed again; never could I have laid a bow across the strings of a violin. My heart would have been sick. And now? Now I have lived to the uttermost; I have loved; I have wronged my love; I have sacrificed! I am no longer ashamed. For my birthday, Teresita, you will give me the old violin. I shall play such music as will make the world stop and listen! Oh, I know! For a little I may leave you here, you and Maxwell, happy together; I may go to the great cities of the world. I will study with masters and in the end I shall be more master than they! Because of you, Teresita Mia, you in whom the sun rises and the stars shine."

He lifted her hand, kissed it and then suddenly ran out of the room.

It was sunset of another day. Under their favorite tree on the King of Spain ridge, hand locked in hand, sat Teresa and Whitney.

Together they saw the Vision. For at last Teresa's eyes saw even as her lover's eyes saw.

Before them in the mellow light lay the King of Spain Valley as it had always been. A valley saved from the mad rush of the world, steeped in peace and quiet, the atmosphere of olden times clinging to everything; the Mission ruin, colorful with romance; wild fields and pastures and hills; old orchards in harmony with the wild, gray and lichenous. The beauty of the untamed.

But as they looked, though the scene was unchanged, its meaning altered. They saw neglect and shiftlessness; they saw man heedless of the gifts that God offered. The valley was like the tramp Jenkins, clothed in outworn rags.

They saw Squalor and Laziness and Ignorance, a trinity, enthroned in the valley, ordering its affairs. They saw small families suffering; they saw Vogel prospering.

Into this they saw a young man come. He was clean and clean cut; there was a golden look to him. His hand was about the hand of a girl with Spanish eyes, eyes which shone and glowed and trusted. These two whispered to each other; they said, "We have a work to do, a responsibility to

317

shoulder. There is happiness in work and we work together."

They saw the King of Spain Valley accepted as a blessing, a rich gift and always a responsibility. They saw wasted waters stored and poured on thirsting lands. They saw reservoirs; long, gleaming irrigation ditches. And they saw this miracle: *None of the older beauty was gone but a new beauty had come!*

Now the valley was changing. There were squared plots and they were beautiful. There were young orchards springing up; grain fields thrusting toward the sky, standing tall, full-bearded and lusty.

They saw, understanding, those parts of the country about them which were sweetly feminine; those which were superbly male. There were the rugged old Santa Lucia mountains standing up against the Pacific; there were the luscious black valley lands; they were husband and wife. From the mountains rushed the tributaries, pouring down fertility; the valley grew fertile and produced. The wide sweep of acres covered themselves in splendid colors, the blossoms of fruit trees, the verdure of spring, the russet of autumn, the bursting purple globes of a million grapes. And the teeming acres enwrapped themselves in seductive perfumes, the odors of a million bursting buds; they wore butterflies like gems.

They saw the Pajaro Azul once more added to the King of Spain Rancho.

Through the valley they saw a man riding. An old man who sat straight in the saddle; who directed everywhere; whose head was erect; who at last knew that the beloved rancho was prospering. Never again for Mentor Olivas would there be talk of the dragging, cruel chains which are mortgages.

And this they saw also: The old forests rimmed the trim fields and were unchanged saving that from the contrast itself their rugged wild beauty was but accentuated. Long, gleaming furrows of black soil flowed behind the marching tractors but never was a hand lifted against an oak tree that might be spared.

They saw before them long years of work, a labor of love. And as the great disc of the autumn sun wheeled down and was gone and the shadows came and the thin voices of singing insects thrilled through the silence, as sweet as a muted violin, they turned from the outer Vision, content, and looked deep into each other's glowing eyes.

Center Point Large Print
600 Brooks Road / PO Box 1
Thorndike, ME 04986-0001 USA

(207) 568-3717

US & Canada:
1 800 929-9108
www.centerpointlargeprint.com